ENGLISH MISS

"YES, let's." That was Harvey's heartfelt response when his fiancée suggested that they should break their engagement, for Julie was half Irish and half French, and her temper matched her heredity. It did not take him long to change his mind, but by that time Julie was staying with her autocratic French grandmother in Paris, and had cloaked her gauche sincerity with exquisite fashionable poise, and extended her experience from sentimental courtship to the Gallic negotiations which are over-shadowed by the words 'dowry' and 'family.' Of course she would welcome his repentance, and of course she would realize that the attentive Charles was the usual superficial Continental with a corrupt past (and present) in which the actress Lucienne figured largely. The outcome was obvious, but then neither Julie nor the author of this gaily entrancing story are people who care for the obvious. Moral : Read the book.

LEWIS COX

has also written

PICK O' THE BUNCH
WHITE ARMS
BANQUET OF LIFE
SOIREE
SOUTHERN RHAPSODY
ANGEL BREAD
NEW LOVES FOR OLD
EASTER SNOW
TALISMAN OF LOVE
THE THOUSANDTH MAN
LOVE IN TWO KEYS
FALSE BARRIERS
LOVELY WOMAN
LOVER TRIUMPHANT
THE TIDE'S TOO STRONG
LEAPING THE RAINBOWS
THE STAR-SPANGLED HOUSE
WHERE THE FIELDS ARE WARM
TO-MORROW'S SUNSHINE
FLIGHT OF YOUTH
LOVE WITHOUT END
HEART OF THE WORLD
WILD HAPPINESS
BROTHERS-IN-LOVE
MAN'S FAVOURITE
RADIANT AND RECKLESS
VOICE OF LOVE
CHRISTMAS MAIL
LAUGHING SPRING
SEEDS OF FATE
WHEN SUMMER BEGINS
LOVE ENCHANTED
OATEN HARVEST
THE KEEPER OF THE TIGER
THOUGH WORLDS DIVIDE
PEDLARS OF PARADISE
NO OTHER TIDE
TAKE THOU THIS HEART
THE CORAL TREE
WEDDING EAGLES
APPLES IN EDEN
ARROWS OF DESIRE
MOORISH INTERLUDE
FRENCHIE
HOLIDAY LOVE
ONE SPRING IN PARIS

ENGLISH MISS

LEWIS COX

The Valentine Romance Club
London

Hutchinson & Co. (Publishers) Ltd
178-202 Great Portand Street, London, W.1

London   Melbourne   Sydney   Auckland
Bombay   Johannesburg   New York   Toronto

This Edition May 1956

Made and printed in Great Britain by
TAYLOR GARNETT EVANS & CO., LTD.
BUSHEY MILL LANE
WATFORD, HERTS.

CHAPTER I

"I HAVE broken my engagement to Harvey," announced Julie, dramatically, to her family one morning at breakfast.

"Did you quarrel last night?" inquired her mother calmly, opening the lid of the coffee-pot and peering inside. She knew from experience how much coffee was in the pot, but she did not want Julie to see the glint of joy in her eyes.

"Not more than usual." Julie began to eat a good breakfast. "But suddenly I was so bored with it all I said pleasantly, 'Let's end it, Harvey.' Just like that."

"And he agreed?"

"He said, 'Yes, let's.' He also told me that if ever I wanted any help to call upon him, and he'd come from the ends of the earth."

"That was a rash thing to say," said her mother. " 'Let's' sounds as though he were breathing a sigh of relief."

"*I* didn't think it silly : Harvey likes being intense."

"So do you, Julie," cut in her father.

"Perhaps, but imagine two intense people living amicably together. We couldn't make a go of it, could we?"

There appeared to be no answer to that.

"Well, I am surprised it lasted for three months," remarked Mrs. Ryan, who was a Frenchwoman. She had the light-hearted French way of looking at everything, but she also had a practical outlook on life, which balanced things finely.

"Are you? Everyone thought that Harvey and I were an ideal couple, who would marry and live happily ever after," Julie told her with asperity.

Her father took a long draught of coffee. Now he put down his cup, saying, "I am Irish and your mother French. You have probably inherited the worst of both countries. Anyhow, you have a temper. You can't get away from that, Julie."

"That isn't fair ; you are blaming me."

"It is fifty-fifty who is to blame. You are totally unsuited to each other. I am glad you found it out in time. It goes to show that you have *some* common sense." He passed his cup. "A little more coffee please, Jeanne."

"Have you returned your lovely ring, Julie?" inquired her mother.

"That's my only regret. I gave it to Harvey last night." Julie looked at her father. "And now you are going to suggest that I take a back seat, find a serious job and——"

"No." Patrick Ryan looked across at his wife and winked. He said mildly, "I was going to say, why not write to Grandmère Lubin in Paris? Invite yourself, at the old lady's convenience, of course, to spend Easter with her. Take a holiday where there is life and gaiety. Fancy Paris in the Spring! Plenty of time to find work when you return from your holiday. You will probably have forgotten Harvey by then."

Julie glanced suspiciously at her mother, but the latter was absorbed in pouring out her husband's second cup of coffee. For several months her mother had made the same frivolous suggestion, but as Julie had been preoccupied with Harvey and the making and mending of their quarrels, it had fallen on deaf ears.

She asked darkly, "Who has been putting ideas into your head, Father?"

"No one," said her father innocently. "I thought of it myself." He honestly thought he had. "Your troublous engagement has been a hectic, nerve-racking time for all of us, but more especially for you. What you want is a complete change."

Julie turned the idea over in her mind. It appealed to her. So to forget Harvey, to avoid her friends who were so curious, and to bridge over a time before she could stage a comeback 'into circulation,' Julie was tempted by her father's suggestion. She wrote to her grandmother, reminding her of a long-standing invitation, and saying that she would like to visit her.

Julie pictured an attractive holiday in the gay city. It would seem like being born again, and after Harvey, she needed a tonic.

In anticipation of the visit, Julie bought an air ticket. If it were not convenient for grandmère to have her, she would still use it. If funds gave out, and that was a probability, Julie thought she might get a job in Paris. She was unaware that though it is comparatively easy to get a three months' permit to stay in France, it is well-nigh impossible for an alien to gain permission to get a *job* in France—unless, of course, a girl is willing to be a show girl, and that did not appeal to Julie. Yet it would be easy, for Julie was of medium height, elegant in looks and manner, and slim, with golden hair, and grey-blue eyes whose beauty was enhanced by dark lashes and pencilled brows. In her heart, Julie was sure she could easily cut all official tape, stay as long as she wished, and do as she pleased.

She had not seen Madame Lubin since she was a little girl, and had only a vague remembrance of her, but Jeanne Ryan had often spoken of her mother as an autocrat. Julie, being half-Irish and independent, had no intention of allowing her personality to be swamped by that of Madame Lubin, who might be old and frail, but who was a kind of matriarch, a power in the family, and indeed, by all accounts, in Paris.

When Madame Lubin read Julie's letter, she sent a cable to the girl telling her to come over by air at once. Also, unknown to Julie, or anyone, she set in motion the complicated machinery of a certain plan which she had decided upon when she first saw Julie as a baby, and which with the years had grown dear to her heart. No one in the world can surpass a Frenchwoman where romantic intrigue is concerned.

The night that Julie arrived at the Lubins' flat, in the Passy district of Paris, grandmère gave a dinner-party in her honour.

She told her unmarried daughter, Nina, that Julie was upset by the broken engagement, and must not be given time to think of her broken heart, but caught up in a whirl of gaiety—hence the dinner-party to which twenty guests were invited.

When Julie, on her knees, was unpacking in her bedroom, from whose closely curtained window she could glimpse a narrow strip of the green trees of the Bois du Boulogne, Madame Lubin knocked at her door, and on being given permission to enter, came in and sat down on a stiff high chair.

"I have invited a few friends to dinner tonight, Julie, and I want you to wear your prettiest evening dress." She spoke in precise English and slowly, which made the words sound impressive.

Julie heard this news with dismay.

"You must please excuse me, grandmère, for I have nothing suitable to wear. I have three evening dresses, but they were not good enough to bring over. I am going to buy a new one tomorrow. Father gave me the money for my birthday."

"I shall not listen to such an excuse, *chérie*. Either you must make do with what you have, or if you have not then you must borrow from Tante Nina. I have arranged a place for you at my little dinner. It is halfway down the long table down the centre of which there is an arrangement of flowers. You shall scarcely be seen. Tomorrow we shall visit my friend, Madame le Gère, who is a famous dressmaker. She has an atelier and salon in the

7

Rue St. Honoré. We shall buy not one evening dress but three, for you will need them during your visit."

"Three !" Julie's mouth dropped open like a fish. "But I am only here for a short while, grandmère. It would be waste of money to buy so many."

"We shall see how long you shall remain in Paris. What sort of a girl are you to talk about 'wasting' money on lovely clothes ! Either your mother has neglected a necessary part of your education, a clothes-sense, or you must be very depressed about this broken affaire with the Englishman. Yes, that must be it. You are broken-hearted, *ma pauvre p'tite*. We must of a certainty cheer you up."

"But . . ." Julie's voice was faint in protest. She was awed by her grandmother's personality, but the prospect of choosing three new evening dresses was enchanting.

"Yes ?"

"Couldn't you excuse me for tonight ? I should love to come down to your party, but I should look a frump and disgrace you. Besides, I really have a headache. May I rest—just this once ?"

"You may not. It is not my intention to give you one moment in which to grieve over the ex-fiancé. I shall not listen. Your headache shall soon be forgotten. Now I shall send Tante Nina to you. She shall tell you what to wear."

Julie retired defeated. Then she looked up from the lowly position on her knees to the old lady, white-haired, sallow-skinned, with high bridged nose and an indomitable look in her brown eyes. So they stared at each other. Then, unaccountably each smiled.

"So, now we understand, eh ?" said Madame Lubin amicably.

Madame Lubin repeated a part of this conversation to her daughter, Nina, who was also a sister of Mrs. Ryan.

"That is what I expected Julie to say. She is partly English, and does not understand our ways," said Nina.

"She will," was the comfortable reply. "The child must not be left alone. Gaiety is the watchword. It does not matter tonight what Julie wears. She has just arrived, and has had no time to buy clothes."

Nina, who was chic and had a cold heart, said calmly, "Julie looks a fright."

"Never that ! With that glorious corn-coloured hair and those oh, so serious eyes, Julie could never look a sight, even after a bumpy plane journey," said Madame Lubin warmly. "She has a headache, and I think perhaps a little cold."

"She has been crying—yes?"

"Then she must be homesick."

"More likely it is for the ex-fiancé," said Nina practically.

"Then the sooner she stops thinking of him the better. Now, Nina, you must lend her one of your dresses for tonight."

"She is smaller than I am," objected Nina, who did not wish to loan a dress to this stranger, though she was well aware why her mother wanted to dress Julie up—to please Charles Patrice.

"Then fix it around the waist with pins and a ribbon," was the sharp retort.

"I should have thought you would want Julie to look her best for Charles. You know how fastidious his taste in women is."

"I am taking a chance on that. All I want Julie to achieve tonight is Charles's notice. Her colouring alone should do that."

"But the dress may put him off?"

"Oh, I give Julie credit for some brain. She does not look stupid. Charles has had such a surfeit of perfection in clothes and manners, that a change shall do him good. It shall certainly attract his attention."

To Julie, accustomed to the haphazard entertainment of two or three guests at a time, the sight of the long table in the *salle-à-manger*, laid with exquisite perfection of detail, the shining chased silver, and polished cut glass; the beautifully arranged flowers made by an artist, and the golden ornaments seemed like a regal banquet.

'Mummy never told me that grandmère lived this way,' she thought.

She seemed a stranger to herself, especially in this dress of dark lace which belonged to Tante Nina, and was drawn tightly at the waist with a blue-grey ribbon.

Everybody was formal in the salon where grandmère received her guests before dinner, their behaviour so stiff and solemn that Julie stifled a yawn. She stood behind her grandmother, beside the door.

'This is going to be the dullest evening of my life,' she thought dismally. 'Even Harvey would be better than this. The worst of it is, in this tight waist band I shan't be able to eat enough.' However, Julie managed to enjoy a glass of sherry. It was then that grandmère turned and beckoned Julie forward.

9

"This is Julie," she remarked quietly. "I have often mentioned her to you—my favourite grandchild."

'That isn't saying much,' thought Julie. 'I am the *only* grandchild.'

She held out her hand and a man took it, bowing low. He did not kiss it as she had seen him do to her grandmother a moment ago.

Meanwhile grandmère was saying, "M'sieur Charles Patrice. *He* is the son of an old business associate. He will take you into dinner."

Charles let Julie's hand drop. He said something, Julie never knew what, and stood back a pace, looking quickly at her in a speculative kind of way.

Julie had no time to question or resent the look, for immediately Charles made his face a blank. But in that sweeping look Charles's eyes had flicked expertly over Julie's figure.

Julie did not know that Charles was the heir to a huge motor manufacturing business. The name 'Patrice' was well known throughout France. The Patrice tractor was met everywhere along the roads. She simply thought of him as a rude young man, and resented the way he had looked at her.

Amongst his friends, Charles was acclaimed as having the most beautiful voice in France—golden and mellow. They said he would have made a fortune on the stage or as a radio announcer. Charles laughed at them. He was not a conceited man, and would have liked to be praised for his business acumen rather than his voice. He wore a dinner suit with a deep red carnation in his buttonhole. He, too, drank sherry, and talked a little while he drank it.

When dinner was announced Charles offered his arm to Julie, and said in careful, precise English, "Shall we go in ?"

Julie's answer was to slip her hand in the crook of Charles's arm, and to rest the tips of her fingers lightly on his forearm. She had nothing to say to this autocratic man with the overbearing look and patronizing manner.

On the short journey through the double-doors, across the ante-room and through more double doors into the *salle-à-manger*, Charles glanced sideways at his partner. He looked thoughtful and puzzled. Then his dark eyes noticed her hair and a queer light came into them. A girl with that bright hair, glistening like gold, could be intriguing—*she could be!*

They were nearly at the end of the line, and as a frequent diner at Madame Lubin's, Charles knew where he would be seated at the table. He did not take long to find their seats.

As grandmère had told Julie, there were flowers in front of her. They stretched away down the centre of the table. Where there were no flowers gold ornaments had been placed, and where neither of these obstructed the plates of people seated opposite, crystal fruit tazzas, laden with fruits and sweets, caught the eye.

Grandmère, seated at the top of the table, seemed a long way off.

Charles said pleasantly to Julie, "You have but lately arrived in Paris, Mademoiselle Ryan ?"

"I only came an hour ago."

"That is a short time ?"

"Yes." And she thought with annoyance, 'Oh, dear, he is talking like a guide book.'

"You have come from England, of course."

"Oh, of course." Julie thought the remark was uncalled for and her voice was cold. It was as though Charles said, 'You look like a tourist—you are badly dressed, but you do not care.' Julie thought passionately, 'I do care. I hate wearing other people's clothes, especially their shoes which pinch; and I did not want to come down tonight, but I was forced to join the party.' She did not tell Charles this, but looking at her he noted the mutinous curve of her pretty mouth, and wondered what he had said to make her look like that.

"You are here for long ?"

"Only over Easter, M'sieur Patrice." And Julie thought, 'I suppose I ought to make the effort.'

"The time will soon pass. Madame Lubin is sure to show you the sights of Paris."

"I expect so." She thought again, 'What on earth can I say to *him* ?'

Charles came to the end of his polite remarks, but persisted a little longer. He spoke tentatively, asking a few more questions, trying to pierce Julie's cool armour of reserve. He could make little headway. He spoke in English, his manner strained and pedantic. Charles knew that he could have made a better impression had he spoken in French.

He did say once, "Do you speak French, Mademoiselle Ryan?"

"A little." Languages had never come easily to Julie. Jeanne Ryan tried to teach her, but Colonel Ryan did not encourage it. "English is good enough for Julie ; she is never likely to live in France. On tourist routes every Frenchman is only too delighted to air his knowledge of English and get a free lesson. Why worry with the language ?" Why, indeed ?

It amused Julie to pretend not to understand all that Charles meant. When he was stuck for a word she made no kind-hearted or laughing attempt to help him out. She did not feel like laughing, anyway. Disliking Charles at sight made Julie think of Harvey, with an added regret that he was not sitting beside her instead of the elegant Frenchman. Yet in her heart Julie knew that Harvey would not have fitted in with this company.

Julie did not know that Charles was a rich man. The rich, seen from Julie's lowlier level in money value, had a certain glamour in her eyes. They were easily forgiven. It would not have made her like Charles to know that he was rich, but it might have made her treat him less coldly. He was getting the benefit of her first impressions. She had not taken to him! Perhaps Charles was too sure of himself—Julie had not though. it out. She was too tired—and her head ached !

At this point Charles took out his handkerchief and mopped his forehead.

"It is warm for Easter—or the room is."

"It is not cold, M'sieur Patrice."

Charles looked at Julie sharply, but her expression remained demure.

"The heating is still on ?"

"It is on."

Now Charles knew that Julie was secretly laughing at him, and it offended him. He did not speak to her again for some time, but paid great attention to his food and wine.

Julie noted with inward annoyance that he drank with knowledge, and ate with relish. He spoke often in French and with much animation to a lovely woman sitting on his other side.

Once Charles turned to Julie saying, "You do not appear to be eating anything, Mademoiselle Ryan."

"I am not hungry."

"You will offend Madame Lubin if you do not eat her marvellous food."

He spoke more naturally, and Julie replied, "Oh, she won't mind tonight."

"Why not ?"

"Because tonight I do not count with her. I am not wearing the right clothes. Indeed," and here Julie allowed herself to smile ruefully, "this is my aunt's dress, made over for me."

Charles relaxed. He understood this kind of remark. Again his eyes flicked over her, and he observed what a natural shyness had not permitted him to see before, that Julie had a sweet figure, and that her skin was young and fresh. She was, in fact, lovely, and in the right clothes would look ravishing.

"You mean that tomorrow night you will be wearing new clothes, you will therefore feel better, and much may be expected of you?"

Julie was not looking at him and so did not see the soft smile that played for a little while about the chiselled lips as Charles added, "You look charming as you are, Mademoiselle Ryan."

That, of course, was an empty compliment, at which all Frenchmen, so Julie had often been told, were adept.

She said almost resentfully, "It is my Aunt Nina's dress."

"And tomorrow it will be a le Gère dress. But *you* will be just the same."

"I think not."

"Then I must meet you tomorrow evening," said Charles. He did not mean what he said. But for once Julie believed him.

The dinner, broken by spasmodic talk between Julie and Charles, seemed like a feast to the English girl. The warmth of the room, the subdued lights, the gay talk and laughter, the exotic flowers and the smell of delicate food and the aroma of wine confused Julie, so that she seemed to be in a dream in which everything had an unreal perfection.

She drank a lovely soft Beaune with her turkey, and sipped a treasured pink Tokay with her dessert, and had no idea that she was eating food cooked by a chef of repute, or that the wine came from a renowned cellar. Julie only knew that what she ate so sparingly was good, and that her father would have appreciated the wine more than she did.

Julie did not know that many years ago, when Madame Lubin emerged from her period of widowhood, she had told her friends naïvely, "I love the society of men, but they will not visit my house if I do not provide fine wines for them. That must be my bait." A highly-paid chef was also installed in the kitchen. At first it was hard work to win a success, but Madame Lubin was ambitious and persevered. With the years she gained an established reputation among the great hostesses in Paris, and people sought eagerly for invitations to her parties. Age curtailed the lists; it also made Madame Lubin choosy. At the time of Julie's visit Madame was well aware of her social value.

The formality of dinner disappeared afterwards in the salon. Some younger guests arrived, boys and girls of Julie's own age who could not be expected to appreciate a banquet. Without ceremony they rolled up Madame's priceless Aubusson carpet and pushed the tapestry and gilt chairs against the walls, so that they could dance. Someone turned on the radio. Dance music came over the air.

Charles bowed before Julie. "Shall we dance, Mademoiselle Ryan?"

Julie hesitated. She was a good dancer, and in London could afford to pick her partners. She was pernickety in her choice. But here it was Charles Patrice or no one.

She rose, aware that Charles was doing his duty in asking her, and pleasing grandmère who was sitting straight-backed in a gilt fauteuil, looking on at the dancing. She did not appear to be looking directly at Julie, but the latter knew that those sharp eyes were missing nothing. It made Julie self-conscious and awkward.

Charles inquired politely, "Do you feel better now?"

"I am feeling all right, thank you."

It sounded silly saying that she was all right, when a short while ago she had pleaded a headache. In fact, Julie's headache was worse than ever as she wondered if Charles danced well or only passably. She glanced at an ormolu and tortoiseshell clock which stood in lonely splendour on the Siena marble surface of a commode, and wished that this party would end and she were free to go to bed. But no one showed signs of going. The older people who had dined with Madame were ranged against the wall, evidently expecting the newly-arrived younger people to entertain them.

Julie need not have feared that Charles could not dance well. She knew by the way he drew her to join the dancers and the easy way he guided her towards the centre of the floor that he was an expert.

Charles had no idea of these fears about his ability to dance. Unless he had been sure of himself he would not have taken the floor at all. He had long known that a man must be capable of steering a mediocre partner three times around a salon before he could decently suggest refreshment. He, too, was quickly aware that Julie was a good dancer, light as thistledown in his arms, her lithe body almost anticipating the slightest pressure of his hand on her back. He looked down, but could only see the top of her spectacularly bright hair which touched his chin. Charles jerked back his head, muffed a step, whispered savagely, "Pardon, Mademoiselle Ryan," and gave his attention to dancing.

Presently Julie saw that other couples had stopped to watch them, and she and Charles soon had the floor to themselves.

The dance was an unexpected joy in the dreariness of an evening spoiled by a weight of dignity. It could have been perfect for Julie if she had not been so dress-conscious, and if her partner had been any other man than Charles, who had played a large part in the evening's ceremony. She might have relaxed a little, and danced with abandon and really enjoyed herself. But no one laughed. Those sitting around the room took their pleasure solemnly. No one spoke, but sat like statues until the end of the dance.

The music came to a sudden stop on an unfinished note, and the voice of an announcer was heard speaking rapidly.

Julie and her partner fell apart, and everyone in the room began talking at once.

"What is he saying?" she asked fretfully.

"It is a sponsored programme. He is talking about somebody's pills. The music will begin again in a moment."

"Fancy breaking in on a dance like that!"

By common consent they walked to the side of the room.

"You dance beautifully, Mademoiselle Ryan."

"I should—I have had a lot of practice."

"That is what I thought. I suppose in England you go to a dance every night?"

"Not every night," Julie corrected, and wished this man were not so formal.

"You dance much with one partner perhaps?"

"How did you know that?"

"I do not. One feels it." He should have guessed that Julie was the kind of girl to do that. Well, what of that? The dancing partners of this English girl were no concern of Charles Patrice.

They stood beside some empty gilt chairs—waiting.

"What happens now?"

"I must leave you with a thousand regrets, Mademoiselle Ryan. I have to dance with others. Shall I take you over to Madame Lubin?"

Julie shook her head. The evening was indeed a flop if a man did not rush to claim her quickly for other dances. Evidently Charles did not like her as a partner, for there was nothing wrong with her dancing. She was chagrined to know that their dance had been a duty one on his part.

"I am tired. I think I shall go to bed," she told him, and glanced up at him forlornly.

Charles said, "Then I will leave you with Madame Lubin so that you may make your excuses."

How correct he was! How stiff and starchy!

Then Charles smiled down at her, and for a moment the smile made Julie almost like him.

CHAPTER II

THERE was a plutocrat in the household. It was Madame Lubin's brother, Michel Pierre. As a successful business man he was fond of ordering the lives of those around him. There were, as a consequence, frequent clashes with his autocratic sister, while he bullied her daughter Nina shamefully. He was a bachelor, and yet a family man, for he disliked the idea of living alone, and brought an iron will to bear on any plans that affected family life.

The evening of Julie's arrival in Paris, Michel was forced to retire to bed with a cold. He gargled frequently, and took aspirin, quinine and whisky as a means of getting rid of it quickly. There were three hot water bottles in his bed, and his windows were sealed making the room like an oven. He had decided that he must be better by the morning. He fell deeply asleep.

He had said to Gilbert, his valet, "Call me as usual in the morning. Tell Madame to see me in the library at nine o'clock—at her convenience, of course."

At nine o'clock next morning not only was Michel's cold better, but Madame, in a trailing house gown, came punctually into the library to see him.

Dressed in a short black coat and the striped dark trousers of a business man, Michel rose ponderously to greet her.

They kissed each other's cheeks lightly, and sat down.

"*Bon jour*, Michel. Is your cold better?"

"Don't I look better? I am. I feel fine. I knew I should," he told her impatiently.

There was a strong family likeness between brother and sister, for both had the same alert bright eyes and high-bridged noses. M'sieur Pierre had a neat Imperial beard, and his spindly legs supported a rotund body which seemed even more prominent because he wore two scallops of gold cable chain across his waistcoat. His manner was impatient because he had asked to see his sister for a purpose, and time was short before he left for his office.

"How did the dinner go off?" he asked.

Madame knew all the questions he might ask, and she had prepared her answers.

"It was a great success, Michel."

"Charles came, of course?"

"Yes. He took Julie in to dinner."

"Ah!"

"He did not like sitting so far down the table, but as Julie arrived with no clothes to wear, I had to place her in a lowly position among a veritable flower and fruit market to hide her a little." She smiled a little at her own description.

Michel's face did not relax. This matter was not a joking one to him.

His sister composed herself. "Charles was much impressed with Julie."

"How do you know?"

"I found time to watch them. I could see it in his manner—in his eyes."

"Well, you know my wish that they must meet often and get to know each other quickly?"

"Yes, Michel."

"You must get busy, Louise, for I intend to announce their betrothal in a month's time."

His sister stared at him. She did not share her brother's enthusiasm.

Michel was accustomed to having 'yes-men' around him. His quick ear was attuned to inflexions in people's voices. He caught one in his sister's, "Yes, Michel," and said irritably,

"Go on, out with it, Louise." He disliked being thwarted.

"You must not be in too great a hurry. If Julie were a French girl it would be understood that you, as head of the family, would desire a suitable marriage for her; but English girls arrange their own marriages with a freedom unbelievable and foolish to us. But do not worry: Charles is amiable—a little spoiled perhaps—but I am sure, when the time comes, he will be ready to fall in with family wishes. It is Julie who is the problem."

"She is half-French."

"But she has been brought up in England."

"She must do as we tell her."

Louise shook her head. "Only if Julie falls in love with Charles."

"That is absurd. But why should she not 'fall in love'? Charles is handsome, debonair and—suitable."

Louise laughed. "One does not order a girl of spirit to fall in love. It is an unpredictable emotion——"

"All right. I have no time to discuss love. For a French-woman you are strangely unpractical. Give Julie every chance of seeing Charles and she must fall in love with him."

"It is possible ; but the start was poor. They did not appear to get on too well last night."

"I thought you said the dinner was a success ?"

"The dinner was."

"You knew what I was driving at. Perhaps you placed them so far from you at the table you were unable to see how matters were shaping. *They* may not have liked the dinner."

"Michel! Of course they did—only imbeciles would not, though I noticed that Julie ate little, and she does not strike me as imbecile." Madame considered for a moment, then she said slowly, "I think perhaps the fault in not making friends lay with Charles. *He* paid too much attention to eating and drinking. They got on better when they danced together afterwards." She sighed. "This is going to be a bigger problem than we thought," she added.

"Food and drink are unimportant to Julie because she is a quarter English."

"Three-quarters, Michel."

"Whatever it is, we must not waste much money on food. Have *you* any suggestions ?"

Madame shrugged. "Julie was dull perhaps."

Michel frowned. "I thought Jeanne said that her daughter was a ravishing beauty ?"

"Julie could be."

"Charles is not blind or insensitive."

"No, but he is fastidious, and spoiled. He seems always to be surrounded by beautiful women dressed in chic clothes."

"Then he may like a badly-dressed woman for a change."

Madame shuddered delicately. "Julie looked ghastly last night in one of Nina's old dresses. I had hoped she would not be noticed, or that those who saw her face would not bother about the rest of her—just for one night, but everybody observed her."

Michel was silent. Then he asked fretfully, "What made you put a fancy dress on the child?"

"Fancy dress indeed! It was one I borrowed from Nina. One could hardly expect Nina to sacrifice one of her best dresses for mutilation. I told you I would have liked to wait until Julie *had* some clothes, but you would not listen."

This kind of talk would quickly have developed into a quarrel, but Michel felt that there was too much at stake to antagonize his sister.

He said, "Put her in le Gère's hands at once. Spare no expense. Those two must marry. It is my wish, and also the desire of M'sieur and Madame Patrice, that the two families with world interests in the motor trade shall marry, and carry on the businesses under one name. As you know, I have already told you, we are building a popular model which I hope to name the Patrice-Ryan car, in honour of the marriage, sacrificing the name of Pierre to Ryan. It will shortly be advertised, when of course the name must have point."

"You are in a hurry, Michel."

"Not at all. It just happens that there is a model nearly ready and waiting for a name. I am an old man. If and when I die I should not like the business to pass out of active family interest."

Madame understood how he felt. She said, "But supposing what you wish for so much does not happen—even as soon as you expect?"

Michel shrugged, spread out his hands in a futile gesture, and looked dismal.

"Then we shall have to wait for a new invention without a name."

But Madame knew that the reason behind this marriage went deeper than that. She guessed, too, that failure of his plans was not worrying him. Michel had never once failed to carry through a project that he had set his heart upon.

"I shall do my best for all of you, Michel," promised Madame, "*but* you must have patience. Such an important event in any-one's life cannot be arranged in a day. There are so many things to consider."

"Patience is not my strong point," Michel conceded. "Buy anything you want to help Julie." Then he added, "I had a letter from Jeanne this morning. She and her husband are willing to help in any way they can."

Michel glanced at the ormolu clock on the ornate mantelshelf, compared it quickly with his wristwatch which kept perfect time, and rose to his neatly shod feet. "I must go now. We both have a heavy day before us. We understand each other, Louise ?"

"*Certainement !*" said his sister, rising too.

Meanwhile, Julie, unaware that her future was already decided and her husband chosen, slept dreamlessly.

She awoke to find that the curtains had been drawn back, and the room was bathed in the golden haze of a sunny morning. A pleasant-faced girl carrying a tray was standing beside the bed.

For a few moments Julie lay still and at ease, among the soft pillows. Then, realizing that she was in a strange bed in an unfamiliar room, and that the maid smiling down at her was not English, she threw back the sheet and sat up, and took the tray that was offered to her.

"*Bon jour*, Mamzelle," said the maid, settling the tray on Julie's knees.

"*Bon jour*, er——"

"Marie, Mamzelle. *C'est le petit déjeuner.*"

Julie's eyes roved over the tray. There was not much to eat —a croissant and a brioche in a small folded napkin, a pat of golden butter moulded on the top with a flower, and two small metal jugs full of coffee and milk.

Julie smelled the air appreciatively.

"I love coffee, and am I hungry !" she exclaimed laughingly.

She began to eat, and Marie busied herself tidying the room. Julie asked her to open the window, but either Marie did not understand, or she dared not open a window and let in the keen morning air.

Directly Marie had gone Julie got out of bed and opened the windows wide. Putting on a wrap she carried the tray over to the window from which she caught a glimpse of the trees in the Bois, and listened with smiling satisfaction to noises alien to her ears—the sounds of a strange city—and foreign smells ! The atmosphere was light and clear. It made her feel gay.

Julie ate the last flaky crust of croissant with relish. She thought, 'I could eat six of these and not feel full.'

Someone knocked at the door, and in answer to Julie's "*Entrez !*" Madame came in. She was still wearing her housecoat, and Julie thought the light colour of the soft material made her look more human than the dark clothes she had worn yesterday.

They exchanged hurried greetings because Madame suddenly saw the wide-open window and broke off to exclaim in horror.

"Never open a window so early in the morning, my child. You will catch pneumonia !" Madame thought, too, while hurrying to close the window, 'My furniture will be ruined !' English failing her in such a moment of stress, Madame broke into French.

Julie laughed.

"I always sleep with my window half-open at home, and I draw back my curtains," she said.

"Such madness ! The cold night air shall kill you. Promise me never to leave your window open all night. Me, I should not sleep a wink unless my window it was tight shut or my curtains across."

"Doesn't the room get stuffy ?"

"Not at all. I sleep well. Did you not sleep well last night ?"

"I was tired. I don't think I noticed whether the window was open or shut."

"But you are rested today ?"

"Yes, I feel fine."

"That is good, for directly you are dressed we shall go to Madame le Gère, who can dress you from the foundation out. By tonight you shall be a stranger to yourself and a credit to me."

Julie flushed with pleasure. "You are wonderfully kind and generous, grandmère. I have done nothing to deserve such generosity. It embarrasses me a little, too, for I can never hope to repay you."

"Do not try. I do not expect it." And to herself, Madame said, 'I shall be well repaid if you fall in with the plans the family has made for you.'

The bath was rather more of a ceremony than Julie would have wished. She was used to having a bath whenever she liked, and taking a chance whether the water was hot or not. Her mother had warned her that grandmère clung to old-fashioned ways. There was carpet on the floor of the bathroom, and several large warm bath towels were brought from the heated linen room, and stacked over the chromium towel rail. Marie ran the water, throwing in a generous supply of scented liquid from a large round bottle which she took from the cupboard. There was a new cake of highly-scented soap, and a box of talc powder with a perforated inner lid, on the top of which was a rose velvet powder puff.

'This is luxury,' sighed Julie, lying in the scented soft water.

It was while lying thus, body and mind relaxed, that Julie thought of Charles Patrice. In retrospect she thought of last night's dinner, Charles's elegance, and the way he had looked at her—like a prospective buyer might look at a filly. At the time the look had flicked her pride, because it seemed to her that his expression was insolent. Now the remembrance brought laughter.

Julie thought, 'I must have looked a sight—like lamb in mutton's clothing.'

It was nice to think idly about the Frenchman, for she was outside the circle of his friends and would never meet him again. They had so little in common—no, that was wrong. There was dancing: M'sieur Patrice had had a good dancing teacher, and an even better tailor, though he did not give the impression of being a dummy. He was masculine and virile, with a facile charm in his clear, bell-like voice that exercised a kind of magic over people. Julie felt it now, but it gave her no pleasure. Indeed, the sense of inferiority he had managed to make her feel served to rouse her antipathy towards him. It struck her as odd she should feel like this, for usually she liked men of personality and character, and intuitively Julie knew that Charles had both.

Then she laughed again. It was Tante Nina's awful dress, of course, a cast-off that she had liked once and had not thrown away. It was fashionless now, and Julie loathed it, but it was difficult to refuse to wear the dress—which was like an heirloom that is also a 'white elephant.'

Julie was roused by the fact that the water had grown cold. She scolded herself for bothering about what Charles said or thought. As if it mattered! This time next week she would be back in England, and the Paris visit a dream. Presently, while she dried and dressed, Julie's mind dwelt on the clothes grandmère was going to buy her. That could be fun, but Julie knew that to her grandmother choosing clothes was a serious business.

When Julie eventually went downstairs she found her grandmother, dressed to go out, sitting upright on a large chair in the marble-paved hall.

She exclaimed at sight of Julie. "I thought you were never coming."

There was an edge to her voice, and Julie guessed that her grandmother was not used to waiting for anyone or anything.

"I'm so sorry, grandmère."

"So!" Madame glanced at her jewelled wristwatch. "We shall be late for our appointment."

A dark-clad figure disintegrated itself from the shadows of the hall, and opened the doors for them. Julie had seen him the night before. He had poured out the wine. She had seen him directing servants, not obviously, but working in the background during dinner, playing an important part, yet not being one of the principal actors.

She said, *"Bon jour,"* to him with a smile, and he replied ponderously, *"Bon jour,* Mamzelle."

Madame waved her hand between Julie and the man. "This is Matras, who has not only been my butler for forty years, but my right hand as well."

Julie smiled at him more warmly, and Matras opened the doors wider for them to pass out, remarking to Madame that it was going to be a fine day. He went out with them to the car, and waited while the chauffeur settled them in their seats.

Julie was glad to be out of doors, for the atmosphere of the house was heavy.

On the way to the Rue St. Honoré, Madame asked, "Did you enjoy the dinner last night?"

"Oh, I did : everything was exquisite. You give lovely parties, grandmère ! Mummy said you gave wonderful dinners, but she didn't prepare me for anything like last night."

Madame nodded, well pleased. "It is not only the food and wine that go to make a success of a gathering, but the guests themselves. Tell me, how did you like *your* dinner partner ?" She spoke diffidently, as though making polite conversation.

"Oh, he was all right," Julie replied off-handedly.

They were driving along the Champs Elysées, and Julie was looking through the window nearest to her at the panorama of the pavements. People were already sitting under the striped awnings outside the cafés, and white-aproned, black-coated waiters were serving them with coffee and drinks. Under the trees was a miniature fair-ground for children, with a man turning the handle of a roundabout laden with children.

On the top of a large building was scrawled in blue neon lighting, 'The Fountain of Youth.'

"What is that ?" she exclaimed, pointing to the sign.

Madame's eyes followed Julie's direction. "It is a beauty parlour," she said. "But you do not need that." And she thought how fresh and sweet her granddaughter was looking this morning. 'She is lovely,' crossed Madame's mind, and she smiled with secret satisfaction. Then aloud, "That is meant for people like me whose bodies are old, but whose spirit remains young."

Julie looked at her grandmother and smiled gently. "Don't *you* change," she said cryptically. "I like you as you are."

"We must not talk about me, but of you. How did you like Charles ?" Madame smiled kindly.

Julie knitted her forehead. "Charles! M'sieur Patrice? Oh, not much."

That was disagreeable news, but Madame still smiled. "That is damning : to dislike anyone at sight."

"My father is like that. He takes instant likes and dislikes, and I am the same," replied Julie gaily.

Madame looked grim. It was bad enough to show Julie the way she should go, and what was best for her, but to have to fight an unseen Irishman as well was terrible.

"So ! Well, one can be mistaken at times."

"Oh, I know."

"Is it not rather unfair, too ?"

"Perhaps." Julie was entirely indifferent.

"You are wrong to dislike Charles, for he is a good son, kind and attentive to his parents. While you have already observed that he dresses well, has nice manners, and he is a fine dancer. Hostesses like having him at their parties, for he is popular, and——" Madame stopped suddenly for Julie was smiling broadly.

"I am sure M'sieur Patrice is wonderful, grandmère. Perhaps I am lazy or should have stayed at school longer, but it is an effort for me to understand what he says, or indeed to make myself understood to him. Unfortunately, this trip there won't be time to learn."

"That depends how long your trip lasts, Julie," said Madame slowly.

"Just a short holiday over Easter, and perhaps a few days afterwards."

"I hope it shall be longer than that. But I shall try to bear it in mind when we order your clothes that you are returning soon to England. If you were here for months I would suggest French lessons for you. There is nothing like living with a French family to learn the language quickly."

Julie nodded in agreement.

"What is this huge square—or is it a square ?" she asked.

Madame looked vaguely about her. It was as though she saw Paris for the first time.

"It is the Place de la Concorde—surely—but no, how could you—what you need is a guide, someone with the time and will to show you our sights. I have seen them for so long that they have ceased to be city treasures."

Then she was silent again, and remained quiet until they reached the great house that was Madame le Gère's dressmaking 'salon.'

A commissionaire in a grey and gold uniform stood on the pavement outside the wide doors of the house.

Julie had thought of new clothes in terms of one—a street dress, and perhaps an evening dress with accessories. Those would have made a worthwhile present for which she would have been grateful. But it was soon evident that a couple of dresses would satisfy neither Madame's nor the great dressmaker's idea.

They had been conducted with *empressement* to a beautiful salon on the first floor, where the colour scheme was a soothing dove grey and the walls panelled entirely with gilt-framed mirrors. Peach-coloured nylon curtains covered the long windows. The frames were hung with dark magenta and grey curtains of Lyons brocade, edged with heavy fringes, which were also on the deep pelmets at the top. The air was heavy with cloying perfume, which was pleasant and exciting to Julie's English senses. Even the spending of money in this tranquil atmosphere seemed deceptively easy.

After some preliminary talk, during which Madame le Gère studied Julie closely from every angle, an assistant was called who measured Julie and made copious notes in a large black book. She went and another assistant came in. It was flattering the attention they paid to the English girl.

Then Madame and Julie sat on a large settee, while an endless procession of models teetered tonelessly across the salon, coming in at one door with a sinister swaying of narrow hips, passing in front of Madame le Gère's critical eyes, and going out at the opposite door. Young men with small moustaches brought in bales of soft-toned silks and velvets. Even furs were modelled, though the season for their need was surely ended.

Julie gazed spellbound, but through her admiration ran a big silent question. What had she, Julie Ryan, to do with all these lovely clothes? She could not wear them. She was not staying long enough in Paris, while they would look absurd at the places she frequented in London. Mostly with Harvey, she had gone to snack bars and medium-priced restaurants. It took an anniversary celebration to make them dine at a place where evening dress was obligatory. As for the furs! Julie sighed inwardly. They would have to remain on the dream list of luxury wants. Furs like these meant a car, and her father only possessed an old saloon which he drove himself, and reserved mostly for country jaunts with her mother.

Madame Lubin noted the cut and texture of every model she saw. She discussed clothes with Madame le Gère with knowledge. The two women argued unsmilingly, and it was clear that whether

25

Madame Lubin gave a big order for clothes today or not, she had been a valued customer in the past.

At first Julie was amused and interested, though she sometimes lost the drift of their remarks, for they talked rapidly in French. Then, having exhausted her stock of ecstatic exclamations as each dress was displayed, Julie relaxed in silence. Presumably, presently, she would be invited to make her choice.

At last the Mesdames seemed to come to some sort of agreement, and Julie was taken to a little room, carpeted in grey, and with the heating on, where foundation garments were brought for her to try on, dreams of peach-coloured satin, lace and fine elastic.

Then a fitter came, and kneeling beside Julie took in gussets and pinned seams closer.

Madame le Gère, a plump woman, came in majestically and offered some suggestions, but she took no more notice of Julie than if she were a dummy.

A little black dress was brought in and tried on. It was simply cut and had so much white drill piping on it that it did not look dark, but chic and youthful-looking. With it went a small hat that depended for its success on the angle at which it was worn.

Julie was asked if she liked herself. The fitters told her the effect was ravishing, then quickly removed the dress for minor alterations. By this time Julie was half-fainting with heat, and saw herself through a haze which blurred her outline. She created consternation by asking to have the window open.

"You will catch cold, Mamzelle," they told her. She knew they would shrug their shoulders after she had gone, and she would go down in workroom history as the mad English girl. They referred the matter to Madame Lubin, who took one look at Julie, and seeing that she really did feel the heat, suggested lunch.

"Obviously, *chérie*, you have high blood pressure, and must see a doctor," she decided.

"I am in perfect health, grandmère ; all I need is air."

"We shall walk to a quiet restaurant close by, where my friends do not lunch. I do not wish them to see you until you are dressed in your new clothes. I must be proud of you, Julie, and first impressions count for so much." And to Madame le Gère, "Dear friend, we shall soon be back."

Julie's heart sank when she heard this. It was not in her mind to spend the whole of her holiday in a famous dressmaker's salon. These people were making too much fuss over her clothes.

26

On the way down in the lift Julie asked, "Must we go back again today, grandmère ?"

Madame Lubin was astonished. "Go back !" she reiterated. "Of a certainty we go back. You do mean 'go back' ?"

Julie nodded, and Madame demanded,

"Do you not like clothes ?"

"I love them, but must it take a whole day to buy all I want ?"

Madame cried, "It would take weeks for me to get what you need. Do you not realize that you have no wardrobe at all, not even the beginning of one ? It is necessary that a girl should look well at all times, but no one seems to have thought of that for you. I am desolate when I think how your mother must have changed, for she had a dress sense when she left France. She *has* neglected you. How does one expect a girl ever to marry well, if one does not present her nicely to her future husband ?"

"Mummy does her best," defended Julie. "But my father is poor, and——"

"So it is want of money ! I might have guessed. You must blame your mother for that. She was wilful, and *would* marry him. I pointed out the mistake she was making *before* she married, but she would not listen. Now we see the result—a daughter without a *dot*."

Julie listened in silence. The fact that she had no *dot* made no impression on her. She was thankful to be in the street where the air revived her drooping spirits.

They walked to the restaurant, which was quiet but exclusive. The service was excellent, and the food and wine of that exquisite quality to which Madame was accustomed.

The maître d'hôtel, the head and wine waiters, the ordinary waiter and two *commis* seemed to hang around Madame, while she chose carefully from the menu, with discernment and taste. Julie was impressed by their manner. It gave her a new respect for Madame. They glanced discreetly, approvingly and with admiration at Julie.

Grandmère ordered champagne, and Julie felt better. No longer did she feel depressed, but gay and excited. The prospect of trying on dresses and the endless discussion that seemed to be a part of the buying alarmed her no longer. It was fun. She was to be envied. She talked vivaciously to grandmère who looked at her with interest.

After lunch Julie returned rather unwillingly to Madame le Gère's. It was not that she had no interest in her new clothes, but it was tiring to have to stand while someone snipped and pinned at a length of white cotton material which was draped

27

and re-draped about her figure; and listen to the endless arguments carried on in rapid French which, try as she would, Julie could not follow. Also, as the afternoon wore away, there was increasing discomfort from the heat. The elation of spirit, which had made her so gay and sparkling, and was called forth by the champagne, had gone. She felt flat, dispirited and tired.

As grandmère pointed out more than once, "We are curing a lifetime of neglect in one day."

At last they pulled over her head again the little black dress, which Julie had tried on earlier, and grandmère said that she could keep it on, also the hat that was its complement, and the accessories that had been produced, fitted on, and chosen in between the trying on of dresses and shaping of the foundation lining.

Julie had made occasional faint protests at the number and expense of each garment for the wardrobe which grandmère was giving to her, but no one seemed to take much notice of what she said. Perhaps they did not understand her halting French, or thought she was admiring their models. Who knows? They were working against time, for it was nearing the close of their working day, and possibly wished that Madame Lubin would stop arguing and go.

Then Julie, seeing the models, salesgirls, and the ubiquitous young men, who seemed to have shadowed her all day, retire, asked grandmère's permission to go outside and look at the shops in the Rue St. Honoré. It was graciously given, for grandmère was pleased with Julie's appearance. Her eyes followed the girl's figure as she walked out of the salon. She was glad that Julie had gone, for it gave her time for a gossip with her friend. All arrangements had been made over the telephone before Madame le Gère had seen Julie. Now Madame Lubin sat back in her fauteuil and waited to receive the fulsome but truthful praise she knew her friend would give.

CHAPTER III

MEANWHILE Julie, conscious that she looked better than she had ever done, scorned the gilded lift and ran downstairs and out into the street, where fresh air and a sense of freedom gave her a quick recovery. She wandered from one shop window to another, lost in admiration at the beauty, delicacy and taste of the window displays. She was even beginning to say to herself, 'If I had the money I would . . .', and 'Oh, if only someone would die and leave me some money . . .', and laugh ruefully at herself for being so silly, when suddenly she was aware that two gendarmes stood together at the kerb, watching her. At the same time she saw that she herself was the centre of a stir, for several young men seemed to have silently attached themselves to her. She stopped suddenly, and they stopped, too ; then she moved, and so did they.

The gendarmes just looked. It was embarrassing. Such a thing had never happened to Julie before. She held her head high and her cheeks became flushed with anger and mortification. She tried staring stonily into the nearest man's eyes, but met such a glint of admiration in his that her own dropped swiftly in confusion.

Julie turned sharply to retrace her steps, her one desire being to reach Madame le Gère's salon, when she saw a familiar face coming towards her. For a few seconds it remained nameless because of the confusion her unexpected entourage had caused, but she hurried towards the man.

She saw him look at her with quickly awakened interest, and even with a swift side glance of amusement at the young men around her.

Almost at once, as he came closer, Julie recognized Charles Patrice, and smiled.

Charles raised his hat and called out, "Mademoiselle Ryan !"

Seeing this, like a practised Greek chorus the young men fell away—and vanished.

Charles grinned. It gave him acute pleasure to witness their discomfiture. "If I may say so, you look puzzled and outraged. Are you lost ?" he asked.

"No. I am shop-window gazing. I was enjoying myself until . . ." She paused expressively.

"I know," said Charles sympathetically. "It is the penalty of beauty and chic—an irresistible double. Were they annoying you ? Or were they keeping their distance—respectful, admiring and sighing ?"

He took her hand in his, bowed low over it and let it drop. Then he stood back a pace and looked at her in a puzzled kind of way, wondering for a moment what was so different about Julie from last night. He had thought her lovely in the light of the shaded candles. She had intrigued him and he had given her all his attention, until he had discovered that she was beautiful but dumb—or perhaps it was the barrier of language that stood between them, his bad English and her halting French, that made even the simplest sentences sound ugly and stilted? She did not seem so dumb today. There was more expression in her face. She was lovelier than he had thought, a colourful personality, and now—— He said on the spur of the moment, "I didn't know you at first—until you smiled at me. You seem so different."

"I am. Can't you see? Last night I was wearing Tante Nina's dress. Now I am wearing a new one. It is my own."

Julie was pleased as a child with her dress.

Charles's face lit up. He liked the new dress. "Ah, I do see. You look charming, Mademoiselle."

Julie laughed and blushed because there was that in Charles's eyes that confused her a little, and for a moment she lost her new poise. The dress seemed to have given her confidence.

She said, "That is what they told me in there," and she nodded her head towards the ornate doors with their heavy bronze furniture.

Charles followed her gaze. "So! Is Madame Lubin inside?"

"Yes, we have been there all day buying a wardrobe for me."

"That is most interesting."

"It was, but oh, the atmosphere!" Julie breathed deeply.

"It would be heavily scented," remarked Charles with some understanding.

"Worse—the scent has gone stale."

"What heresy! You must never say that."

"Only to you."

That was charming of her. It implied the confidence of friendship.

"I will keep it a secret."

Julie went on, "Grandmère in her house, and Madame le Gère in her salon, are determined to shut out fresh air on the pretence of keeping out draughts and preventing colds. It makes me feel stupid and faint."

"And you, being oh, so English, like the fresh air. Is it not so?" Charles remarked quizzingly.

Julie retorted boldly, "Don't you?"

"I am a renegade Frenchman, for I sleep all night with my windows thrown open. My parents despair of me. They are so sure I shall die young of pneumonia."

"You don't look a bit delicate."

They both laughed. Then Charles said quickly, "If Madame Lubin is gossiping with her friend, she will be there for at least half an hour. Shall we take tea together in a *confiserie*? It will do you good."

"That will be lovely," Julie sighed thankfully.

Charles seemed more approachable this afternoon. His manner was not so formal as it had been last night. He looked younger, too, and Julie had discovered that he liked fresh air and could sympathize with her for being shut up in a hothouse.

"There is a good one close by."

Julie turned to walk with him, and they went down a turning into the Rue de Rivoli.

Even with an escort many people turned their heads to stare at Julie. Charles was well aware of the admiration she was attracting. He felt proud and pleased. He knew that men envied him his companion. It made him more attentive to Julie.

The atmosphere of his world was suddenly sweet, and everything combined to make life right and agreeable.

The little round tables with their spindly legs in the *confiserie* were crowded, but influenced by Charles's commanding personality, one was brought out and laid with a fresh cloth. The two were by that time the cynosure of all eyes.

When they sat down Charles asked, "Would you prefer chocolate?"

"I should love it."

"With cream?"

"Oh, yes, please."

Charles ordered two chocolates with plenty of cream. While this was being prepared he took Julie to the counter, provided her with a plate and fork, and helped her to choose some cakes.

"You must have one of these 'Mont Blancs.' This place is famous for them," he advised. For her second cake Julie chose the plainer 'palmier.' Charles chose a couple of 'Baba au rhums' for himself. They returned to their table, which was so small and intimate they were obliged to sit close to each other.

Then followed a delightful half-hour for Julie. Never had she enjoyed so much attention as Charles gave her. She told herself that only a Frenchman, with his instinctive knowledge of woman, knew how to flatter and make her feel pleased with herself. 'If I were a queen, he couldn't be nicer,' she thought. Harvey could be kind and nice, too, and when his temper was not ruffled he was a good companion. They had had some lovely times together —fun, he called it; but Harvey at his best was not so good as

Charles's worst. After the months with Harvey and his unreliable temper, when he was apt to shower horrible home-truths on her head, it was a relief to sun herself in any man's admiring glances.

"I cannot ask if you like Paris," said Charles. "You have seen so little of it."

"There will be no chance of sightseeing this trip," Julie told him. "Grandmère is in a shopping mood. She is convinced that I came across in rags and she is trying to dress me properly to go back."

"Already you are speaking of going back?"

"I only came for a week."

"But that is absurd. One week in Paris is a waste of time. Now that you are here you must stay for months."

"With grandmère leading me around I shall never see Paris. She appears to think that not only do I need new clothes, but a guide to show me around Paris, and French lessons from an expert," Julie told him laughingly, with a gaiety of spirit Charles had not dreamed she possessed, and which he found intriguing.

"To do all that you must change your mind and stay for a long time."

Julie shook her head.

"Why must you hurry back?"

Julie did not reply because confronted with such a question there was no answer.

"Perhaps there is a fiancé in England?" Charles asked, and was surprised to find that his nerves were tensed while waiting for her answer. It was a relief when Julie said, "No—not now."

"There was once?"

"Yes."

"I see. Have you any regrets?"

It struck Charles that he had asked a pertinent question which Julie might refuse to answer.

Instead she sighed, looked remarkably young, childish and innocent, and said, "Not one."

"That's good," Charles said.

He was disconcerted when Julie said crisply, "Why?"

"Why?" It was his turn to look stupid. "Because it is not fun to talk to a girl whose mind may be politely with her, but whose heart is elsewhere."

That was an involved statement, and to make himself clear Charles spoke half in French and half in English. Julie translated freely, and so amusingly that he was forced to laugh at himself.

"Oh, well, I make you laugh," he said. "It is better to laugh, is it not so? But it points one way: you must stay here and improve your French. Don't ask me why again because I shall not tell you this time, even to make you laugh. I have it. You stay and learn French; and while you are here, I will practise my English."

"So what?"

"So what?" Charles repeated.

Julie grinned. "That is just my slang."

"I like it. 'So what!' It is most expressive. What you mean is . . ."

"Where do we go from there?"

Charles looked puzzled. "I do not understand. You go too fast for me." Then he said in different tone, "Then it is settled that you stay a long time."

"Oh, I can't."

"Why not? Is there a job waiting for you?"

"Not *waiting*, but I hope to land one."

"You only hope. Well, stay here."

The 'Mont Blanc' was melting deliciously in her mouth. Julie could not talk, so she gave him a provocative glance, and was astonished when he answered it seriously, saying in an urgent sort of voice that was quite out of keeping with the subject, "I beg of you . . ."

"Why should you?" she teased. "It is no business of yours."

"It could be."

"How?"

"I could leave my office early, and be your guide around Paris. I could even teach you French."

"You are a busy man."

The retort was so obvious that they both laughed. "Not too busy for you."

Julie had no desire to waste her short holiday learning French, but she said amiably enough, "The effort would bore me; but I am quite willing to help you with your English."

"I should very much like that, but it would not be fair unless we make of it an exchange." It was only afterwards, when thinking over their meeting in retrospect that Julie realized how easy it had been to talk to Charles. There had been inevitable misunderstandings and she had laughed at him. He had taken it all in good part, and had even been amused with his mistakes.

But there were serious moments. One was when Charles said, "It would be stupid for you to see the sights alone. I saw what was happening when I met you. Wherever you go there must be a trail of admirers. You could not enjoy yourself with so many unofficial guides standing on your toes. If I am there no one will bother you."

Charles did not say all this easily. There were pauses when he searched for the right word, or when he lapsed into fluent French which Julie tried in vain to follow. She even spoke in French, when Charles remarked,

"You have an adorable accent, Mademoiselle Ryan." Then he added quickly, "What is your name?"

"Julie."

Charles smiled. "It is romantic, as you are."

"I don't feel a bit romantic."

There was a pause, then Charles said, "You have not asked me my name, but I shall tell it to you just the same. It is Charles. Surely we may call each other by our Christian names. It is so much simpler."

Julie nodded. "I don't mind—Charles."

"Julie!"

It was Julie who remembered Madame Lubin.

"I quite forgot grandmère," she exclaimed, picking up her bag and getting to her feet. "She will have the gendarmes out looking for me ; she will think I have been stolen." She spoke carelessly, in the same light vein that being with Charles called forth.

He grew serious. "That must never happen to you. Please, be careful. It would be a terrible thing if misfortune overtook you. Your family in London would never forgive Madame Lubin."

Charles was a little excited. Julie's looks, her gay manner and amusing talk, even the way she laughed at his mistakes, had aroused his emotions, so that he felt moved and tense, his nerves not quite under control.

So they returned to the Rue St. Honoré, and Charles cupped her elbow in his palm while crossing the road, a gesture that made Julie smile wisely to herself. She was elated and triumphant, too, because last night she had failed to rouse Charles's interest. Today everything was suddenly different. She was a success.

There was no sign of Madame waiting impatiently for Julie's appearance. Charles asked Madame's chauffeur, who was gossiping idly with the grey-coated commissioner, if Madame were still in the house, and was told that she was.

Julie did not wait with Charles, but bade him 'au revoir,' and ran up the steps and through the door, taking the shallow staircase two steps at a time. There was happiness in her heart because she had talked to Charles, who was so aristocratic-looking, as though he were Harvey, and she knew that what she had said had made him interested in her. It was funny she should feel like that, when less than twenty-four hours ago she had taken an instinctive dislike to him. This time yesterday she had not known of his existence. Now it was Julie and Charles. She was returning to England in a week's time, but both grandmère and Charles had already asked her to stay on.

At the top of the stairs she paused, composed herself, and prepared to make a decorous entrance.

Even as she did so, grandmère came out. The latter paused and looked at Julie, who, no longer bored, appeared to be lively and alert. She decided it was Julie's reaction to the new clothes.

She smiled and said, "I am just coming home, Julie. I have cocktails at six o'clock. You must meet some of your relatives, the most important of whom is Uncle Michel."

Julie turned with her, but this time the attendant was waiting to take them down in the ornate satin-padded lift, which looked more like an old-fashioned sedan chair than a business lift.

Directly they were seated in the car and were driving away, Julie turned impulsively to her grandmother. She stretched out her hand and put it, warm and soft, over Madame's gloved bony hands that were folded together in her lap.

"I haven't thanked you for my lovely dress—in fact for anything that you have bought for me today. I love them all— though as yet, I am not sure what 'all' means," she said softly, and glanced at some cardboard boxes which had been brought out and placed in the seat beside the chauffeur. The old lady's hands trembled, and then she flung off Julie's clinging fingers.

"I do not wish for thanks. Dress means much to a Frenchwoman ; it plays an important part in her life. I blame myself that your dress sense was not cultivated when you were very young. I have bought you but three evening dresses, a day dress, the one you are wearing, a silk cocktail suit and a couple of cottons. That, of course, is but a beginning. As I said this morning, it would take months to provide you with a suitable wardrobe, the kind of clothes thought necessary by every French mother for a grown-up daughter to wear if she hopes to marry her suitably. The old days when families inter-married because it was wise and politic have passed. But there are still dutiful sons who, if they are attracted to a girl, are willing to contract an alliance. . . ."

Julie only half listened to this, but she understood the gist. Grandmère was riding her hobby. She was living on past ideals which old people clung to so pitifully, perhaps because they felt the insecurity of the present.

She said, "A beginning! But, grandmère, even these are too much. We do not live the kind of life in England that you do over here. Our lives are simple compared with the grandeur of yours. I shall never wear the clothes you have given me, lovely as they are. Please, be sensible, and rest content that you have already given me far more than I have ever had before."

Grandmère compressed her lips. "*Ingrate!*" she cried. "You shall have many more clothes."

"Darling grandmère! You are kind and I am grateful, but we must be sensible, too. What should I do with lots of expensive clothes?"

"Why, wear them."

"But where?"

"How do I know where. You wear clothes not only to please yourself but your husband."

"I haven't one," Julie laughed.

"No, you have not. You can laugh now because you are young and beautiful. But it shall not always be so. You want a husband, do you not?"

"Well—yes, I suppose so—some day."

"Some day! It must be soon. And because I try to help you by dressing you in lovely clothes, you tell me to be sensible and not to buy you any more. It is absurd."

"I said I had enough," said Julie firmly, but already a suspicion was forming in her mind that grandmère might have a possible husband in view—perhaps a Frenchman. She said, "You mustn't worry about me so much, grandmère. I am all right."

"Are you? I doubt that. I see that you have so much to learn, our language, a dress sense—why, you do not even know Paris which can teach you so much. It is a tragedy that you have been so neglected. I do not want to ruin your confidence in yourself, but dear child, you are gauche. You have no poise. You walk like an athlete, you——"

Julie put her hands to her ears.

"I won't listen, because if I do I shall run back to England tonight—a failure," she cried.

"You shall not do that. You shall stay here. If I have to beat the knowledge into you, Julie, you must stay in Paris until you speak French well, you wear your clothes with an air, and you do not blush every time anyone speaks to you."

"Then I shall be staying here forever," said Julie, not believing Madame Lubin, but determined to keep her end up with the old lady. To herself she added, not without spirit, 'If you beat me, I shall return it with interest.' But she dared not speak her thoughts aloud for fear of the old lady's temper.

Madame Lubin replied more quietly, "I shall not lose my temper. But you must have confidence in me when I am doing my best for you. Even if you do not like your dresses, and do not wish to accept them from me, please do me the kindness of wearing them without further comment."

"I'm sorry, grandmère !" Julie whispered humbly. She made no further protest. It was impossible to explain how embarrassed she felt. Grandmère either could not or would not understand. The visit, so far, had not been a great success, unless she could call flirting with Charles a success. Anyhow, it would soon be over.

Then Madame recovered, and she said, "When we get in, I shall make you a cup of tea. You will feel better after that."

"It sounds lovely," said Julie, "but please, don't make it especially for me because I've already had some tea."

Madame Lubin turned her head in astonishment to look at Julie. "You have had tea ! Where ?" She spoke slowly and deliberately.

"Yes, while you were in Madame le Gère's salon."

"Where ?"

"I don't know," Julie expressed. "It was somewhere in the Rue de Rivoli."

"Alone ?"

"Oh, worse ! With a man." Julie strove to speak lightly, hoping that her grandmother would see the matter in the same light. But one look at the set face beside her dispelled Julie's airy mood. It looked as though she were to be scolded, for the atmosphere was brittle.

Madame Lubin was alarmed. "I beg of you, Julie, nevaire do such a thing again. If you want tea so early in the afternoon please ask *me* to take you out." Then she asked quickly, hoping by the swiftness of her question to surprise the truth, "What man ?"

Julie laughed. "You've got it wrong," she said. "As a matter of fact it was M'sieur Patrice—Charles."

Madame Lubin gave a little gasp, and Julie, looking at her, saw that the tenseness of a moment ago was gone, and grandmère had relaxed.

"Charles !" the old lady repeated. "Already you know him well enough to call him 'Charles' ?"

"I call all my friends by their Christian names."

"It is a habit—yes ? Where did you meet Charles Patrice ?"

"Just outside the salon—in the street."

"Was it prearranged ? But no, that was impossible. Why did you not tell me at once ?"

"I meant to, but we were so busy talking about clothes. Don't you remember ?"

"I remember well."

Then grandmère was silent, turning the matter over in her mind.

Julie said demurely, "I'm sorry if I did wrong, grandmère. It is the sort of thing I would do in England and not think twice about. I know it is different here."

"Do not be sorry," said Madame graciously. She was recovering her poise which Julie's news had disturbed. "For once you have pleased me much. For a long moment I imagined you having tea with a complete stranger, or even an English friend, perhaps the ex-fiancé. I never thought of Charles. He happens to be the one man in all Paris that I would choose to be your friend."

She felt rather than saw that Julie looked at her quickly. As she did not want to frighten the girl, or to force her emotions in any way at this moment, Madame Lubin explained more calmly, "Charles Patrice is the son of an old friend of our family. In a sense we are business rivals. I have known him since he was born, and I love him." Grandmère did not say, 'Charles is the reason why I have bought you so many new clothes, because I want you to look well in his eyes. I wish for you to attract him strongly so that soon, when his parents suggest certain wishes to him, he shall readily fall in with their plans.' But she thought all that and more.

"Oh ! Then you won't mind if I go sightseeing with Charles ?" ventured Julie.

"Mind !" Madame repeated stupidly. Then she said, "But you must be careful." She saw that her eagerness might be mistaken, and that Julie might guess how much this friendship meant to her and draw back. She thought, too, that if she warned Julie *against* Charles it might spur this girl of spirit to win his friendship. So she went on talking quietly in a reasonable voice, "You are in my care, Julie, and I must remind you that Charles is only human. He has a great reputation with women, though I do not know how true it is. I have never questioned him. I have not the right. He has always been charming and kind to me. But I have never seen Charles among his girl-friends. I cannot judge how he behaves with them, or what he would be like with you."

38

"Don't bother; I can look after myself," Julie assured her.

"That is as I thought when I first saw you."

"Yesterday."

"No, long ago, when you were a baby."

"I must have been a hateful child."

"A child with a personality!" Then suddenly Madame Lubin laughed gleefully, for was not Fate arranging everything better than she could have wished?

Julie was puzzled by her grandmother's manner. She inquired, "Was I so funny?"

"Funny! Oh, yes. But we were talking of Charles. You were asking my permission to go out with him. *Certainement*. You are young. It is only natural that you should wish to see Paris with someone of your own age. Go and enjoy yourself, my Julie."

In the evening Julie met Uncle Michel. He was ponderously solid, took his pleasures heavily and was entirely humourless, so different from her own father, who joked even at breakfast. He looked long and intently at Julie, observing her unusual colouring and admiring the vitality of her expression. He thought, 'This little one, she should go a long way. Charles is a lucky man, luckier than I imagined.' Then, because Julie evidently expected him to say something, he asked, "How do you like Paris?"

"It is marvellous—what I have seen of it, Uncle Michel."

Julie's eyes had not been idle. She had been watching him, too, and thinking how fortunate her mother was to live out of France, right away from her family.

"You will love it, this time next year."

He spoke gruffly and in French. Thinking that she had translated what he said wrongly, Julie asked him to repeat the words. Uncle Michel spoke loudly as to a deaf person.

Then laughingly Julie shook her head. "I shall love it when I go home next week," she told him with assurance. "It is a feminine city."

His brows beetled heavily and his jaw set as though someone had hurt him. Julie guessed that her answer had annoyed him. She did not care, for he had just said something silly.

Madame had overheard, and presently drew her brother aside. "Why are you shouting at Julie? You must not upset her or you will ruin everything."

"I only said——"

"I heard you, and it was foolish."

"You go too slow. I had to make a start, especially as the girl has got it into her head that she is going home this week."

"That may yet happen," said Madame Lubin calmly, "but

39

she will come back. Do not interfere with our plans, and all will be well."

Michel shrugged his ample shoulders. "One must help Fate."

"Fate is helping us," Louise remarked smilingly, so that some of the gloom was lifted from his face.

"How ?"

Madame told him what had happened, and Michel looked happier, rubbing the palms of his hands together, showing that he was pleased. "So ! It goes well. She is a lovely child. That should please our fastidious friend."

"Everyone has congratulated me on her appearance. Madame le Gère was enchanted. Julie is so young and fresh—so different."

"You bought beautiful clothes, I hope ?" Michel had confidence in his sister's mature taste.

"Everything a girl could wish for—only a beginning you understand, but it took us all day."

"*That* put Julie in a good mood."

"You are wrong, Michel. Julie was *not* pleased. Do not look so astonished. It is not surprising, for the child has no dress sense, and was merely embarrassed by my gifts. She sees no reason for clothes which she cannot wear in England and will have little time to enjoy here. At present, Julie has made up her mind that she goes home in *one* week."

Michel thrust out his jaw. This was evident by the way his 'imperial' quivered.

"That is a stupidity I find it difficult to forgive in a woman."

"But it is delightful in Julie. So many girls take as their right—Julie is grateful, but full of an embarrassment. She has had so few gifts in her life."

"You are taking her part. You like her."

Madame paused before she replied quietly, "Yes, so much that I wish I had known her before. It was senseless of me to keep up a quarrel with Jeanne simply because she had married the wrong man, against my wishes. I have missed much over the years. Now I want to keep Julie in Paris, not so much for Charles's sake, but for my own. This morning she came downstairs singing. Julie has not much of a voice, but it is sweet and flute-like. I could have imagined a bird was in the house. She seems to have brought a new life into this old home, for even the servants appear to feel it and already are happier. I knew, directly I heard Julie's voice, that it was Spring."

Michel stared at his sister. For one moment he thought she had drunk too many cocktails, but he knew that was impossible. She was not that sort of woman. While surely only several drinks would cause her to show what was in a heart that had been locked against life for years.

He said, "I have never heard you speak like that before. It sounds unbelievable."

"Perhaps I have not felt like it. Neither of my children ever aroused such foolish emotion in me. It may be a sign that I am really old."

CHAPTER IV

JULIE was wearing the silk cocktail dress at the party. It was grey, and the cut so simple it showed every line of her slim figure. It would have dismayed her to know how many francs the dress had cost.

Julie came down late because she had spent much time admiring herself before the long glass in her room. Also, grandmère had arranged for two of the cousins, André and Hubert, to take Julie, with Nina as chaperon, to the Comédie Française that evening. They were to dine first at Chez Blenheim, one of the most exclusive restaurants in Paris, which was having a vogue among the young set. After the theatre Julie was to visit a night club, to see something of the night life of Paris.

Julie was excited at the prospect, especially as grandmère had told her to wear the evening dress they had brought home with them that afternoon. It was a dream of cream corded silk trimmed with sprays of diamanté lilies that glittered and sparkled with each movement. The dress was spread across the bed, and Julie had stroked its rich folds, aware of a sensuous pleasure as her fingers contacted the soft material. There were sandals, too, consisting of a sole, heel and nylon straps, and the thinnest of silk stockings. Nina had brought in a fur cape for Julie to wear. It lay on the bed curled to look like a white rabbit.

When the visitors crowded in the great painted and gold salon saw Julie standing in the open doors, a sudden silence fell over the room. Everybody turned to look at Julie, who made an unforgettable picture with her glorious golden hair and haunting grey-blue eyes set in dark lashes, hesitating shyly when she found so many people staring at her. Some women, in their envy, thought that Julie was deliberately late, to make an entry. But from the men, after that first silence, there were exclamations of surprise and delight. It was not only Julie's looks but her clothes. Was this the little English girl they had heard about who looked, in her simple dress, more French than the French ? With her dramatic hair and the dark fringes of her eyelashes which looked more artificial than real, she might have been a comedy actress. It was intriguing. They called her 'Ravissante !' among themselves.

Grandmère went forward, took Julie's hand and drew her into the room, introducing her to everyone, saying simply, "This is Julie. The party is for her because I want you all to know my granddaughter."

Most of the guests were young and near Julie's age. The men surrounded her, claiming Julie as their cousin, when it was their privilege to have first right of friendship. By that time Julie was exultant with success, and remarked laughingly, "I had no idea mine was such a large family. Half of Paris seems to be here."

She spoke in English which happily most of them understood, while many had visited England. Julie was quickly the popular centre of a crowd of young men who made no pretence of hiding their admiration.

Everyone was asking, "Where have you been hiding ? Why haven't we met before ?"

Someone thrust a small glass of amber liquid into Julie's hand.

Charles was not at the party. He had been invited, but to Madame's chagrin had refused, pleading a previous date. That had not worried Charles until this afternoon, when he had seen and talked to Julie. He had tried to cry off the engagement, but it was too late.

Julie did not give Charles a thought until one of her numerous cousins, André, said he would like to show her the sights of Paris. Then Julie recalled Charles. He had made no definite arrangements. Perhaps he would give her a ring and name the day. She did not turn down the cousin's invitation. She said vaguely, "I will let you know in the morning."

They called Julie by her name, but there were so many of them she could not place them individually. She only knew that she had never talked and laughed so much in her life before to such friendly people. She had never been made such a fuss of by men whose motto seemed to be 'Gaiety is the Watchword !'

Julie knew that her first appearance in the family was a success, for grandmère joined in the laughter that seemed to break out at any and every opportunity, while Uncle Michel, who looked dour enough to be anybody's killjoy, seemed to have softened too. He stood on the fringe of the enchanted circle that was about Julie, and though he did not understand all that they said in a mixture of English and French, he could see Julie, sparkling and brilliant as a jewel in the centre of an admiring throng. When she laughed, which was often, youthfully and whole-heartedly, he laughed, too.

The restaurant was warm and softly lighted. Everything was muted, from the shaded lights to the service, even the music played as a sort of backcloth to the gay voices and laughter of the youthful clientèle.

André insisted that they must not rush in. He was emotional without experience. He had just finished college, and was at loggerheads with his family. His parents wished him to join his father's automobile business, but André, a lover of beauty and nature, longed to be an artist. The battle was still on. In the meantime, with funds provided by his doting mother, André, while making up his mind to fall in with his father's wishes, was enjoying himself.

"Why must we go slowly?" inquired Tante Nina.

André stared at her in pained amazement. "Tante Nina, have you forgotten that Julie, our English cousin, is with us looking *ravissante* in this exquisite dress? Naturally I want all our friends to see her."

"Are you thinking of Julie or yourself?" Nina asked drily. "You are wanting your friends to envy you."

"*Naturellement*. I wish you to stand talking to the maître d'hôtel, while I, with Julie beside me, look around the room. I shall be thinking, 'Look, boys! See whom I am with?' It will be a sensation."

Nina tossed her head. "Only a very young man would think of such nonsense. I shall not do as you wish. I am hungry, and I think Julie is, too."

"Are you, Julie?" André was crestfallen.

"I am rather."

He clapped his hand theatrically to his forehead. "I have been thinking of you in terms of nectar and crumbs, and you tell me that you are hungry. How mundane! How earthy!"

Julie laughed. André amused her by showing off for her benefit.

Though Nina led the way into the restaurant, and partly obscured people's view of Julie, the latter, in her beautiful dress, stole the show. Within minutes of her arrival everybody was asking who Julie was. Even André, deprived of the shock entrance he had planned, was youthfully pleased.

Between them, pretending to consult Nina and Julie, but actually guided by their own tastes, André and Hubert ordered a young, silly, gay sort of dinner beginning with iced cantaloup, Lobster Newburg, then chicken Perigord, and ending with an ice. They drank champagne.

"Will you like that?" Hubert asked. He was at the Foreign Office and spoke English well.

"It sounds lovely."

The choice seemed to suit the three young people, though it was too 'partified' for Nina, who, at her age, preferred a more solid meal.

Though she did not complain, secretly Nina found fault with the food, but Julie said it was delicious.

As Nina thought, 'Poor Julie does not know any better.' That was true; also the atmosphere of luxury about her appealed to Julie, so that everything seemed right this evening and nothing wrong—except perhaps Tante Nina's occasional sour pricks.

Once Nina remarked sourly, "You laugh easily, Julie. I do not see that there is so much to laugh at."

"Julie laughs because she is happy," said Hubert, who appeared to be so fascinated by Julie that he could not tear his eyes away from her, and ate little. The girl was like a magnet to the susceptible Frenchman.

They did not linger over dinner, but drank their coffee quickly and were impatient to be off. Only Nina felt hurried, cheated out of that extra ten minutes she needed after a meal to keep her digestion quiet. But tonight, she, too, was forced to rush. It made her disagreeable suddenly and angry.

"Are you really happy, Julie?" inquired Nina pointedly, when they were titivating in the powder-room after dinner.

"Of course, who wouldn't be tonight?" But Julie thought the question strange. It roused a small maggot of worry at the back of her mind. What it was she did not know, unless it had been called to life by Nina's sour, disapproving expression.

"Because of André and Hubert?"

"Everything. They are so nice to me. Perhaps it is my dress. Frenchmen seem to notice how a woman dresses. They are not afraid to say if it is nice. They give one confidence."

"You seem to have forgotten what happened in England so quickly."

"What?" Julie wondered what Nina was driving at.

"I thought, Maman certainly told me, that you were grieving for your ex-fiancé ; but you do not seem to mind."

Julie shook her head smilingly. "I do not mind. Why should I ? All that is in the past. I wonder what made grandmère think I was upset ?"

Nina looked puzzled too. She thought, 'Maman only said that to arouse my pity for Julie.' And aloud she said, "Maman has a plan for your future."

"Has she ?" said Julie lightly. "So many people have."

Nina thought, 'Maman is hoping to marry J. to C. Perhaps Julie knows this and will not say. Something is going on that I do not know.' It made her feel unfriendly towards Julie.

She was quiet, too, in the taxi on the way to the Comédie Française, and sat back while the others talked gaily to one another.

The theatre was crowded, for the celebrated actress Charmian was appearing in a good farce. André tipped the woman who showed them to their seats. He tipped the attendant who took away their coats. He tipped the programme seller.

Julie's eyes widened, and she asked Nina, "Do you have to tip ? It makes such an expensive evening."

Nina told her, "It is the custom. The tip is small, but a few sous."

Hubert and André sat on either side of Julie, explaining what was going on. There was the usual bedroom scene which the French always do so exquisitely, and Julie was entranced. It was not only what was happening on the stage which mattered, but Julie had the feeling that the audience counted as much as those they had come to watch.

During the acts it was a delight to listen to the flexible accents of Charmian, Lucienne Jeanson's understudy, who acted so magnificently, and who seemed to have so many entrancing feminine tricks at her fingertips. But between the acts Julie found pleasure in looking at the audience, the women so beautifully dressed, so much more distinguished-looking than their escorts.

After the theatre came the high spot of the evening, the worldly elegance of a smart night club. Julie had been to them in London, but here it was like learning the world all over again. Hubert and André vied with each other in pointing out the celebrities who filled it. Their reason for coming to this one was that they liked the band, which worked hard to amuse them, and seemed hypnotized by the personality of the band leader, Sulka Knizburg, an Austrian. He was a colourful man, with red hair which was crew cut, revealing his prominent forehead, white skin and burning eyes.

Suddenly Nina, who had been silent for a while, put a detaining hand on Julie's forearm, and asked in a loud whisper, "How well do you know Charles Patrice?"

Julie's eyes mirrored her surprise at the question. "I only met him yesterday."

"Do you like him?"

"I think so—yes—why?"

"Because he is sitting at a table on the edge of the dance-floor."

"Oh!" Julie looked about her. "Where?"

"There."

By this time André had caught the drift of these remarks and said, "Charles is having supper with Lucienne Jeanson."

Julie had already spotted Charles and his companion and stared in silence.

"Who is she?"

André explained, "An actress, considered to be the best-dressed one in Paris."

Julie thought that was not surprising for Lucienne was elegantly dressed, and undeniably attractive in a fierce dark way with lovely raven-dark hair and clear pale skin like a magnolia petal. She had pretty hands, too, for she was gesticulating to emphasize what she was saying to Charles. Julie felt gauche, even in the new dress which everyone had praised and which gave her so much confidence. Lucienne's magnetic personality put all other women's attractions in the shade.

It was something of a shock, too, to see Charles, who was in full evening dress, with a white tie and waistcoat, looking sleek and elegant, talking animatedly with Lucienne. Julie had not expected to see him. He had been out of her mind. It was obvious that the couple were on terms of easy friendship. Julie knew now why Charles had made no new appointment with herself. His thoughts were occupied elsewhere. So that was the maggot, not Nina at all, but the fact that Charles had forgotten her for a while. Why not? Why shouldn't he? But Julie had felt so sure that he was interested in her. It was a shock to find that Charles's interest was but a passing one.

Julie stared at the back of Lucienne's neat head and wondered what her face was like. She saw Charles's head bent towards Lucienne. There was something intimate in the gesture, and Julie said hollowly, unable to keep the disappointment out of her voice, "They are great friends."

"She is his best friend—for the moment," Nina told her. "Charles is not constant in his friendships."

There was something in her aunt's voice which made Julie turn to look at her. She guessed by the way Nina was watching her that there was a definite meaning in her remark. Carefully Julie made her face a blank.

"Why do you say that ?" she inquired.

"It was but a passing thought."

André ordered a light supper, a cup of iced consommé, a veal cutlet and a dish of *petite pois*, and a variation of the ice-cream they had eaten at dinner.

While they ate Sulka's band played, the maestro himself leading the violins. While eating and listening to the music which André told her was the latest thing called 'Rhapsody by Moonlight,' a part of Julie's mind was busy turning over what Nina had said about Charles. It surprised her to hear that Charles was fickle.

Suddenly, without warning, Sulka, still playing his violin, came down from the platform and threaded his way among the tables. There was purpose in his progress, and many heads were turned to watch and speculate where he would stop. He paused before Julie, and bending towards her, looking soulfully into her eyes, he continued playing his voluptuous music. Everyone turned in their seats to look at Julie, who sat, embarrassed and flushed, bathed in the beam of a gleaming arc light.

Julie looked at Sulka and smiled uncertainly. Her glance fell away from his glowing eyes, and she found herself looking into the enormous, flashing dark eyes of the actress, Lucienne, who was Charles's partner. She did not see Charles.

Breathlessly, involuntarily, Julie cried in English, "She is lovely."

Sulka paused in his playing. "Say that again, Mademoiselle ?" he whispered.

"I only remarked on Mademoiselle Jeanson's eyes," Julie replied.

"Ah ! Mademoiselle Lucienne Jeanson is of an unbelievable enchantment. I have often noticed it. But what man in his senses looks to Autumn when Spring with its youth and freshness is here ?"

Julie stared stonily at him, but Sulka, known for his bold

47

and pertinent remarks, only laughed and went on playing. For some reason he did not finish his sweet music, but paused and gave a signal to his band, and presently he led them in a wild tarantella. Sulka bowed while he played to Julie, and she smiled her thanks. He moved away.

André, bubbling with a new enthusiasm for her, asked, "What did Sulka say to you?"

"Oh, nothing much."

"Julie would not know," said Hubert.

Julie did not mention that Sulka had spoken in English.

"That was a great honour for you, Julie," André told her. "Sulka seldom leaves the dais to play to clients."

"It is a new face. Sulka has a weakness for blondes. He is so dark himself," Nina told them.

The band now swung into a one-step, and André asked Julie to dance with him. He was not a good dancer, but liked showing off. Julie soon found that he was a menace, for he had no idea where he was going, and it was a strain upon her. André had to give so much attention to his footwork that they made erratic progress, and often people scowled at them.

Though Julie did not actually look at Charles, she was acutely conscious that he was watching her. She could have looked at him and smiled a greeting, but something within Julie would not allow her to be friendly. It was only long afterwards that Julie recognized the feeling as jealousy. If Charles had been with any other woman it would not have mattered so much, but his companion was elegant and sophisticated, one who not only had lovely clothes but who knew how to wear them. That was an importance which Julie, up to now, had not fully appreciated.

She pretended to give all her attention to André, who danced with zest, chattered while he danced, and said that he was bursting with pride, the envy of every man in the room.

"I can't believe that," smiled Julie.

"It is true. Everyone is watching us. You are beautiful. Your dress, it is beautiful, too. And you dance so well. Together, it is perfect."

André was in high spirits. He, at any rate, knew the full meaning of his success. In response to his mood, but also because Julie wanted Charles to know that she was enjoying herself, Julie acted with a gaiety and abandon, which gave her an added brilliance, but which shocked Nina.

Once, unable to control her gaze in passing, Julie's eyes met

48

Charles's for one bare moment. She appeared not to know him, for her glance slid away indifferently. She was quickly laughing at one of André's apt remarks.

When she returned to her table, Julie thought, 'Now I have offended Charles.' It should have caused her some elation, but instead she felt flat.

The dance was a long one, and at the end Julie was glad to sit down.

Hubert had risen at her approach to the table, and said hopefully, "It is my turn next."

Julie refused laughingly. "Let me rest for a moment," she cried. "This is my first day in Paris—and what a day!"

André glanced quickly about him. He saw that many of his friends were gazing eagerly at Julie, and that it was only a question of time when they would approach him for an introduction and perhaps take Julie away from him. He said, "You may dance with Hubert, for you are *our* guest, but you must not dance with anyone else."

The arrangement was agreeable to Julie. "All right." But she looked ruefully at the soiled straps of her shoes, and decided that she would not be in a hurry to repeat the evening with such a poor dancer.

As André had thought, their table was soon surrounded by his friends. They begged Julie for a dance, but she refused them all.

Then, presently, Julie heard Charles's voice, mellifluent and deep, and knew by the swift beating of her heart that she had been waiting to hear it. With Charles's coming the youthful, lighthearted men around Julie seemed to melt away.

"Hello, Julie!"

"Oh, hello!"

"I have been watching your success."

"Do you call it success?"

"Oh yes—the dress, Sulka's distinction, which has made every woman in the room envious of you—your dancing. You will see your name in the social columns tomorrow."

He left her to take Nina's hand and bend over it in courtly fashion. They chatted for a few moments, then Charles turned again to Julie.

"I have been meaning to give you a ring," he told her, "but I have been too busy."

André grinned. "So we see," he remarked pointedly.

Charles scarcely noticed the young man. He said to Julie, "May I call for you tomorrow morning at ten o'clock?"

Hubert's jaw dropped. "Are you not going to business?" he inquired.

"I am taking a holiday," was the calm answer.

"You are always taking holidays."

"Am I? But you cannot say I neglect my work. Tomorrow, it is going to be a special holiday. I want to show Julie the sights of Paris."

"*We* can do that," said André, and glanced at Hubert.

"Perhaps."

It was Julie who refused regretfully, saying, "I am so sorry that I cannot go with you, but I have already promised André."

The latter looked surprised and pleased, and said swiftly, "I asked Julie at dinner."

Charles still smiled, but his expression was a little fixed. "I had invited her earlier."

"Only vaguely, Charles. We arranged nothing definitely," said Julie.

"That was impossible for me to do at once because I had to cancel dates and rearrange business interviews." Then with a hint of reproach in his voice Charles added, "You might have waited a little, Julie."

She shook her head, smiling up at him. "I thought you were just being polite."

"I hope I was, but I certainly meant what I said this afternoon. However, let André take you around."

"But——" Julie was beginning, wishing that she had not turned Charles's offer down, and feeling disappointed, when Charles cut in.

"Please, there is nothing more to say."

"Nothing."

"I hope you will have an enjoyable time."

"Thank you."

When Charles had gone the party fell flat, and though the boys tried hard to whip up Julie's enthusiasm again, they failed. Presently, she admitted feeling tired, and suggested that she would like to go home.

She sat silent in the taxi while the boys wrangled between themselves as to which one should take Julie out next day. It was decided that as Hubert was working for an examination, André should go with Julie.

CHAPTER V

Nina must have repeated in detail to Madame all that had happened during the evening, for the old lady came into Julie's bedroom later in the morning, while the latter was eating her *petit déjeuner*. Seating herself upright on the hardest chair in the room, Madame, after polite preliminaries, asked, "How did you enjoy yourself last night, Julie?"

"It was a wonderful evening, grandmère."

Julie poured herself out a second cup of coffee, and Madame Lubin said quickly, "That is luke-warm. Ring the bell for some hot coffee."

It had not occurred to Julie to do that, and she giggled.

"Have I said anything so funny?" was the stiff remark.

"Oh, no, grandmère. I was just thinking that at home if I wanted any coffee at all I should have to get it myself or go without."

"We do things better here. Life is easier for women. Ring the bell, Julie."

The girl did as she was told, and when Marie answered it, Madame ordered more coffee, very hot and at once.

While waiting for the coffee Madame said abruptly to Julie, "I hear that Charles was at the night club, too."

"Yes."

"And that he had arranged to stay away from business to take you out today?"

Julie nodded.

"You refused to go with him."

"Did Nina tell you?"

"Yes. It is the truth?"

"I suppose so."

"Do you really prefer to go with that boy, André?" Madame asked curiously.

"Well—he is easy."

"Too easy! He is not worthy of you. André should be working."

Julie looked at her grandmother helplessly. "If I had known you disapproved I should have refused, but it is too late now."

"Oh no; it is not too late. Already I have talked on the telephone to André's father, and he has told his son to stop playing the fool and go to business."

Julie flushed. "You should not have done that, grandmère," she said coldly.

"Why not? We are not in England. In France the parents have much to say how their children shall work or play."

Julie did not answer. She was too angry to pick the words to make her grandmother understand how she felt about such interference. While she was wondering how quickly she could write to her father and receive an answer telling him that she would be leaving Paris immediately because she did not like the Lubin family, the coffee arrived, and afterwards the old lady said,

"As soon as you are dressed, Julie, I shall be glad if you will come down to the library where a noted professor is waiting to give you a French lesson."

Julie opened her lips to say that there was no point in taking such a lesson as she would not be staying in France long enough to make it worth while, when she saw the determination in her grandmother's face, and closed her lips with a snap. There was a glint of battle in the old lady's eyes, and without being downright rude Julie knew that it would be impossible to make her understand.

'But I shall not learn one word,' Julie decided to herself. 'It will be waste of money.' At the same time she was aware that money did not count for so much with grandmère as it did with her.

She did not reply, and the old lady said "Good," and seemed well pleased. She went on amiably, "When the lesson is over, Charles Patrice will call for you——"

"He will *not* call, for I have already turned down his invitation."

"Poof! That was no answer. I have also spoken to Charles this morning, and explained that you did not understand."

"You interfered, grandmère?" Julie was pale with anger. This was going too far. "What will he think of me?"

"Much, I hope."

"He will think I am a fool."

Madame shook her head.

"You do not know me, Julie, or you would not imagine me capable of making you look a fool in Charles Patrice's eyes."

Then Julie asked sharply, "Why do you wish me to be friendly with a stranger like Charles Patrice, and you do not wish me to make friends with my own cousins, Hubert and André?"

Madame smiled wisely. "You have great intelligence, and so I will explain to you a little. You are here on a visit, Julie. I have promised your parents to give you a good time, to give you the chance of meeting the right people, and to do the best I can for you. Why should you be angry with me for trying to do that?"

She spoke patiently. It said much for grandmère, who was an impatient woman, that she replied so kindly to Julie. It was a disarming explanation, though it evaded the question, and Julie was sensible enough to realize that grandmère, who was old and had no special interest now in her own life, had suddenly taken a fresh lease of existence through a newcomer to the family circle.

But Julie was also puzzled. It made her wonder what was in her grandmother's mind that she made such a point of Charles's friendship. Julie was afraid of this kind of friendship. Sometimes, in the past, her mother had invited men to the house whom she thought would make suitable friends for Julie, but the result had been failure, for Julie had not liked her mother's choice.

Charles, of course, was a nice companion for any English girl in France, because he seemed to know his way about. But he was nothing like the ideal that had grown up in Julie's heart of the man she meant to marry some day. She had made a mistake about Harvey, and was not going to be caught like that a second time, especially with someone of her grandmother's choice, and a Frenchman.

But how to explain all this in the limited English that grandmère understood, or to say it in French, was beyond Julie.

She shrugged—and then laughed.

"I am used to making my own friends."

"You would have a poor time in France if someone did not arrange some friendships for you," said grandmère.

"I did not expect to make any friends over here. I came to see you," Julie pointed out. The effort to make herself understood by mimicry and gestures, with a few words in English and French was tiring.

Perhaps it was the same with grandmère.

She said, "We waste too much time in quarrelling. Fools do that. Be quick and dress, *chérie*."

When she had gone, Julie stood for a moment looking at the door, her forehead knitted in thought.

'Now I wonder what she is up to?'

To Julie's astonishment, the Professor who waited for her in the library, and who rose to greet her was a young man. He

53

was tall, thin and bespectacled, with a mop of unruly hair, a clean white linen collar, and much-worn clothes.

When Julie, with fine impertinence, bade him a cheerful "Good morning" in English, he bowed deeply and replied in French.

Their eyes met—the brown and the grey—mild, disarming looks screening warlike thoughts.

"I am so sorry you have been put to the trouble of coming here today," Julie told him smilingly. "It is my grandmother's desire and not mine that I should have lessons. I have no special wish to speak French."

The Professor looked owlish. He shook his head sadly, and when he spoke it was to inquire in French if she had a pencil and exercise book.

Julie affected not to understand him. She thought wilfully, 'Two can play at that game.' And again she thought, 'It won't be me who goes down first.'

She meant that, until suddenly Julie looked down and saw the frayed edges of his shirt cuff.

She was shocked to realize that this man needed the money earned from these lessons. After a long pause she said impulsively, "Okay, you win ! But I warn you you'll need all the patience in the world to teach me two consecutive words."

Julie's mouth widened generously. She sat down at the round leather-covered drum table and waited for the Professor to begin the lesson.

The hour passed quickly. The Professor certainly had a genius for imparting knowledge. He did not speak a word of English, yet it was improbable that he did not understand her language. Listening to his voice, Julie found the French language intriguing and pretty. She who was considered unteachable was soon absorbed in learning, but not so absorbed that she found time to wonder if the Professor ever smiled.

Julie kept her eyes fixed on his face while he read to her, to get her used to the 'sound' of the language, though what he said was unintelligible to her.

No sooner had the Professor left the room than Charles arrived at the house.

Julie met him in the hall.

"Who was that ?" Charles inquired curiously, taking Julie's hand in his and bowing over it.

54

"He has just spent an hour with me in the library, trying to teach me French," said Julie, withdrawing her hand.

"A whole hour! Poor man!" cried Charles.

"Poor me, you mean. However kind the fairies were to me when I was born, they forgot to give me the gift for languages," said Julie.

"I was not pitying him for that reason," was the meaning answer. Then he asked more formally, "Did you enjoy your lesson?"

"Oh, yes; the Professor read to me most of the time."

Charles seemed impressed. "Is he Madame Lubin's choice? But he must be."

"What is wrong with him?"

"Nothing. I am sure he is very nice—if young."

"That's not a crime. I like it."

"You would."

Julie laughed. "I assure you he is a most proper young man."

Charles agreed lightly. "I am certain that as Madame Lubin engaged him, he must be." Then he changed the subject abruptly. "Are you ready to start?"

"I am ready except for my hat."

"Then I shall wait here for you," said Charles.

Actually Julie remained upstairs for twenty minutes.

Grandmère was waiting in her bedroom. A dressmaker was with her. A dress had to be tried on. It was an ordeal.

Madame said, "Charles Patrice is downstairs."

"I know: I have seen him."

"I want you to enjoy yourself with him."

"Oh, I mean to."

"He is a worldly young man."

"I am sure he is—spoilt."

"As all rich men are by women—especially Lucienne Jeanson." Madame Lubin knew by Julie's answer that the fact that Charles was rich had not registered at all.

"I could see they were friendly last night. Anyway, everybody said they were."

"That friendship, it is not good for Charles. It is a worry to his mother."

"She need not worry," said Julie kindly. "I am sure that Charles can look after himself very well."

"I want you to take him away from her," said Madame deliberately.

"Me ! I couldn't. I shouldn't dare. Mademoiselle Lucienne is a beautiful and experienced woman. I am no match for her." Julie smiled at the foolishness of such an idea.

"What nonsense you talk ! You, too, have a ravishing beauty. You are not experienced, but you are fresh. Lucienne Jeanson is stale beside you. There is no reason why you should not teach Charles to forget her."

"Is that why you invited me here, grandmère ?" asked Julie abruptly.

"No—but since we have met and I have seen you, I shall be pleased if you will do what you can. It should please you, too."

"Why ?" Julie asked directly.

"Do not ask me—just do as I say."

Julie shook her head. "I won't do it," she decided.

"Why not ?"

"I am not that sort."

"Do you not like to feel you have the power to win a man ?"

"No—I prefer them to win me."

"You shall not fight ?"

"Never. Men must fight for *my* favours."

"We do things differently in France——"

Julie nodded. "That's right," and she thought, 'If grandmère says that again I shall scream.'

She put on her new hat, and grandmère tweaked it forwards. "Forget what I have said," she advised. "As you say, you could not make Charles forget Mademoiselle Lucienne, you do not even know how to wear a dress properly yet—so gauche you are."

Julie gave a sigh of relief. "Then that's settled," she agreed cheerfully. "Is Charles taking me out to lunch ?"

"I do not know. I do not care," cried the old lady. "Just go."

Julie kissed her grandmother's forehead. *"Au revoir !"* she cried blithely.

When Julie came downstairs Charles was pacing impatiently to and fro in the hall, his movements watched by Matras, the butler, who stood discreetly quiet in his black garb, by the front door.

The stairs were thickly carpeted, but Charles heard Julie approaching.

He stopped at the foot of the stairs and looked up, and saw a shaft of sunlight striking Julie's corn-coloured hair, that part of it which showed from under her small hat. The reflected light from the polished banisters, and white marble floor of the hall illuminated her face which was excited and eager. She looked so gay that Charles, who a moment before had been telling himself fiercely what a fool he was to accept Madame Lubin's explanation of a misunderstanding on Julie's part about his plan to go sightseeing with her, smiled, too, his impatience at being kept waiting vanishing.

Julie felt a little self-conscious as she came down, for the uneasy memory of her grandmother's last words still remained with her. She had a sudden panic of being left alone with Charles, and said the first words that came into her head.

"I am so sorry to have kept you waiting," she told Charles gaily, speaking rapidly because the sight of him made her feel shy, "but a dressmaker came to fit a dress for me, and grandmère is so fussy about my clothes." She said nothing about the lecture grandmère had given her. That was something she could never discuss with Charles.

"It is as nothing. I do not mind. Clothes are an education in France," Charles told her as they went together to the door which Matras opened for them.

"Like the language," said Julie wickedly.

Charles bent his head to look down into the laughing face upturned to his. He found Julie's expression provocative, and for a second his eyes gleamed in response.

"They are small hardships bringing in big returns," he said. And as they crossed the broad courtyard to the huge double doors which led to the street, he asked, "Shall we walk in the Bois before taking a taxi for our grand tour ?"

There were few people about and not much traffic in the Bois, where the leaves of the chestnut trees were unfurling, a tender green against the blue sky. The sun was warm and the air light.

They walked slowly, talking about themselves, their lives and likes and dislikes, often laughing over language misunderstandings. Oddly, since her lesson with the Professor, Julie found it easier to understand Charles's French.

Julie felt suddenly happy, though why, she could not say. More than once Charles had looked at her directly, a curious light shining in his dark eyes. He was so easy to talk to, so ready to laugh with her.

With a certain air of secrecy, Julie took a letter from her handbag saying, "I want to get this to England as soon as possible. I bought the air mail letter when I reached Paris, just in case. It is to my mother telling her to write that she expects me home at the end of the week."

She had treated Charles as an intimate friend, though she scarcely knew him, and in a sense she had cast a slur on Madame's hospitality, something she recognized as soon as the words were out of her mouth, but which she had not meant to do. She added quickly,

"Everybody is most kind to me. They could not be kinder, only—I guess, I am homesick. Grandmother is wonderful, and Paris is lovely, but I do not like staying for long so far from home."

There was an awkward silence. Then Charles said,

"Madame Lubin wants you to stay here for a while : is that what is worrying you ?"

"In a way."

Charles smiled sympathetically. "Then do not worry any more. I shall arrange that you leave at the end of the week."

"I don't see how."

"It shall be done."

"I will try to believe that, but—I don't know you very well."

"We are friends—yes ?"

"I suppose so."

"You only suppose. Do you not know ?"

"Well—yes."

This kind of talk—Charles trying to fall in with her wishes— was confusing.

Charles suggested easily, "I do not know of a post office that is near, but after lunch we shall make a point of finding one. Will that suit ?"

"Oh yes, that will do nicely." Julie replaced the air letter to her mother in her handbag. Oddly enough, the incident made them seem friends. She liked Charles now. When with him she had the feeling of being wrapped with care. The way he looked at her, as if she were the only person in the world who mattered, and the things he said, ordinary enough in themselves, half in French and half in English by Charles in his caressing voice, made her feel important. Julie's head was not turned. She knew that only a Frenchman could possibly make any woman feel so wanted and important, when in reality she was ordinary and of no importance at all.

They had lunch on the glass-covered verandah of a restaurant in the Bois, which was surrounded by lime trees in young leaf.

It seemed that Charles was known here, for the maître d'hôtel himself, bowing deeply to Charles and his companion, brought

58

them the huge gold-printed menu-cards, bearing the choice of many dishes, some of which were bound to appeal to and please most palates.

Julie remarked smilingly, "You seem to be well known about Paris."

"Why not ? I am a bachelor with a fondness for entertaining. I should be lonely eating and drinking by myself."

He studied the menu seriously, inquiring searchingly about Julie's likes and dislikes in food. It pleased him when she said at length, "You choose ; you seem to know so much better than I do what is good."

There was a *bisque écrevisse*, a grilled sole, some veal cooked with mushrooms, and, "Because I know you have a sweet tooth," a chocolate basket with a layer of ratafia crumbs, and mixed candied fruits soaked with brandy and covered in cream.

"That will do to go on with," said Charles, "unless, Julie, there is something you like better on the menu."

"No ; what you have chosen sounds perfect," and Julie sighed blissfully.

Charles gave his attention to the wine waiter. "We shall drink champagne because it is our first lunch together. It is an occasion."

When it was brought, wrapped in a snowy napkin, leaning at a crazy angle in a pail of ice, Charles had it opened at once, and insisted on toasting Julie.

"To our next meeting."

Laughingly she raised her glass and drank some of the amber liquid which stung her palate slightly, and tasted so clean.

"May it be soon," said Charles. "Perhaps tomorrow." He spoke tentatively and there was an inquiring look in his eyes as they rested on her radiant beauty.

"I shall have to find out first what grandmère has arranged for me," Julie told him guardedly. She wanted to go out again with Charles, who was such a kind and attentive host ; but some instinct warned her against becoming too friendly with him, for Julie knew that the older the friendship the more difficult it would be to break.

He replied, "Oh, Madame Lubin will not mind."

"Why not ?"

"Because she happens to like me."

"She likes André and Hubert, too," Julie told him demurely.

"*Naturellement*. She is their grandmother."

It was then that Julie's mind harked back to the previous evening, when she had seen Charles sitting with his girl-friend at the night club. He had seemed as friendly with the French-woman as he was with her, Julie, now.

With her head turned towards the scene outside, her eyes fixed on the crumbling broad walls of the old city, Julie was quiet for a while, not liking the recollection, but unable to stop herself thinking about it.

Charles asked quickly, "Is anything the matter, Julie?"

She recalled herself to the present and looked at him, "No, what should be?"

"You look rather solemn, a little distraite, not like yourself."

"Oh, I have my solemn moments."

"What is it?" he persisted quickly.

She sensed the obstinacy that would probe for the truth until it was revealed.

"As a matter of fact, I was thinking of the night club I went to last night."

"It is a good one."

"I know—you were there. . . ."

"Yes?" He sounded puzzled.

"With a famous actress."

Again Charles said, "Yes," but his tone was distant, and discouraged further talk on the subject.

Julie drank her champagne when an attentive waiter refilled her glass. She knew how Charles felt, but something rose within her, a curiosity too strong to be resisted, the need to know how friendly Charles was with Lucienne. Both André and Hubert had inferred that the actress was a special friend of Charles. Grandmère had told her that his family thought the friendship undesirable.

With her heart beating overtime, and with a sudden, daring, absurd frivolity that was characteristic of her temperament, Julie said,

"She is remarkably lovely; but then I can't imagine you being very friendly with any girl who is not outstandingly attractive."

Charles listened in angry astonishment.

Seeing this, Julie gave an impertinent little gasp of laughter. Charles thought her gauche and lacking in good taste, "Oh dear, how serious you are suddenly," she cried.

The tension lasted a few seconds longer, then Charles relaxed.

"That is interesting," he said easily, "but now you say so, and I look at you, I see that it is true. Shall we say that I am fastidious, and conceited——"

"All of it—and condescending and spoilt," Julie interrupted

quickly, voicing her keen disappointment in Charles. He had twisted her words so neatly. She had been hurt, too, by the look of anger in his eyes. She could not bear that Charles should be angry with her.

"You, too, have your faults, Julie," retorted Charles with spirit.

"Oh, that isn't being kind."

"You asked for it."

"Thanks." Again the tension rose between them.

"Do not look so crestfallen. These truths are but the gleams and reflexions of our growing friendship," Charles consoled smilingly. "It is natural that you should feel inquisitive about me."

But he had not answered Julie's question. Obviously he had no intention of doing so, and Julie's curiosity secretly increased. She would not at the moment risk a second snub. She wanted to tell him quickly, 'You see, I am growing to like you. That is why I feel so curious about you.'

But she only smiled brilliantly and said, "I'm sorry."

Charles laughed. "Forget it," he advised. "I am in danger of forgetting that you are terribly young."

The tension slackened, and Julie regained her usual confidence.

After a while she said softly, "And I was in danger of imagining that we were greater friends than we are."

"Oh, please—do not punish me." Then Charles looked at her plate and said swiftly and with some concern in his voice, "But you are not eating anything. Do you not care for veal? Perhaps you would like chicken——"

"I have already eaten a feast."

"It is not enough. You will starve. I will tell them to take this away. You——"

"No, it is delicious. Really, I mean that."

They wrangled intensely over the *filet* of veal.

Then came a brief moment.

Charles accepted her word. Julie's eyes met his. . . .

The world seemed to spin about her darkly, and presently stood still again.

Julie felt breathless.

Something quite unexpected but inevitable, as though pre-destined, took shape then and there. Julie came to bright reality. Everything about her seemed oddly quiet. She felt stunned.

Yet there were noises in the restaurant, for it was a gay place, and there were, as usual, much chatter and laughter.

Seeing that Charles was staring at her strangely, a deep colour suffused Julie's cheeks. His look, inquiring and gently amused, steadied her, so that she heard the sounds around her—the talk and laughter, the subdued clatter of plates, and the popping of corks.

"What is it now?" asked Charles, and to Julie's ears, alert because of this new emotion that had stirred within her, the sound of his voice was like a caress.

"I can't tell you."

"I need not remind you that I am your friend," and again she was stirred by the deep, sweet notes of his voice.

"No, but I can't tell you just the same."

"Will not?"

"If you like."

Charles did not press her further, and Julie thought wildly, 'If only I could tell him what is in my heart!' and again she thought, 'If I did I should probably scare him away forever. He belongs to Mademoiselle Lucienne. He would have no use for a girl like me.' In spite of this Julie recognized that it was impossible for her to go back to England at the end of the week.

She had the chance to stay longer and she must take it. 'I could not bear to leave Charles now. Just one more week,' Julie prayed fervently of the fates, forgetting that an hour or so ago she had prayed quite as fervently to leave Paris.

As though Charles read a part of her thoughts he said, "As you are going away this week, we must arrange to give a really big party before you go, and make it so exciting that you will never forget us, and perhaps want to return some day."

It gave Julie a queer and unaccustomed pain to hear Charles speak so because it implied that Charles expected her to go. In his self-sufficiency Julie knew that Charles could manage to live quite well without her. It was she who did not want to leave him. It was unbelievable that she could have changed her mind about Charles in so short a time. Yet it had happened—dramatically and suddenly.

"Besides," added Charles thoughtfully, his eyes not leaving her face for an instant, "I often travel on business to South America, and I might not be here when you come back."

Stung to retort, Julie cried, "I may never return."

"That is a sad thought. I am sure that once you get to know Paris, you will never be happy away from it."

But Julie was not thinking of Paris, but of one man living

in it—the man who was sitting opposite to her at their small table, who was gazing at her so admiringly, and giving her the whole of his attention, flattering her not only with his caressing voice, but with the gleam in his eyes.

"Oh," she said, in that light deceiving tone which she found useful to hide her deeper emotions, "I shall return some day, of course, perhaps for a part of my honeymoon."

"Honeymoon!" Charles exclaimed sharply, and Julie never forgot the look in his eyes. "Then you are betrothed? No one told me. I understood from you and Madame Lubin——"

"Grandmère knows little about my private life. She believes that which she wishes to accept. It is often far from the truth."

"Then you are not free?" Charles's brow clouded.

Julie wanted to say, 'How dare you question me about Harvey, when you refused to talk about your Lucienne.' But she knew that that kind of remark, pert and snappy, would get a girl nowhere. Besides, she did not resent Charles asking her personal questions. It showed that he was interested; or could it be that he was jealous?

She said, "I told you that I was engaged, but it is all over now."

His brow cleared swiftly. "Are you sure?"

She nodded.

"And you have no regrets?"

"None."

Julie wanted to ask Charles why he was so anxious to know if she were heartwhole, but she was afraid of wearying him by seeming gauche, as grandmère had taunted her with being.

It was Charles himself who said, "I do not like being friendly with a girl whose thoughts are full of another man."

Julie smiled. She said, half-impatiently, "Oh, you want everything."

CHAPTER VI

CHARLES and Julie spent the afternoon driving about Paris. They went up the Eiffel Tower, and Charles pointed out various landmarks to her. It seemed natural that he should throw a

63

protecting arm across Julie's shoulders, in case she should feel giddy at the height. When Julie shrank instinctively from the familiarity, Charles said, "Pardon," and removed his arm. But a few moments later, with a warning, *"Prenez garde,"* his arm was back again, and this time Julie did not appear to notice, though every nerve in her body thrilled to his touch.

They talked about Charles, his work and his hopes—his flat, his cars, and his family who lived close by. Charles adored his mother and saw her nearly every day, but he had a separate *ménage* because his was an independent spirit.

After tea at 'Marquise' where they drank chocolate, Charles took Julie to the Louvre. They went no further than the first salon, but sat on a window seat and took no notice of the pictures or the view of the Tuileries gardens, but, half-facing each other, talked about Julie.

Charles listened intently, though he had been giving her his close attention all day. The admiration in his warm, full glances went to Julie's head. As the minutes sped by she knew herself to be hopelessly and irrevocably in love with Charles. Sometimes she felt so emotional it was difficult to hide her feelings from him. Then it seemed as though she cast caution to the winds. Emotions drowned her commonsense and made her careless of consequences. She could have left him then. To spend the day with him sightseeing did not mean that she must dine with Charles. It was dangerous for her peace of mind to dally any longer. Yet Julie felt a kind of bitter-sweet ecstasy in being with Charles, meeting his glowing eyes occasionally and listening to his softly-modulated caressing voice which made her think what a wonderful lover he would make, and what heaven it would be to be loved by him. In vain Julie tried to still her fast-beating heart by reminding herself that Charles, being French, knew by instinct how to make a woman think she was in paradise ; and that because of his nationality, which made a fetish of worshipping women, he was the same to every woman. There were just those shades of deference in his manner to her which Julie adored.

It was Julie who noticed the quietness about them. The visitors had gone and the salon was empty except for the uniformed attendants who were gazing speculatively at them, not liking to disturb them but wishing they would go.

Julie sighed, and gathered up her bag and gloves. "I suppose we must go," she said regretfully, "or they will be turning us out in a few moments."

"But we haven't seen the pictures yet," Charles objected, but he rose to go and held out his hand to help Julie.

"Some other day."

"That is vague ; and you are returning to London so soon."

Julie smiled. "Perhaps I will change my mind and promise to come back."

"Why not go further and stay now ?" Charles suggested boldly.

"Why not ?" They turned slowly to leave the salon.

Charles squeezed her arm. "That is what makes you such a fascinating person, Julie."

"What ?"

"You are so feminine." Then he sighed. "One has only to look at you to know that you must have had many admirers. I wish I could be sure that you are heartwhole."

"I have told you."

"Still, I am not certain."

"What difference would it make between us, anyway ?" Julie asked provocatively, but there was a yearning for him in her heart which was almost frightening in its intensity.

"Quite a lot, I assure you. If I were talking to a French girl I should know many things about her at once ; but English girls have a greater freedom than ours. It must be—how do you say it ?—worrying to the nerves, to the family, to wonder with what man they will spend their lives."

"Harrowing ! What *do* you mean ?" Julie said with astonishment.

"You will pick and choose your husband—which or what man among your friends ?"

"Yes ?" Her voice held a question. Julie looked puzzled.

They were outside the Louvre now and walking in the gardens. On the other side of the road was the arcaded Rue de Rivoli where many people were gazing into the brilliantly-lighted shop windows, at the masses of bijouterie displayed there.

"In France neither men nor women like us choose whom they shall marry. That is our parents' responsibility—theirs and the lawyers'."

A queer little pain tugged at Julie's heart. What had seemed so simple and straightforward throughout the day, making herself so attractive to Charles that he would fall in love with her and want nothing better than to spend the rest of his life with her, was easy no longer. They might flirt and play at being in love as much as they liked, but marriage was another matter. It involved pleasing others, practical parents and still more practical lawyers. Marriage was not simply a binding together of two people in love, it was a contract between families.

She asked in a flat tone, "Do *you* like it so?"

Charles shrugged. "I do not know about 'like.' I have always respected our customs. They are wise."

"Would you agree to marry a girl of your parents' choice, even if you loved another girl?"

Charles was silent for a few moments, then he said slowly, "I shall probably do as my parents wish when the time comes for me to marry."

Julie's blood ran cold. 'How could he speak so cruelly,' she thought wildly, unaware in this fresh anguish that Charles could not know how deeply she cared for him already.

She said crisply, "You are certainly old enough to know your own mind, and to tell them what you want in a wife." But Julie knew she was butting her head against the rock of Charles's national habits.

"*Certainement!*"

"Perhaps your parents have already decided whom you are to marry?" Julie's voice was forlorn.

"Yes."

"Who is she?"

Charles hesitated. Then he said quietly, "I have been told there is a girl, and that I must marry and settle down soon. But I do not know her name."

Julie shivered. "You are obedient," she remarked harshly.

"I am content," he conceded. "But until that time . . ."

"You are willing to play with me?"

Charles laughed suddenly. "As you are willing. Shall we say I am sowing a few wild oats."

'Beast!' thought Julie angrily, and she said, "Perhaps your future wife is occupied in the same way."

"I sincerely hope not. I should not care for her to have too many men-friends, or as you would say, boy-friends, before we marry."

Again Julie caught the faint but unmistakable note of reserve and hauteur in his voice that she had already heard today. It made her shiver. It was like looking through a window into a warmly lighted room, one that she would never have the privilege of entering.

"Why not?" she cried tartly. "It is only fair that if you play she should."

Charles refused to accept this. "It may be fair, but it is not right."

Julie's eyes were hostile, not to Charles, but against his country's customs, and she said, "Your wife must be kept in a glass case, not because you love her, but simply because your parents and hers have chosen her to be your wife."

"I have put her on a pedestal, and so she must be above reproach," he told her calmly. "I believe that she will be wonderful and divine. I hope we shall make each other very happy."

"How odd, when you don't even know her."

"There *is* a girl who is to be my wife. I have great faith in my mother's choice."

It was obvious that Charles adored his mother.

"What are you waiting for?"

"My mother has been very ill. She is convalescing in the South. Directly she returns the important preliminaries will open." Charles spoke in a matter-of-fact voice. He said, "This girl *is* on a pedestal and must remain there always."

"You sound absurd to me."

"That is because you are English."

"Your poor wife! How I pity her!" Julie cried, but in her heart she was saying, 'Wretched girl! I could tear her eyes out! I envy her.'

Charles grinned. "You need not. As my wife she will need no one's pity."

"I expect she will be unhappy. What girl could feel happy with a loveless marriage?"

"She will be happy."

"She won't. Even you can't love to order."

"Yet I shall love her."

He spoke so firmly that Julie, listening to the determination in his voice, could have screamed with despair.

She said instead, "That kind of passive love wouldn't suit an English girl. She would want something more than that to make her happy and content. I know *I* would."

Charles did not reply for some moments. He continued to look smilingly at Julie, and the glint in his eyes which had made them seem so beautiful and luminous all day deepened.

At last he said, "Say it again! You look adorable when you are talking about love, Julie."

He was laughing at her.

Quickly Julie talked about something else. She refused to listen to Charles talking about his future wife and love any longer. She felt curiously depressed.

The day which had begun with such promise, joy and unreasoning happiness, was swiftly passing into an evening of disappointment. There were times, in the next half-hour, when Julie had to exercise all her self-control to stop herself from bursting into tears.

She thought, almost bitterly, 'Charles is enjoying my friendship to pass the time agreeably. He is that kind of man. If he is friendly with a woman she must amuse him or he drops her. It flatters him to be seen with an English girl dressed in French clothes. But after this week he will be quite willing for me to go away and never see me again. Marriage with me would never occur to him, for his parents have already taken care of that side of his life, much as parents in England arrange what schools their children shall go to. It is all cut and dried for him. He expects me to be intelligent enough to understand this. In the meantime, now that he has made the position clear to me, he is willing to play at being in love with me. I'm sick of playing, and I won't play. It isn't fair of him.'

While Julie was thinking like this, her eyes fixed moodily on the gaily-lighted shop windows in the Rue de Rivoli, Charles looked at his wristwatch and exclaimed :

"I have kept you out rather late. I hope Madame Lubin will not scold you. What time is she expecting you home ?"

Julie's eyes came back to Charles's face.

"She did not say."

"For dinner, anyway. I have an engagement or I would ask you to do me the honour of dining with me."

"Thank you," Julie said quickly, anxious that he should not think she was hoping for such an invitation, "but I have a date." She thought angrily, 'I suppose Charles had a date with his play-girl, Lucienne ?'

Charles looked long and curiously at Julie, as though he could not quite make her out. She seemed to blow hot and cold without reason. He did not ask further questions about her date.

"I have tired you," he said with some compunction.

Julie shook her head. She felt too depressed to speak normally. But even if Charles had been free Julie had no intention of going out with him tonight. She had to have some time to herself to think things out. Her mind and heart seemed overcharged with the increasing emotions of the day. They were full, excited and confused. Everything must be sorted out, and some code of behaviour arranged with herself before she met Charles again.

It was Charles who remembered to ask, "What about that party tomorrow evening ?"

68

"Let us drop the idea," Julie told him roughly. "I do not really care for parties."

"You said you did earlier in the day."

"That was this morning."

"And this is tonight, and you have completely changed. Why?"

Julie shrugged. She had forgotten what she had said about the suggested party. What had she said?

"I guess I am too lazy to dress up and make myself pleasant. I don't know many people to make a party—only my cousins, and the Professor whose face is so stiff he cannot laugh."

"I cannot imagine the Professor at a party," Charles remarked lightly.

"He might be amusing."

"I doubt if he has any suitable clothes."

"If he had they might smell of mothballs. But I would be willing to make the effort to humanize him."

"Then let us have a farewell party *à deux*," Charles said eagerly. "I should prefer that. Perhaps you would like that, too; would you, Julie?" His voice dropped to an enchanting whisper.

She shook her head. Then with an effort she told him in what she hoped was a light voice : "We have already talked too much today, Charles. Let us wait for a few days. It would be a blot on our friendship if we should bore each other."

"There can be no danger of that with me. Each moment I find something new in you to amuse and interest me."

"It is nice to hear you say that," said Julie, but she spoke without enthusiasm, accepting the compliment as mere words, Charles's usual expressions when talking to a woman.

"You think I do not mean what I say," Charles exclaimed.

"Of course. It *was* very prettily said."

There was a little silence, and Charles said, "There are times, Julie, when you exasperate me so much I should like to shake you."

Julie glanced about her.

"Try it," she dared. "This is a public place."

"If you continue to madden me I shall be in danger of forgetting it."

Julie laughed at him. It was a taunting, mocking sound and for a moment Charles stiffened, saying, "I do not see anything at which to laugh."

"Don't you ? I do. You. Us." She continued laughing so gaily that presently Charles began to laugh too.

They took a taxi back to Madame Lubin's house, where Julie took a brief leave-taking of Charles.

CHAPTER VII

JULIE went slowly up the wide staircase, Charles's image in her mind's eye, remembering Charles's look, his soft caressing voice, his personality, his stumbling English, his explanations in French, his expressive hands—*everything* about him. He was so close to her, memory was vivid, painful and more than she could bear with equanimity. She took long steadying breaths, then hurried so that she could reach the safety of her room before finding exquisite relief in a burst of tears.

At the top of the staircase she literally ran into Uncle Michel, who stretched out podgy hands to steady her.

He smiled in kindly fashion, apologized for their unexpected meeting, then asked, "Did you have a good time with Charles ? But of course you did. All the girls adore Charles."

So he knew with whom she had been all day ! Julie supposed that the entire family was aware of and had criticized her doings.

"Very nice, thank you, Uncle Michel," she replied politely in French, for the old man made no attempt at compromise by speaking in English, or even miming to make himself more clearly understood.

"You look pale, child," he said, noticing the signs of strain on her face.

"I am tired. Sightseeing *is* tiring."

"But yes ; what did you see ?"

Julie reeled off the names of well-known places.

"You saw all those ?" He sounded disappointed. "Charles *must* have been a bore. Have you brought him back with you to dinner ?"

"No, he could not have come, anyway. He had a previous engagement." She spoke French slowly and with effort, then tried another approach to her difficulty with the language.

But the old gentleman interrupted fractiously. "I understand.

I remember now that Charles dines at home every Tuesday, *en famille*. It is a habit with him."

Julie nodded and sighed. "Charles seems full of old French customs," she said unkindly, then recalled that if Charles were dining with his family, he could not be entertaining Lucienne. It brightened Julie's horizon slightly.

"You will feel more rested tomorrow, and will enjoy going out with Charles some other day."

"Perhaps."

But it was an effort to make herself understood, and Uncle Michel was not co-operative.

Julie passed on to her room ; and Michel went along the carpeted corridor to his sister's boudoir, and reported what Julie had said, what he feared, and asked for her advice.

"I have just met Julie on the stairs. For a slight young woman the impact was of a violence unbelievable." He rubbed his waistcoat, catching his fat fingers in the gold cable chain that was looped twice across its breadth, and which he thought added to his dignity. "She seems put out. I do not think she has spent a profitable day with Charles. I hope Julie benefits quickly from her lessons in French. It tires me to talk to her. Though her accent is execrable, I would have complimented her upon it, only she did not stop to listen. She ran away from me."

His sister listened in silence. "You are inclined to be impatient and rush things, Michel. The child has but just met Charles !"

"I think you are making a mistake, Louise. It would have been wiser to arrange matters in our own way, without having to please Julie's whims first."

"Julie is half-English. She has been reared there and naturally understands English customs better than she does ours. She is a high-spirited girl and would resent being told, 'We have arranged this for your future—it is for your good.' She would refuse to carry out our wishes, hate Charles and probably take the next plane to England. I prefer that she meets Charles and grows to like him. It should not be difficult. One *leads* a girl like Julie, not drives her. Tonight I am speaking to Jeanne on the telephone."

"Ah !"

"I must keep Julie longer in Paris. I have asked her to stay and she has refused, so I must try to work it some other way."

"Well, you seem to know what you want."

"I have dreamed of these plans for years."

"Does Julie suspect your plans ?"

"I hope not. But I think you are unduly nervous and imagine obstacles in the way of success. Julie is tired. Presently I shall go to her room and find out why she is as unhappy as you say she is. In affaires of the heart one moves delicately."

When Madame Lubin did go to Julie's room it was to see that the girl's eyes were pink-lidded.

Julie was recovering from one of the most violent fits of crying she had indulged in for years. She had been too troubled to open her windows, and the room was closely-curtained as Marie had left it earlier in the evening. It was stuffy, but the softly-shaded lights were kind.

Wisely, Madame pretended not to notice anything amiss. She said, "Did you enjoy your day?"

"Very much, thank you, grandmère."

"Are you too tired, *chérie*, to go to the opera tonight?"

"I should love to go." Julie spoke without enthusiasm. She would have liked to be left alone, but that would have invited questioning. Perhaps anything would be welcome that would take her away from her thoughts.

"My loge is unoccupied. They are playing *Carmen*, with a Spanish prima donna in the title rôle, which is as it should be. We must dine early. I should like you to wear your new dress. It will be a well-dressed house. We shall stroll in the foyer between acts, for I want you to be seen and to meet all my friends. Is there anything you would wish me to do for you?"

Julie could have said that Charles, at that moment, was the only person she wanted in the world, the one wish she could not have.

Julie shook her head. "There is nothing more," she said. "You have done so much already—too much."

"Nonsense! I please myself."

At the last moment, after dinner, when Julie was just leaving her room after titivating to go to the opera, Marie brought a message that she was wanted on the telephone in Madame's boudoir.

Julie did not wait to ask who it was. She knew instinctively that it was Charles.

With wildly-beating heart she ran down the corridor and through the door that had been left ajar, into the boudoir, and picked up the receiver. What did Charles want?

72

"Hello !"

"Oh, 'allo. Is it you, Julie ?"

There was a sudden restriction in Julie's throat as she replied, "Yes."

"I want to ask your pardon for forgetting to post your letter to England. You remember I said I would find a post office after lunch ?"

"Oh, it doesn't matter. I forgot myself."

"Good ! Then we are both to blame." He paused, then asked uncertainly, "Is anything the matter ?"

"No."

"You sound different, so depressed. Your voice is usually clear, but now it is thick, as though . . ."

Charles hesitated, and Julie interrupted swiftly, "Your voice sounds odd, too."

"Does it ?" His spirits rose. "Then it must be the telephone."

"You seem terribly businesslike."

Charles laughed. "I do not feel so, but elated and happy. I have spent a wonderful day with you. I hope you feel the same way."

"Of course."

Julie spoke lightly. She managed a laugh. Suddenly it came to her that the right way to deal with Charles was not to take him seriously, but to be light and gay, radiant and reckless, to laugh at and with him, to have fun. He would like her better that way.

"But you are tired," Charles persisted. "I have walked and talked too much. If you had not been so kind you must have told me so. Go to bed early and rest."

"I can't do that. I am already dressed for the opera."

Julie knew by the sudden pause which followed her remark that the idea of her going out for an evening's enjoyment did not please Charles.

"Why am I not invited ?" he inquired.

"I do not know."

"You are dressed ? What are you wearing ?"

And when Julie told him Charles cried, "You sound adorable, Julie."

She laughed. "Several times today I have wondered whether you admire me or the clothes I am wearing which, I am told, are le Gère at her best ?"

"It is both."

It was Julie who, with a courage born of desperation, ended the talk abruptly and hung up the receiver.

She was quiet during the drive to the opera, thinking of Charles. She had not known him for long, yet already she was experiencing the aches and yearnings of falling in love.

At the opera Julie met many members of the Patrice and Lubin families. Their manner was cool at first. They eyed her with direct and curious glances. Julie felt that they watched her closely, criticizing her looks, manners and clothes.

Apparently they liked what they saw, for they spoke approvingly of her to Madame Lubin, who appeared to enjoy her granddaughter's success immensely. Occasionally, Julie caught Charles's name, or it may have been a cousin of that name they were talking about. But even hearing the name, pronounced 'Sharle,' awoke a poignant emotion in Julie and it took all her efforts to appear unconcerned. The word '*dot*' cropped up, and suddenly Julie was aware with fresh anguish that here was another unsurmountable barrier between Charles and herself. She should have guessed that lawyers discussed *dots*—but she had no money at all.

Between the first and second acts, Julie and her cousins went into the great oblong foyer, its great crystal chandeliers glittering with blue-tinted lights. Here, women were dressed in exquisite clothes and wore sparkling diamonds, and moved in an atmosphere of heavy cloying scents which Frenchwomen affect, and Julie was introduced to many more members of the family, so that she thought, 'These people could populate a village.'

The first awkward minutes over, having accepted Julie, the cousins vied with one another in showering invitations upon her.

Madame Lubin would have known how to deal with these invitations, especially as she was determined to keep open dates for Charles, but she had already booked a call through to her daughter Jeanne Ryan, in London, and she was told that the line was clear earlier than she had anticipated. She had excused herself and hurried away.

It was during her absence that Fate worked against her. Julie was full up with engagements for a week ahead. She wrote them down on her programme.

In the second act, though Julie's eyes were fixed on the stage, her mind wandered, and fell into a dreamy state of despair because added to her first reason why Charles could not marry her was the added drawback that she had no *dot* to bring to any marriage. Though she knew that Charles had plenty of money, she realized, too, that he would expect his wife to bring a substantial sum to the marriage.

74

She allowed her thoughts to drift to Charles, wishing that instead of being brought up in England, her mother had married one of her own countrymen and settled in France. 'Then I should have understood the French way of life. I might not be suffering now,' she thought.

Julie did not know that someone had opened the door at the back of the box and had slipped into a vacant chair behind her, until she felt a light touch on her arm. At the same time she heard Charles's whisper behind her, "Julie !"

Startled, her pulses leaping madly, she turned and saw his face close to hers.

"Charles !"

The chorus sounded strongly on the stage.

"I had to come, Julie, to see for myself."

"See what ?" She strained her ears to hear.

"Whether you had been crying."

"Crying ! What an absurdity !" She turned her head further away from him.

"Is it not ? Look at me, Julie."

Nervously she said in a low voice, "Hush ! How can I ? It is so dark."

"I can see. . . . Julie, what have I said to make you cry ? It is all right. No one can hear us above this noise."

"Nothing. I never cry." The clamour on the stage was terrific. She glanced sideways at him, and knew that he *saw*.

"But you did tonight. Because of me ! Your voice on the telephone was thick with tears. I was desolated. I would not harm a fly. Why should I hurt you ? Imbecile that I am, I would rather die than cause you to shed one tear."

It was wonderful to hear his voice. Surely he would not have come here did he not like her a little, thought Julie.

So great was her revulsion of feeling that Julie was on the point of shedding many more tears, but of joy this time. She remembered that she was at the opera and must control herself. She recalled, too, that it was unwise to be intense or dramatic with Charles. He could never have any serious intentions towards her because his family had already booked him for some other girl. If she could not remember to play his game she must take the consequences, and get hurt and be miserable.

Julie made a great effort to behave as though Charles's presence did not affect her, as though her heart were not beating wildly because of his nearness, and as if she were not near to fainting with ecstasy and wretchedness combined.

She said, with an assumption of lightness, "Please don't die for me. I would prefer you to live. If I was silly enough to shed tears, Charles, it was not because of you, I assure you. It was a private matter in which you could not possibly have any part. Anyway, I am all right now."

"But——"

"Don't I look it?" The orchestra and choir joined with the principal singers, splintering the atmosphere with harmonic sound.

Charles paused, then he said warmly, "You look *ravissante*!" The curtains swung together on a burst of applause. The lights went up then, and everyone looked around to see what restless, alien presence had invaded the box. Charles was discovered, even as the curtains swung to and fro to renewed clapping and "Bravos."

There was an awkward but revealing silence. Julie had the feeling that Charles had done something unorthodox which shocked the older people, but she had no idea what he was supposed to have done wrong. He stood up, a fine figure, and faced them quietly, bowing to them all.

Someone asked, "What are you doing here, Charles? I thought you always spent Tuesday evenings at home."

"So I do," he assured the speaker, and his charming voice, which had held a deep note of feeling a moment before, was expressionless.

"Then what brought you *here*? Of course . . ." Here the speaker paused. She was a dark woman, and looked at Julie with speculative eyes.

"I came to speak to Julie," Charles told his tormentor calmly. "Now that I have done so I shall go home again."

"When is your mother expected back?" inquired another woman.

"In two weeks' time."

"Her health, is it better?"

"She assures my father that she is now perfectly well."

"Impossible, after all she has been through. You will have to take care of your mother for a long time, Charles."

"I mean to," was the fervent response.

Julie looked at her grandmother to see what she thought about all this.

Grandmère had not spoken, but she looked like a benign goddess, her eyes resting approvingly on Charles. Julie's cheeks were flushed a lovely wild-rose colour. She looked like an exquisite piece of rare china. Her eyes, which a short while ago were dull and lifeless with a hidden grief, were now sparkling with a new life.

Charles said to Julie, "*Au revoir*, Julie. I will give you a ring in the morning."

"What time?"

"About eight-thirty, or is that too early? I must not disturb the morning sleep."

"You won't. I have my French lesson at nine. You will not be permitted to disturb that."

"Oh, the Professor! I had forgotten him."

In a debonair manner Charles kissed the older ladies' hands. He bowed low over Julie's and pressed it reassuringly.

There was more whispered talk about Charles when he had gone. It might have been revealing to Julie, but the lights were lowered and the buzz of conversation ceased.

Julie sat still for a long time, not listening to the opera, but in a kind of daze, and she was happier than she had ever been.

On the way home Julie said to Madame Lubin, who was dozing in the semi-darkness of the car, "Grandmère, why do you want me to be so friendly with Charles Patrice?"

It was out now, the maggot of suspicion which had been at the back of Julie's mind all day.

For once, the suddenness of the question surprised the old lady into saying:

"Your mother and his were school friends. We have known Charles's family for many years, and have close friendly and business relations with them. Also, if I had had a son, I should have wished for him to be like Charles—intelligent, courageous, and kind to women and children."

Her confidence exhausted, Madame was silent again.

"But that doesn't explain why *I* must be friends with him," persisted Julie, with a blunt purpose which secretly annoyed Madame. "Is there a reason?"

"Oh, dear, am I to be catechized by a chit at this hour of the night? I do not know. All I can say at present is 'because I do'." She spoke rapidly in French and Julie was not sure whether she had translated it correctly and was afraid to ask.

Then Madame sat upright, and roused herself to say, "I had a talk with your mother tonight on the telephone."

"Is she all right?" asked Julie quickly.

"*Certainement!* She has asked me to keep you here for a little longer. She and your father are closing the flat and leaving at once for a holiday in Ireland. She said, 'It would be like a second honeymoon. We have never been away without Julie before.'"

Julie was quick to see the point. She said readily, "Then of course she does not want me. But isn't it rather a sudden arrangement? There was no question of their going away when I left England. Daddy said that it had taken all his spare cash for pocket money for my stay here."

Grandmère shook her head. "I know nothing about that. Our talk was short. She inquired how you were, if you were having a good time, and to give you her love."

"Thank you." And Julie added, "Then I am to stay here?" and did not know whether to be glad or sorry. One half of her was delighted at the thought of seeing more of Charles—the wilful, selfish and emotional side of her that was willing to risk anything for a few moments' reckless joy; the other half recalled the danger, pain and unhappiness which must come if she continued to see more of him, knowing that the break must come some day.

But grandmère was still speaking.

"For a little while longer," she said. "Apart from anything else, it will give you a chance of improving your French. I shall not find it easy to forgive your father for neglecting to have you taught French correctly. I think it is important that everyone should speak at least one foreign language." Grandmère said nothing more about Charles.

"This is what you wanted?" Julie said.

"Yes, but I thought it would please you, too, to hear such news."

"It does, only—I am a bit surprised."

"But I would not force you to stay if you wished to return to England."

Grandmère sounded hurt, and Julie hastened to say that she loved the idea, and was having the time of her life, adding, "Anyway, if the flat is shut up, there is nowhere for me to go."

"Nowhere to go!" replied Madame Lubin, and her eyes gleamed with hidden laughter in the darkness. "All I can say is that you do not *seem* pleased, Julie."

CHAPTER VIII

JULIE did not sleep well that night. She spent the hours of darkness sorting out the chaos in her mind, trying to subdue those emotions which meeting Charles and falling in love had aroused within her. She lay on her back between the sheets, her window wide open and her curtains drawn back. Occasionally the darkness of the room was lit up by the beam that came from the searchlight on the top of the Eiffel Tower, changing the black and grey shadows to grey and white.

It would have been hard enough to hide her emotions if the way ahead had been comparatively easy—if Charles were free to love and marry her as she wished with all her heart it could be. But to know that however much she charmed Charles they could never be happy ! His future was already arranged. He was willing that it should be so. To have fallen for him was indeed a major misfortune.

At first, Julie rebelled at the fate which had dealt so badly with her. It was wrong for any man to have his marriage arranged for him by people a generation older, who might be wise and experienced, but who had outlived the warm emotions of youth. Charles was neither mad nor too young for his age, or even inexperienced. Even she could see that Charles knew his world very well. He would know how to pick the right wife. He had sufficient confidence in himself not to choose unwisely.

After a stormy rebellion, during which she cried copiously, Julie felt sorry for herself for having had the misfortune to fall in love with a man who seemed to think he was not morally free.

Then Julie decided to fight for Charles's love ; but even as she thought like this Julie knew that she was butting her head against a wall of iron convention.

She retreated defeated from this belligerent attitude.

And so it went on throughout the night, her thoughts milling around rebellion, pity, fighting and defeat. It was dawn before, tired and weary with thoughts that seemed to turn in circles, getting her nowhere, she fell into a deep sleep of exhaustion.

She awoke to find it was daylight. She felt lighter and better, her thoughts no longer chaotic, but clear and at peace. Some time in her sleep, subconsciously Julie had conquered her experience. She still loved Charles. She would never change. But she was not going to allow herself to be broken by it. She was not the kind to sit down long under defeat, and because she had been unlucky in her love affairs allow herself to be disillusioned and emotionally lame for the rest of her life. She was a girl of courage and spirit. She would go back to England in a few weeks to a new future. She refused to be morbid or pity herself.

She got out of bed and opened the pretty handbag she had

carried last night and took out the folded programme of *Carmen*, and read the list of dates she had made for a week with the new cousins who seemed friendly disposed towards her. Grandmère would be annoyed if Charles asked her out and she could not go because of these dates. Grandmère might even try to cancel them, as she had done so ruthlessly with André and Hubert before. But she, Julie, would be strong and not allow this.

Later, Julie sat in a French bergère chair at the telephone in the boudoir, listening to Charles's voice, with the bright gleam of morning sunlight striking through the windows on to her hair. He had asked at once, "Are you better today, Julie?" and she had replied:

"I feel fine, but it is terribly hot in this room. All the windows are sealed. They don't seem to like fresh air."

He had laughed sympathetically, then he said eagerly, "What is your mood?"

"Oh, light and gay!"

They both laughed self-consciously.

"Then you will want to dine at that kind of restaurant in keeping with your mood." He was silent a moment, then he announced, "I know the very place. It is chic and you must wear that lovely white dress which makes you look like an angel. What time shall I call for you?"

Julie caught her lip sharply in her teeth. She had remembered the list of dates with the various cousins. She could not cut them so easily as they had been made. Now she could not go with Charles. The realization of her position was heartbreaking. It was all she could do to prevent herself crying out with rage and disappointment. What a fool she had been!

She cried briefly, "Oh, stop! It sounds so exciting, but I can't go."

There was a pause. Julie felt that she had dashed cold water in Charles's face.

"Why not?"

"Because—I have another date."

"You made it last night?" Charles asked curtly.

"Yes."

"But you knew I had something for us in mind. There was no privacy to make arrangements last night. That was why I suggested phoning this morning."

"I—forgot. There were so many cousins, all asking me to go out with them."

80

"I am sorry." Charles spoke stiffly.

"So am I." Julie sounded so genuinely regretful that Charles relented a little.

"Then I suppose it must be some other night."

"No, Charles, not the next or the one after that." Julie spoke firmly. "I am booked up for a week."

"Do you mean that?"

"I'm afraid so."

There was a silence. "I see," Charles said slowly then. "Pardon. I did not understand. Obviously you do not wish to go out with me again or you would not have booked up every evening until you leave for England."

Julie could tell that he was angry by his voice. She thought, 'It hurts Charles's pride not to get his own way.' She tried to harden her heart by remembering all the resolutions that had formed themselves in her mind in her sleep, but it was harder than she had expected.

Striving for self-control, to pretend a nonchalance she did not feel, Julie did not speak for a few moments. It was awful having to deny him. Julie's eyes looked hopeless, and the sun gleaming through the window on everything in the room was a mockery.

Charles did not seem to notice her silence. He was too full of his rebuff.

"So this is the end," he said.

Julie thought, 'He is taking it calmly'; and she thought again, 'I don't believe he really cares if he never sees me again. It is his pride that is hurt.'

"What do you think?" Julie managed to ask flippantly.

"You know how I feel."

"Do I? I am not a thought-reader, you know."

"No. Then I shall not be seeing you again."

How could he speak so quietly when there was so much at stake? She felt anguished, but made herself say demurely, "That depends on you, Charles, for I am not returning to London so soon as I thought. I am staying in Paris with grandmère."

The announcement appeared to put a different complexion on matters.

"Julie!" There was no mistaking the gladness in Charles's voice now. "How cute of you to arrange it." He had obviously thought she had done something to please him, and took himself to task for having been so unkind to her.

"I didn't. Grandmère and my mother seem to have done that on the telephone last night."

"And I was thinking you did not wish to see me any more, and meant to go away and never return, and that you would forget me as quickly no doubt as you have forgotten many other men in your life."

"Would that matter much to you?"

"Why of course. All day yesterday we were together. And you can say that!"

Julie laughed. It was an odd sound. "Well, you can be sure of one thing, Charles. I won't forget you ever."

"Is that a promise?"

"Yes."

Charles did not make the mistake of arranging a new date a week ahead. Presently he rang off. Julie felt herself to be left in the air. She wanted to see Charles again and soon. Yet she had deliberately arranged matters so that she could not see him. It left her strangely dissatisfied and disappointed, yet she had only herself to blame.

As Julie had no excitement for the rest of the day except some sightseeing and a cinema with Nina, she thought, 'I may as well take a longer French lesson.'

The Professor read to her for a short time. She had no idea what he read, but it amused her to watch his face, and to wonder idly what she could do to make him laugh. Julie even made a bet with herself that she would have him laughing at or with her, it did not matter much which, by the end of the week. The effort to do so might assuage a little of that loneliness from which she was suffering and which was an entirely new sensation to her. To make him interested in her, to encourage him, would perhaps give her back some of the self-confidence that Charles had robbed her of, for Charles was not easily conquered. Though he made her feel loved, admired and wanted, he reserved his own emotions. It made her feel vulnerable and powerless.

So Julie worked hard to rouse the Professor's emotions, but at the end of a long, exhausting lesson, she was still in the dark as to whether the Professor had any emotions to arouse.

Some time during the day a cellophane box arrived from the florist's, full of lovely La France roses. Julie lifted them gently from the box. She knew, though she had not read it, that the bit of pasteboard pinned to one of the roses, belonged to Charles. She stood for a long time with the flowers lying in her arms, thinking of Charles.

In the evening Charles rang up. Julie had been feeling bored but now she was full of joy.

"This is to remind you of my existence, Julie."

"You have already reminded me with the flowers you sent me."

"Do you like them?"

"I adore having them. How sweet of you to think of me!"

"It is as nothing. I know you are going out this evening with the cousins. What are you wearing?" When she told him, her heart leaping, her eyes dancing and every nerve in her slim body quivering, he cried, "*Charmante!* Are you dressed now?"

"Oh yes, and waiting."

"I can imagine you."

The following day some starry white stephanotis came, and with them a box of chocolates with an absurd French poodle tied to the cover with the tricolour of France.

Oddly, Julie missed Charles's telephone call. She would have preferred to hear his voice than to eat the wonderful chocolates he had sent.

Grandmère was well pleased these days. At first she had been annoyed to learn that in those few minutes of absence from the family box at the opera, Julie had found time to do the wrong thing in making numerous dates with her cousins. That was offset by the flowers which had arrived during the day from Charles.

Madame lunched with her brother, Michel, at his favourite restaurant near the Bourse. There, away from Nina and Julie, or the ears of servants, they could talk freely. At the moment, Michel was only too ready to spare time from business to listen to his sister. He could not afford to be patient much longer over this plan that had taken shape in his mind. There had only this morning been a meeting with the advertisement manager about the best way to present the new Patrice-Ryan car which was now ready for the home and foreign markets. When he heard that Julie had refused to go with Charles, pleading other engagements, he was angry.

"You are going the right way to making a mess of everything. It may not matter much to you, but *I* shall look a fool. I have tried to keep my plans from the family, but I find they know more about them than I do myself. It is common talk in my club that the lawyers have been told to prepare contracts of marriage."

"You know we cannot make a decisive move until Charles's mother returns from the Riviera. She must be consulted, and then only if she is well enough to discuss business."

Michel snorted. "Business! Such a business is pleasure. She is quite fit, I am sure, to speak openly to her son. He expects her to arrange his future. He must be waiting for her to say something."

Madame Lubin did not believe that. Charles was obviously enjoying himself at the present time, not only with Julie, but with Mademoiselle Lucienne Jeanson, and perhaps other women, for he was popular. But she said nothing of this to Michel, who was an irascible man and easily upset.

She said placatingly, "Charles is clever—telephoning, sending flowers and chocolates, and keeping his personality before Julie. It will do them no harm not to meet for a few days. They will come fresh to each other. I do not worry."

Michel was easily mollified. He said, "Perhaps Julie is even more clever. In making arrangements with her cousins she is keeping aloof from Charles. He always gets his own way, I notice. It cannot be good for him. By holding back, Julie will spur him on. That is human nature. But——"

"You want them to hurry. *Bien !* A little more patience, and you will find yourself president of the biggest car combine in France, with a bigger fortune and greater power than ever before."

"Shall we drink to that ?"

"*Certainement.*"

CHAPTER IX

Much happened in the next two weeks. After the round of pleasure and entertainment with some of her cousins Julie went out again with Charles. They spent wonderful evenings together, at the theatre or cinema, or dancing at various night clubs— Le Chat Noir, L'Oiseau, L'Ange Bleu, and Fleuris. Charles did not stick to one club. He liked change. He had noticed that Sulka Knizburg was attracted to Julie, and for some reason he did not understand himself, wanted to keep Sulka from being too friendly.

Julie had acquired a small wardrobe of exquisite model clothes. The beauty and the simplicity of their line gave her confidence and poise. With those came tact.

She did not ask Charles any more questions about his friendship with Lucienne Jeanson, though there were times when Julie was seized with a fierce burning jealousy of the actress. Once she coaxed André and Hubert, who were frequent visitors to the house, to take her to the theatre where Lucienne was playing lead. In spite of a feeling of bias, Julie was bound to admit that Lucienne, if not a great actress, was exceedingly good. She had personality and charm, and Julie was fascinated and able to understand why Charles was so attracted. She was depressed, too, realizing how she must fail in comparison with Lucienne. She had no charm, personality or graces. It was useless hoping to win Charles away from the actress. She had tried to amuse him. At first Charles had shown a tolerant amusement to her efforts, which had changed lately to an alert interest—but no more.

But Julie was no longer content with being noticed. She wanted something more. Charles was kind enough to give his evenings to her, and Julie put this down to her good dancing and marvellous clothes. It was no effort for Charles to dance with her, while he liked being seen with a well-dressed woman. Also Charles, having been asked by grandmère to take her about and give her a good time, was doing his part.

There were times, however, when Julie allowed herself to think that Charles's glinting eyes were telling her a deeper message than just a man's admiration for a pretty girl, and that Charles might be falling in love with her, but they were only fleeting moments, for Charles was too experienced, too debonair, too much a man of the world ever to allow his emotions to run riot, out of bounds of will power.

Julie knew that for her own serenity of mind she was seeing too much of Charles. Soon there would be a terrible price to pay in agony of longing if she continued to meet him, and dance in his arms, feeling the strength of them, but without any passion in the grip. Yet she continued to give herself up to the enjoyment of these precious evenings, which, with the return of Charles's mother from the South, might come to an abrupt end. When with him, it did not seem to matter which night club they visited, or what friends she met there. There was no reality in the world outside Charles and herself. Indeed, only Charles existed.

Later, of course, after they had said their brief 'good night,' there was the rest of the night to be got through somehow—and alone, in the semi-darkness of her room, when bitter-sweet memories and regrets crowded in to haunt her.

As the days passed, Julie grew more beautiful, but her body

became thinner with strain. Madame le Gère complained that if a dress fitted Julie's figure like a glove one day, the next it hung upon her like a sack.

Secretly grandmère was worried. She recalled that Nina once went into a decline because she was prevailed upon not to marry the man she loved, for her family had already chosen another man as her husband. That milestone in Nina's life had meant two years spent in a clinic in the Swiss mountains. Nina had never been the same since.

Perhaps Julie was still in love with the Englishman? It might be so. Jeanne had written that the man, Harvey Robins, had asked for Julie's address. That could only mean that he wished to make it up with her.

One dawn, when Julie tossed about sleeplessly in bed, there was a knock on the door, and Nina came into the room, looking like a ghost in a trailing white gown, and carrying a small tray with a teapot and teacups on it.

"I heard you moving about," she said to Julie, who had switched on the light when Nina knocked. She put down the tray. "I came to see why you cannot sleep; and bring you some tea—English fashion."

Julie sat up in bed. "I should love some," she cried. "You can't think how often I have longed for an old-fashioned cup of tea. I am sorry I disturbed you." She remembered the open window and threw back the sheet ready to jump out of bed. "But you must be cold. I will close the windows."

"Do not. I like them open."

"Do you really? I thought your family liked everything sealed against fresh air."

Nina smiled slightly, as she busied herself pouring out the tea. "I learned to like them open when I spent two years in a clinic in the Swiss Alps. I had no choice at the time."

"What was the matter with you?" Julie inquired, taking a cup of tea from Nina, stirring it slowly and then tasting it.

The tea was weak, tasteless, and to Julie, horrible, but she sipped it courageously.

"Is that how you like your tea?" asked Nina, watching her.

"It is just right, and so refreshing at this hour."

Nina sat back in her chair, well pleased with her effort. "They said I was going into a decline."

"'They' ? Do you mean doctors or grandmère ?"

"All of them."

"And were you ?"

"No, I had a broken heart."

"Oh, Tante Nina !" Julie cried sympathetically. "Do you feel able to talk about it ?"

"Oh, yes. It is old history now. It happened fifteen years ago."

"What happened ?"

"Nothing. I fell in love with one man, and my parents wished me to marry another whom I hated."

"Well ?" Julie inquired curiously.

Nina shrugged. "I had the strength to refuse the man I hated. . . ."

"Then why didn't you marry the man you loved ?"

"I do not know. He had no money. I had none, because naturally my parents would give me no *dot*. He vanished. I never heard of him again."

"What a shame !"

"Perhaps. But if I had married the man my parents wished, possibly I should have been happier."

"But not if you hated him ?"

"Why not ? It would have been a life for me instead of existence. But I was young, and youth, though valiant, is not far-seeing. That belongs to older people."

"What became of the man you hated ?"

"I still see him occasionally. We do not know each other now. When I refused him I wounded his pride mortally, and now, between the two, I am lonely, sour and—exist."

Julie looked long and owlishly at her over the teacup. Nina recognized herself—unwanted, embittered and just existing. Dull, with no zest in life, she had allowed one bad experience in her life to spoil it completely. She had permitted her spirit to be broken and to die under disillusionment. Julie looked at her in dismay. Nina had a depressing halo of hopelessness about her. Then the girl said vigorously :

"I think you're looking at this from the wrong angle, Tante Nina."

"What is the right angle ?"

"I am not sure ; I am only certain that yours is wrong. You have changed inside in fifteen years. You don't even know where the man you loved is. It does not interest you. You don't appear to care. I do not blame you. It is wrong to look back and never forward. Why not make an effort, snap out of the past, let it go and start afresh ? You are still young. You are pretty, and you could be prettier if you liked."

"I could not do that," Nina told her flatly.

"Why not ?"

"It is too late."

"No, it isn't. You only talk like that because it is easier. You won't make the effort."

"I should not know how to begin. It would seem unorthodox. People would talk, and say, 'Look at Nina Lubin. See the mutton skipping about like lamb.' I should look a fool. People would laugh at me. My mother would be ashamed. There is no comeback for women like me."

"Let them laugh. There *is* a come-back. You start one. Come out with me. I'll help you."

"What ! Go out with you and Charles Patrice ? That would never do."

"Charles would not mind. He's a good sort, and always ready to help people." But she thought, too, 'I'll explain to Charles. He will understand.'

Nina laughed. It was her first genuine laugh for years. "It does not matter whether you or Charles mind. It is my mother who would care."

There was a short silence.

Julie put down her cup and saucer on the bedside table. Her face was sobered as she said, "Why should grandmère care so much, Tante Nina ?"

Nina had already realized that she was talking too much. Now she said, "Not only Maman, but everyone would say that I was the unwelcome third. They might suggest that I wanted Charles for myself. People have such quaint ideas."

But both she and Julie knew that the answer was weak.

They talked about Nina for a long while, and reached a point where Nina was content to speak about her future and forget the past.

But long after Nina had gone, taking the tea tray with her, Julie lay on her back and pondered about Charles and herself. Julie thought, 'Grandmère likes Charles. I think she wants him to like me. Perhaps it is in her mind that we may marry.'

But Julie knew Charles's secret, that his future wife was already chosen for him. This was something which evidently grandmère did not know, and would surprise her when she did.

Julie's mind see-sawed back to Nina, and she had a passionate wish to help her forget the past and regain her emotional health. 'Sitting at home and moping about what is over and done with will get her nowhere,' thought Julie.

That evening Julie dined out with Charles. They did not go to a theatre. Charles was not in the mood for dancing, so he said :

"Let us go somewhere quiet, away from our friends and crowds," he said to Julie. "I want to talk to you."

Yet when they sat down to dinner the atmosphere was too quiet, so heavy that they were aware of the sound of their voices which destroyed privacy, too conscious of each other, and had nothing much to say—not one of those things that seemed tonight to fill the hearts and minds of both to the exclusion of all else.

As usual, when out together, they drank champagne, not sweet or dry, but a taste between the two, pricking the palate and lightening their spirits. But somehow even the effects of the wine did not last, and lingering over the coffee, Charles sighed heavily more than once.

"What is the matter with us this evening that we are not so gay ?" he asked at length.

"I am enjoying myself."

"So am I in a way. But we are not like ourselves. There is something wrong."

"No, there isn't," denied Julie, "unless it is you."

"It cannot possibly be me. I am very happy. I am alone with you, which is what I like ; and my mother is coming back from Cannes tomorrow, very fit and well."

"So what ?" cried Julie, in English. She had been talking in French. It was quickly becoming a habit with her. She was not fluent, but the pauses and broken accent were fascinating to Charles. If the sentence were too involved, or her vocabulary gave out Julie would break into English. Her progress with the language had been astounding, and when people commented upon it, Julie generously passed on the praise to her French professor who was a genius at teaching.

Charles repeated the slang. He knew how expressive it was. "So what !"

Charles knew what was depressing him, what lay like a dead weight upon his spirits. His mother's homecoming was the signal for a family conclave about his marriage. He had looked forward to this arrangement of his life with calm, and even pleasure— before he met Julie. Now he wondered how he could postpone what was beginning to be irksome to him. With his heart else-where, marriage with a strange girl whom he might respect but could now never love would mean a life of misery. He had not got so far as refusing to fall in with his parents' wishes. He was a good and dutiful son and had no desire to hurt them or cause them worry. But he wanted to be happy in his marriage. It was not much to ask. Charles debated whether he could confide how he felt about Julie to his mother, and if he did whether she would understand. She was sweet, kind and loving, not over-blessed with intelligence, but a perfect housewife, this last some-thing which Charles knew his darling Julie was not.

His mother was hidebound by tradition. She had a great respect for the size of a girl's *dot*, and Charles was well aware that Julie had not a sou. She was quite frank about it. He did not care about it either way himself. It was the family who cared. These things carried weight with his mother. She might therefore be blind to what he considered his happiness. She was feminine, chic and pretty, and knew how to use all her womanly arts to bend his father to her slightest whim.

If—supposing she were on his side. . . .

Charles abandoned the idea. It was no use. Somehow, he knew his mother could never be won over. It was foolish and unpractical to suppose she could.

But the prospect of the near future, and the changes con-templated in the state of his life, depressed Charles so that he could not hide the heaviness of his spirits. It made him irritable and impatient.

Julie was looking ravishing tonight. Her hair gleamed under the shaded lights. Her personality was vivid. Her lovely grey-blue eyes looked mysterious and dark under the thick fringe of lashes. Her skin——

Why go on with a list of this wonder girl's charms? Charles caught himself up sharply. He smoked his cigarette thoughtfully, his eyes fixed contemplatively on Julie, his thoughts, confused and emotional, milling about until his head ached under the strain.

Julie, too, was feeling emotional. She knew well what the homecoming of Charles's mother meant, for he had told her laughingly in the early days of their friendship, when they were able to talk about love in an abstract way, or as though it were a game. It was only lately that they had discovered love was a serious matter, and that there was no game about it.

Now, thinking of all this, realizing that the end of a perfect friendship was in sight, slowly the joy and pleasure of the evening seemed to ooze out of Julie, leaving behind such a load of depression that nothing could lift. It came to her then how much she had hoped that something would turn up—and it had not.

She felt suddenly isolated from Charles. They had been close friends, but now he seemed withdrawn and remote. The warmth, bordering on something more intimate, that had been between them like some living thing, binding them together, was there no longer. It did not exist.

Charles said swiftly, "What about some more champagne ? Perhaps we'll feel better after a drink."

"No, thank you. I've had enough, but you have some more if you think it will do you good."

"Drink alone ! That *would* bore me."

"Well, I don't want any more."

"All right. But we must try to get back quickly to normal. Tell me something to amuse me."

"I don't know anything especially amusing—unless," and here a bright idea struck Julie, or rather she remembered how earlier in the day she had promised to help Nina, "you asked me to dine with you again ?"

Said in that deprecatory small tone, it brought forth an immediate response.

"Oh, yes—again and yet again." It was as though Charles would never let her go out of his sight.

"Then, next time, shall we go out as a foursome ?"

"A foursome !" Charles frowned. "Are you talking about golf ? What do you mean ?"

Julie smiled faintly. She said in a bold tone, "Why not take Tante Nina with us ?" Charles's frown deepened, and Julie rushed on, "She has rather a dull time at home. It would do her good to get out sometimes with people like us."

Charles stared uncomprehendingly, "You mean, you want a chaperone ?" and his tone was cold.

"Of course not." Julie was not so sure of herself now. Charles could be stupid when he liked. "I thought, if you invited Nina, and a suitable friend of yours—a man about her age—someone not tied up in any way . . ." Julie floundered on. She was stopped suddenly, frightened at the icy glare that had crept into Charles's eyes. She thought in despair, 'I knew he would not understand.'

"So," Charles said, and his eyes glittered with anger, "you find it boring to dine alone with me ?"

"I did not say so."

"No, you thought it."

"I didn't."

"Are you afraid of me?"

"Good gracious, no."

"Have we exhausted everything we have to say to each other?"

"I don't suppose so."

"Suppose! Why do you not answer 'yes' or 'no'?"

"No."

"Then why do you wish to drag Nina Lubin into our friendship?"

"I wanted to do something to cheer her up."

"You were thinking of her?"

Julie nodded.

"Not bothering whether *I* should like it."

"I do not like it much myself."

"I do not like it *at all*. No, Nina shall not come out with us. I refuse to have her."

Julie shrugged her slim shoulders. "Okay, it is as you wish— your dinner party! I thought we were friendly enough to make a suggestion, but it seems I was wrong."

Julie was relieved that Nina was shut out. It would be rather a big sacrifice for either of them to have her because Nina had acquired the habit of criticism and suspicion, and could not be expected to change her nature in a moment. She would have a bad influence on them.

Charles asked suddenly, "Did Nina make the suggestion?"

"Don't be silly!" Julie replied testily. "Of course not. She knows nothing about it."

"That is what I thought. She would be too sensible to make herself unwelcome."

"You mean *I* am foolish."

"Foolish! That is hardly the right word. Imbecile would be better."

"Thanks." Julie's mouth trembled a little.

Charles saw it and softened. He stretched out his hand placatingly across the table.

"I am right. Everything is wrong between us. It is not your fault, but mine."

"No, it is mine. It was stupid my suggesting that Nina should join us."

"It was silly, but I suppose you had your reason."

"I have tried to explain."

Clearly Charles did not believe her.

"Yes, I know." Charles smiled. "I am a brute with a pain in the head—not myself. Indeed, I have never been so difficult before, not knowing what I want, but sure that I want something." He paused, then said, "The truth is I am harassed."

Julie put her hand in his outstretched palm, and Charles's thin, steel-like fingers closed over it.

"I knew you were worrying about something."

"Yes, and the trouble is that I can do nothing about it—or I can, but I shall upset many people in doing so."

Charles looked at Julie with heavy moodiness across the table for some minutes. Julie had never seemed so beautiful and desirable to him as she was at this moment, when Charles had to face up to the fact that the end of his friendship with her was in sight, or decide to hurt his family as never before by refusing to carry out their careful plans for him. If he did the latter it might possibly mean parting from them, something he did not wish to do.

Yet this new emotion, which Charles recognized as love, was powerful and dominating. It could not be put aside or forgotten or disregarded in any way. It was a part of himself, his very life, so that Charles felt existence would not be worth while if he could not enjoy his love. He would feel dead without that vital love.

It was an issue Charles knew he would have to face, if not this week-end, then certainly some time next week.

There had been time to hold back before the emotion had grown too strong for him to withstand it, but somehow Charles had let it pass, believing somehow in his strength to put the affaire behind him when he chose to do so. He had deliberately avoided making a decision. Now, it was too late. The emotion had not only caught up with his will-power, but had swiftly mastered it, and was with him always and forever. He could not forget because it was now a part of him. He felt suddenly helpless. It was this helplessness which made him irritable, even with Julie whom he loved so deeply. While this new idea which had been sprung upon him, that she was bored with him, or did not delight in his company, wishing to drag Nina along with them, was frightening. It might mean that Julie did not love him in the same measure as he loved her. It would be Charles Patrice who would suffer when they parted. It was an unbearable thought. It would be bad enough if they both regretted parting, but if he was going to be alone for the rest of his life, then he was going to be an unhappy man. Charles had no tolerant thoughts for the girl who had been chosen to be his wife. At that moment he hated her.

Charles tried to tell Julie something of the muddle that was in his mind, a confusion which had begun over a week ago, and gained momentum when she went about with her cousins and left him to his own devices and thoughts—and Lucienne, whom he had liked once, but who now bored him. But the words refused to be said. The English was beyond him, and the French was meaningless to Julie, and lost point when he explained. He broke off in the middle of a sentence, crying with the impatience of despair :

"Oh, what is the use of talking."

Julie sympathized with Charles. She was feeling wretched herself, not knowing how deeply Charles cared for her, or indeed if he cared much at all, certainly not enough to oppose his parents' wishes.

'But it wouldn't be any good if he did,' she thought. 'We couldn't be happy. There would always be the shadow of his parents' displeasure between us. They would tell Charles that I had forced him to do something unorthodox, and at the first disagreement he would remember this and blame me. Later, he might taunt me with it, and where would our happiness be ?'

So she said quietly and with some philosophy, "It is useless sighing for something you can't have."

Charles turned on her. "It is all very well for you to talk. You will go home to England and soon forget me. You may even marry that man you were once engaged to."

That, too, was a nagging worry at the back of his mind : Julie might still love her ex-fiancé.

It was infuriating when she agreed calmly, "I might. One never knows."

"There, I knew it," cried Charles. "You have not forgotten him."

"How can I when you remind me of him ?"

"Oh, you are impossible tonight, Julie. I like you so much that I am jealous of your shadow if only because it is always with you."

She laughed lightly, not because she felt like laughing, but to save herself from crying, when she would create a scene in the restaurant, something she knew the fastidious Charles would dislike intensely.

Julie strove hard to make the remainder of the evening with Charles bright and happy, and partially succeeded, for Charles rallied and took a hold on himself. They agreed, by tacit consent,

94

to speak of pleasant things. But the shadow that all was not as it should be remained.

If Charles had intended to take a tender leave-taking of Julie that evening, he was baulked. For just as he drew his car to a standstill at the kerb outside the Pierre-Lubin house, Madame Lubin arrived home from a card party. She greeted Charles warmly and invited him into the house, but knowing what that meant—a half-hour *en famille*, talking platitudes, and not being left alone with Julie, he refused. Under those conditions, seeing Julie was too great a strain, especially tonight when his nerves were so ratched by his confused thoughts.

He went to the door with them, his eyes meeting Julie's for a brief moment, when they were eloquent with feeling. Then kissing Madame's hand, and bending over Julie's, squeezing her small hand convulsively in his thin, steel-like fingers, he waited until they were inside the door and it was closed. Then he went away.

On the other side of the door Julie stifled a sigh. The events of the evening had left her frustrated, dissatisfied and discontented. Whatever Charles had intended talking about this evening had not been said. Julie would have liked Charles to make love to her, something he seemed always on the point of doing, yet had never done—unless one counted such abstract lovemaking as was possible with his eloquent eyes and caressing voice. With grandmère his manner was perfectly correct.

In the dim light in the hall, grandmère looked sharply at Julie.

"You look heavy-eyed, *chérie*," she remarked. "Late nights do not agree with you."

Julie did not answer. She appeared not only tired but dispirited.

Grandmère opened her mouth to speak, but thought better of it, and closed her lips again. Grandmère thought, 'It will all be over in a few days now, and I think Julie will be happy once more.' Then remembering the shadow of that man who lived in England, and who had once played an important part in Julie's life, and might still possess a part of her heart, she thought again, 'At least, I hope so.'

Looking back over the last month, Madame was quite content with the progress of her little intrigue.

They went upstairs arm in arm, for grandmère these days was showing quite an affection for Julie.

"Have you any engagements for tomorrow, *chérie*?" she inquired.

"André and Hubert are taking me to a dance in the evening," said Julie, half-afraid lest grandmère should object because the cousins were taking her out and not Charles.

"Where?"

"It is at Georgette Roth's flat." (Georgette was a married cousin.)

"That will be very nice," was the gracious answer.

'Perhaps she knows that Charles's mother is coming home, and he must be there to meet her,' thought Julie. 'Otherwise I am sure grandmère would have raised some objection to my going out with Hubert and André.'

Grandmère went on, "I expect to be busy over the week-end, but Nina will look after you. On Tuesday I am giving a small dinner-party. It will be a family affair."

"Am I to go to the party?" Julie asked, and hoped that Charles would invite her out that evening.

"Yes. I especially desire that you shall be with us," said grandmère impressively. "And I want you to wear your best dress."

There was nothing new in her saying that. It was becoming a habit for grandmère to say, "I want you to look your best. All your cousins here seem to have the idea that English girls have no dress sense. You must show men by your example that they have."

"If they haven't," Julie had remarked, "it is because clothes are expensive, and for years they haven't had the chance of buying anything decent."

Grandmère had answered, "Well, never mind. Wear your *best* dress."

Julie did not hear from Charles over the week-end. She waited for Marie to come to her room and tell her that she was wanted on the telephone. No letter arrived for her. No flowers were delivered from the florist bearing Charles's card. It was as though a door had been closed suddenly on their friendship.

At first Julie told herself that she could not expect Charles to spare her any of his time or thoughts over the week-end. He was devoted to his mother whom he had not seen for some weeks, and they would have much to say to each other. The fact that mother and son would have much in common to interest them caused Julie a sharp prick of jealousy, because Charles's mother had a right to enjoy his company, while she had not. It passed quickly, however. Later, when the silence between them seemed long, continuous and unbearable, Julie became anxious. It was useless telling herself that Charles had spoiled her lately. He had paid her so many little attentions that when they ceased she missed them. More than anything Julie longed to see Charles and to hear his voice.

Neither grandmère nor Uncle Michel happened to mention Charles's name, though it had often been said during the last weeks.

After a short period of anxiety came pique, and then anger.

Charles had no business to neglect her like this, making much of her one moment and appearing to forget her existence the next. It was unfair.

Once more Julie felt that curious helplessness whenever she thought of the position between them, for she could make no further plans to attract him. Charles was not free. What could happen in the future was up to him and no one else. Yet what he might do only Fate knew.

Julie thought fervently, 'If only Charles would say, "I love you," or "Do you love me ?" ' She would know then what to do. So great was her longing for him that she might even fight for him. It was the uncertainty that was so unnerving. It undermined her confidence in herself and her power to attract men. She felt unsure and nervy. Once a sickening thought came to her that perhaps this absence was Charles's way of letting her down by degrees when saying 'Good-bye.'

Well, it was her own fault. Charles had been quite frank from the beginning. She had only herself to blame for any pain and worry.

Not once did it occur to Julie that perhaps Charles was suffering a secret misery because of her. He was always restless and alert, his mind working with a Gallic swiftness which she admired, thinking, 'In England such quickness would be called impulsive, but in France high spirits, vitality and rapid decisions make up the usual national tempo.' He was usually gay, debonair and overflowing with physical activity. Even lately, when Charles had been worried, he had used laughter as a kind of armour to hide the real state of his heart from Julie, and also his feelings from his friends. So no one knew what was in his head or heart. Certainly Julie, occupied with her own longings, did not. She only hoped—and there are times when hope seems faint and the human spirit droops.

CHAPTER X

As often happens with well-laid plans, the unexpected setback came. It was Madame Lubin who felt it first.

It was Monday. The week-end had gone well. Everything had taken place according to plan. The old gentleman, Michel Pierre, seemed to spend the day rubbing his hands together, the outward expression of inward pleasure. Madame Lubin's voice had softened. Her eyes were soft when they rested on Julie before lunch. The girl was going out to Versailles, to spend the day with some Americans who had rented a villa near the Palace. The French lesson had been postponed until the early evening, and she was not to be expected home until six o'clock. Julie looked lovely as ever when she set off. If her eyes were a little tragic, her face paler than usual, and there was a quiet languor about her which meant that she was either overtired or sad, Madame Lubin ignored it.

When Julie had gone, Madame herself went out to lunch with Charles's mother, and spent the afternoon talking to her of Julie, the granddaughter whose existence Madame had barely recognized until lately, but who now occupied a large part of her heart and life.

When Madame Lubin arrived home soon after five o'clock she was told by Matras that a gentleman was waiting to see Mademoiselle Ryan.

"Who is it, Matras?"

"An English gentleman, Madame."

"Oh!" Madame's worst fears were realized, and she said quickly, "What is his name?"

"Monsieur Robins, Madame."

"Ah! I hope you told him that Mademoiselle is out, and that we have not the slightest idea when she will be in?"

"I did, Madame, but he did not go away. He said he would wait to see her."

"You should have got rid of him."

"I did try, Madame, but the gentleman said he had come a long way to see Mademoiselle. It was important and he would wait."

Madame nodded absently to show that she had heard. Then she decided, "I will see him. He is in the library, you say?"

"*Oui*, Madame."

Madame did not wait to go upstairs to remove her things. She took them off in the hall, with Matras's help. They were placed carefully on a chair. She opened her bag and with a deftness born of long practice repaired the damage the day's wear had done to her make-up. Then slowly and deliberately, her mind working rapidly, she crossed the wide hall to the library door.

When Matras would have preceded her and opened the door, Madame waved him aside. She entered the room swiftly, hoping to surprise the young man who waited to see Julie. She was anxious to find out as much as possible from his manner and the expression of his face, what kind of man he was.

She looked across the room at Harvey who, hands in trouser pockets, was pacing to and fro in the room. He was just finishing a promenade and was about to turn when the door opened. He stopped and looked expectantly towards her. Madame had time to catch the glad expression in his face before Harvey realized that the person standing in the doorway was not the one he had come so far to see, and his muscles sagged with keen disappointment.

Slowly Harvey drew his hands from his pockets. He bowed slightly.

"Madame Lubin?"

Madame took an instant dislike to his voice, which was harsh and overbearing and grated on her sensitive ears. She did not like the coarse red hair which covered his massive head like a thatch. She thought, 'He could be clever, but I am afraid he is a fool. He let Julie go so easily. Now I suppose he has tumbled to it that he had a treasure within his grasp and wants her back. If I can possibly help it he never will.'

Harvey had no idea of what was going on in Madame's fertile brain. Her gentle, aristocratic look gave him no indication of the adamant will-power that existed within her.

It was now Madame Lubin's turn to bow slightly and distantly.

"Yes?" Her tone was cool.

"You do not know who I am?"

"Matras, my butler, tells me you have just come from England. Did you come by plane or boat and train?"

Harvey moved impatiently. He had not come to talk about his journey.

"Does it matter?" he demanded roughly.

"Not at all. It was merely a polite expression." Then Madame sat down in a large chair, and indicated another close to her. "Please, sit down. It is easier to talk."

Harvey sat down with more force than elegance. He felt impatient with this old Frenchwoman.

Madame folded her hands, and crossed her legs at the ankles. She looked demure, unpretentious and disarming. Actually she was alert, on her guard for Julie's sake, and anxious to get rid of this young man as quickly as possible before he had time to do any mischief.

"You are a friend of my granddaughter."

Harvey regarded her in silence for a long moment. For the first time, hearing this old lady claim kinship with Julie, he realized that Julie had foreign blood in her veins, and it must be this which made her so unpredictable, often unmanageable, and sometimes unaccountable to him. There had always been something about Julie which he did not understand, but which lured him back to her whenever they quarrelled, and it was her fault, which he could never put a name to. Now he knew what it was. It was that part of Julie which was alien.

"'Friend' is putting it mildly," he said shortly. "I was Julie's fiancé—Harvey Robins."

"Julie told me so."

"Oh, she did!"

"But you are not now."

"No."

Harvey stiffened. He hated having to admit that he was nothing to Julie now.

"How did you find your way here, M'sieur Robins?"

"That is an easy one, Madame," said Harvey, respectfully enough, but with just that amount of looseness of speech which he usually found strangers liked, for it made them more approachable to each other. It had the opposite effect on Madame. Her jaw stiffened as though someone had hurt it. She would have spoken, if only to keep this man, whom she disliked so much, at a distance, but Harvey continued speaking:

"I could not stand life any longer without Julie, and decided to see her and make it up again. I went to the flat and found Julie's parents standing with their baggage in the hall, waiting for a taxi to take them to the station. It was luck for me that I arrived in time to get Julie's address from them. As I had a holiday owing to me I came across at once to see her."

So far they had talked in short sentences which both could

understand, but Madame could not get the meaning of all that Harvey had just said. He had to repeat it several times, and then make pantomimic efforts which would have amused Julie could she have seen him, before Madame Lubin caught the gist of what he was telling her.

"My daughter, Madame Ryan, gave you the address ?" she asked disbelievingly.

"No. Julie's father did."

"Oh !" Then Madame inquired, "Where are you staying ?"

Harvey mentioned a cheap little hotel somewhere behind the Opera House. Madame had never heard of it, but she knew from Harvey's graphic description of the district, the crumbling façade of the hotel, its owner looking after the guests himself, that it was the kind of hotel she would never know.

"I was recommended to go there," he explained. "I don't know anything more about it than you do."

"Who told you about it ?"

"Well—as a matter of fact, it was a porter at the Gare du Nord."

Madame's eyes were fixed on his face, though she scarcely saw him.

Harvey was uncomfortably aware that she considered him poor, and unworthy of Julie. It was shattering to Harvey's self-esteem to observe the comfort and luxury with which Julie was obviously surrounded, quite different from her home-life in England and what she was used to there. He began to wish he had not come. Perhaps he should have written to Julie and told her how he felt, leaving her to invite him across, as she surely would.

Anxious to get this horrible interview over, Harvey said, "May I see Julie ?" He felt that if only he could see Julie all would be well. Together they would prove more than a match for this ridiculous old woman with her old-world airs and graces, which were out of place these days.

"But of course. . . ."

"Your butler said she was out, but I didn't believe him," said Harvey confidently.

"Matras spoke the truth. Julie *is* out."

Harvey did not believe Madame either. He had got it into his head that Julie was in this house. Perhaps the old girl was deliberately keeping her a prisoner, away from him—somewhere upstairs. . . .

Harvey looked suddenly belligerent, the veins on his bull-like neck standing out like whipcord, his hands hitherto loosely clasped, clutched each other convulsively.

But Madame, unaware of the tenor of his thoughts, met his fierce look with wide-eyed innocence.

"Out !" he repeated.

"Why not ? She is visiting Paris. Is it not natural for her to wish to see our lovely city ?"

Harvey had not thought of that, but he replied, "I suppose so."

"Indeed, I have been at pains to show Julie the best in every way."

Again this sentence had to be repeated, this time by Madame, amiably, until Harvey caught the gist of her remark.

"That is kind of you. I bet Julie lapped it up. She is a greedy creature, and knows what is good."

Madame shrugged as though to say that everyone was greedy. She said kindly, "Perhaps you will join us this evening at dinner ?"

It would be policy to keep an eye on this young man. Better to have him at the house, under her watchful eye, than that he should take Julie out and spend the evening with her goodness knew where.

"I am sorry. I haven't a dinner jacket with me. I left in rather a hurry."

"Then you do not expect perhaps to stay long ?"

"No, I shall return soon—possibly tomorrow. But I had to see Julie if only for an hour." And in case the silly creature did not understand, Harvey said again, "I simply had to see her."

"Was that not impetuous ?" How condescending she was ! Well, he was not going to be patronized by anyone, least of all this stupid old woman.

"I am that."

"Would it not have been wiser to write the letter ?"

"I'm no letter-writer. My thoughts are too quick for my pen." Then Harvey said, "Will Julie be long ?"

Madame glanced at her little jewelled wrist-watch, a treasure that once belonged to Queen Marie Antoinette.

"Not long," she said, thinking, 'As he had to come, this *bête*, how much better to get the sorry business over tonight, instead of upsetting things tomorrow.'

"I hope to persuade Julie to come out with me tonight. We could get a snack somewhere. I don't feel much like company until I know which way Julie is going to jump," Harvey said.

Madame smiled dimly. She loathed this young man who, for all his obvious poverty, might, if only because of a certain attractive animal handsomeness, upset all her carefully laid plans.

She said quietly, "Perhaps Julie will take pity on you. It is for her to decide."

"I don't want Julie's pity. I don't even want her to come out with me unless she really wishes it."

Harvey found himself mentally counting the small amount of money in his wallet. He wished he had worked harder or saved more last year, but he had not bargained for a trip like this. He had not contemplated being engaged then.

"Julie likes fun," Madame told him enigmatically.

Harvey laughed. He was glad he *could* laugh in this stuffy room. It released some of the tension that knotted his nerves so that he wanted to hit out at somebody.

"You bet she does. We used to have wonderful times together. If we both had money we'd 'blew' the lot. If I had some tin, I paid ; and if she had a few shillings, she did. But we managed to enjoy ourselves."

"I understand," Madame nodded. "But that was yesterday."

"I know. Yesterday ! It seems ages ago, like a lifetime. Don't rub it in, please. Yesterday ! And today and tomorrow are other days. But whatever happened, in spite of everything, our love, hate and differences, I still love Julie, Madame."

"Do you ?" she asked gently and curiously. "That sounds a little sad, for in the meantime Julie may have changed towards you."

There was a long, uncertain pause. "You mean she has ?" Harvey asked anxiously.

"I do not mean anything so certain because I do not know ; but Julie has met so many cousins of our large family, and she has made many new friends. It is possible that amongst so many people she may have found one special friend."

"Perhaps you hope she has." It was dawning on Harvey that this old woman, far from being feeble and frail, was a demon of mischief. If she were disposed to be friendly there was much she could do for him, but if she hated him, as he felt she did, then Madame could make a formidable enemy.

She said now, "I have tried to create a fresh interest in life for Julie. When she arrived in Paris, Julie was a poor, peaked little thing, frightened as a mouse, afraid to speak, with no poise, no joy and no clothes."

"Oh, my poor Julie !"

"Not yours any longer, M'sieur."

"Surely that is for Julie to decide."

Madame nodded.

"But that isn't my picture of Julie, Madame."

"No ? Then yours is wrong—I do not know how you say it ?" she gesticulated prettily.

"You mean mine is out of focus ? Go ahead." His voice was tense now. He feared the worst. Julie was lost to him for good. . . .

"It is as nothing. Julie had, I saw, great possibilities—so many good points—but so many horrible clothes. I have attended to them all. I think you will find her changed."

Harvey sighed with relief. He thought, 'Is that all ?'

"I'll recognize her, Madame, don't you worry," he told Louise Lubin.

Madame rose abruptly. It wasted time to talk to this man. She said, "Julie may be a little late. I have an appointment and cannot stay with you. Perhaps you would care to call later."

"No, thank you. I should only mooch around, not knowing what to do with myself, and probably miss her. If you don't mind, I'll wait here."

Madame did not want to watch the two meeting. Julie, too, would expect some privacy in meeting her old friend. 'But I wish I could stay,' she thought, 'or that I dared send him away.' She knew, of course, that these were vain wishes. She must leave them together and hope for the best—the best being that Julie herself would send him away for ever.

Aloud she said, "You will find some papers on the table. I am sorry they are all French, but I did not know you were coming."

Harvey replied frankly, "It would only puzzle me trying to read French. But don't you bother about me, Madame Lubin ; I'll find something to amuse me until Julie comes." But what, Harvey asked himself grimly, could possibly amuse him in this great mausoleum of a house, a relic of old France ? It should have been burned down years ago. He was as anxious to get rid of Madame as she was to go.

She apologized many times before leaving him.

But when she had finally gone and he was free from her silent criticism, Harvey also had time to think with growing anxiety about Julie. More than once he thought, 'I wonder now what Julie has been up to since she left England ?'

It was bad enough to think that the old lady had filled Julie's mind with foolish ideas, encouraging grand ideals and setting a standard of living that was new to Julie, and which he could not possibly carry on in England.

'The old fool,' he thought with some annoyance, 'does not understand that we have had such a dose of utility it will take a full generation to want much else.'

Only ten minutes after Madame had left the room, but seeming like twenty years to Harvey, he heard voices in the hall outside the door and recognized Julie's light tones speaking in French. There was no time for him to feel disquieted, for within seconds the doors of the library were thrown wide open and Julie, laughing excitedly, stood on the threshold.

It was a dramatic entry. To Harvey, turning to stare at her in awe, she appeared to be the loveliest creature on earth.

He exclaimed loudly. It was a cross between a cry and a greeting.

"Harvey! They told me you were here, but I could hardly believe it." Here was a familiar face, an old friend, someone who spoke her language and who understood her—someone who *liked* her. Throwing her handbag down on the nearest chair, Julie ran towards Harvey and gave him both her hands. She was suddenly overjoyed at meeting one of her own countrymen, and one she knew well, too.

Harvey tried to meet her in a dignified manner. But somehow he could not stop his feet from running to meet her. The result was the ponderous playfulness of a big bear.

"Julie!"

He took both her hands in his large ones. He would have drawn her close to him and kissed her not once but many times, as he used to do when they were engaged, and as he had the urge in his joy to do again.

It was Julie who held back, and dashed some of his ardour. She cried hurriedly, anticipating a warmer welcome and rejecting it, "How did you get here? Why have you come?"

There was time now to feel dismayed at his arrival, for Harvey was not a man to take hints, and his presence might prove a nuisance, especially if Charles saw him. Not, Julie thought sadly, that there would be any danger of that at this hour. The only person who might interrupt them would be her Professor, and he seemed so inhuman he did not count.

Harvey said, "I came by train and boat. You can ask me why I have come? Oh, Julie! Surely you know?"

"Well, I don't." No sooner were the words said than Julie guessed the truth, something she had no wish to face. "Have you been waiting long?" How strange she sounded—so sure of herself!

"Just long enough to get cold feet."

"That is one thing you do not suffer from, Harvey," retorted Julie. "You should have warned me you were coming and I would have hurried back to meet you."

"You know I am a rotten letter-writer."

"Then you should have telephoned."

He could have done that, but Harvey forbore to remind Julie that telephoning cost money, and she would know, if she stopped to think, that he never had a penny to spare.

"Yes," he said slowly and sadly, "I could have phoned. It did not occur to me. I was in a hurry to see you ; and I wanted to surprise you."

Since meeting her he was conscious of a disturbing quality in this new Julie. Not only did she look different in every way, with smart clothes and an assured manner which made him feel like an immature schoolboy, but there was a delicate, indefinable and heady scent about her—powder, soap or scent. He did not know if it were any one or all of these, but the effect on Harvey was to confuse his senses and make his head swim a little.

Their hands fell apart, and Julie sat down on a hard, stuffed, walnut-framed settee, covered with a beautiful tapestry depicting French hunting scenes. It was uncomfortable, and would probably have looked more at home in a museum. Harvey sat gingerly on the edge beside her.

"Anyway, I've got more to say than I could possibly put clearly in a letter," he told her, not looking at Julie, whose great eyes were on his face, but at the books on the far wall opposite to him, which were neatly arranged in serried rows from floor to ceiling, and which looked in immaculate condition as though they were never used—as indeed was the case.

"Yes," Julie said flatly, sensing what was coming and wishing she could avoid it, but realizing that the sooner it was said the better for both of them. But how he bored her !

She was looking at Harvey with frank, critical eyes, wondering with some dismay what she had ever seen in this big, red-headed man to like or admire. He looked coarse, uncouth and rugged. Or did he seem so in comparison with the debonair Charles ? Harvey's hair was too long, the ends drifting over the edge of his collar. He appeared unruly and undisciplined. Something in Julie withdrew from him. She hoped he would not want to touch her. Harvey slipped two fingers within his collar, as though to ease its constriction. Then he said plaintively, "It isn't going to be as easy as I thought it would be in London. You might at least meet me a quarter of the way."

"How can I, when I am in the dark ? I expect it is the effect of a strange city—or even this room. Go ahead." That was meant for encouragement. It did not help Harvey.

"Maybe," he agreed, "but I think, too, it is you."

"Not poor me?"

"Yes, you've changed. It certainly isn't *poor* you."

"I haven't. Perhaps it is my clothes."

"They're grand." His tone said that the clothes were too grand for Julie. She resented such silent criticism from Harvey, who knew nothing at all about clothes.

After a pause Harvey complained, "You don't seem to want to hear what I've come so far to say."

"Oh, I do! What is it?" Julie sounded artificial.

"There you go again. 'What is it?' You are too blunt, too forthright. *I* am speaking about love."

Julie tried not to laugh. There was something funny in Harvey's approach to love.

"Why didn't you say you had made the journey especially to talk about love?"

"I inferred it. You are sharp enough to know."

Quickly he took her hand in his, and though Julie tried to draw hers away, disliking the contact, Harvey clung to it.

"Julie, I love you." His voice was a croak. He was feeling the strain of seeing her again and finding it so difficult to speak of his emotions. It was out now, what he had followed her to say, and he waited breathlessly for her answer, for the first time not sure whether it would be favourable or not.

"You didn't think like that when we parted," Julie told him unexpectedly, giving him a respite in which to regain some of his courage. Unfortunately she might be discussing pigs or cake, not love.

"I know, but I've changed since then."

"Until we squabble, when it will be the same all over again."

"That's a nasty thing to say when I've just told you I love you."

"Well, I can't forget that you once said you hated the sight of me."

"I said a lot of stupid things ; people do when they are in tempers, and I don't profess to be better or worse than other men. Besides, I wasn't in love then. It is different now, I've had time to think, and to realize that I am in love with you now."

Julie smiled. "I doubt it. Even if you love me it would make no difference to you when in a temper. It would be the same as before in no time at all."

"No, it wouldn't. I promise you I'd control my temper. I know I've been a fool, but I've learned my lesson. It shall never happen again. Give me a second chance, Julie, and I'll prove to you what a decent fellow I can be." His voice changed. He spoke more persuasively, "Let's get married at once, Julie. Cut out all thought of a white wedding, such as we had planned. We won't bother about a flat, but live part of the year with your people, and the rest with my mother. It won't matter to us so long as we are together, and it will save no end of expense."

Julie was silent for a moment, then she asked, "Where should we have our children ?"

Harvey bit his lips. Then he said, "I hadn't got that far in my thinking."

"I thought not." Then she added clearly, "What should we live on ?"

Harvey frowned. He had not dreamed that Julie was so practical. He said glibly, "If we live in the present the future will shape itself. . . ."

"On how we live in the present." Then she demanded, "Have you got a new job ?"

Harvey shook his head gloomily.

Julie sighed. "Money is so necessary," she told him. "If you love me . . ."

"I do."

"All right, but how could we possibly marry on a pay packet that won't keep *you* ?"

"You think it clever to be smart about cash. I would rather talk about love."

Julie ignored this. "We should soon lead a cat and dog life, because I, too, have a temper."

"You are creating difficulties."

"Marriage is for two people—two mouths to feed, two minds, two——"

"Your share would be to be a good companion and to spur me on to success. I could take my troubles to you to solve."

Julie laughed lightly. "I—I—I—Oh, dear, that sounds too much like hard work for me !"

Harvey paused. He did not like the sound of Julie's laugh. He did not even like her ideas. She had grown selfish and thoughtless. If he did not love her so much he might feel sorry he had made the trip to persuade her to change her mind.

"You've changed," he accused bitterly, "and for the worse."

"No, I haven't. I don't believe either of us has at heart. It isn't possible."

"Then it is those grand clothes you are wearing — this luxurious way of life that your grandmother appears to enjoy and that she has forced upon you."

"Oh, I wouldn't say *forced*. I like it."

"You look as though you enjoyed it. All these things have combined to change you from the Julie I know, and honestly, it isn't for the better."

"Does that mean that you do not like my lovely clothes?"

Harvey gave her a cursory glance—at least it was meant to be that, but somehow his eyes would linger on her lovely face. It drew him like a magnet. There was far more life and meaning in her expression than was usual when in London. In spite of everything he tried to do to please Julie she had often looked bored.

"You look all right," he admitted grudgingly.

Julie smiled. "That is scarcely a loverlike tone," she complained.

Harvey stared at her moodily. He had felt elated before this talk, thinking that if he exerted a little pressure Julie would consent to going back to London with him. If she could not go home to an empty flat, she might be willing to stay with his mother. Now he was depressed. Julie was not in a temper. He knew how to deal with that. She was difficult, wilful and unmanageable.

Then he had an idea.

"What's behind all this?" he demanded suddenly.

"What do you mean?"

"For years your grandmother ignored your existence. In fact, I had no idea there was a French grandmother in your family."

"You knew my mother was French."

"Of course—well, I didn't know her mother was alive. It was your father who put me wise when I called at the flat a couple of days ago. Now I find you installed in this palatial house, dressed up like a doll, changed out of all recognition. Even your hair-do is different."

"Everyone says it is an improvement." Julie's voice was cold.

"Do they? I liked you as you were. They've trimmed you up like a fine lady, given you a taste for all this which you will never forget—made you vain, conceited and selfish—and for what? That's what I'd like to know."

"My grandmother was shocked to see a country bumpkin. She has done her best for me," said Julie stiffly.

"Right. Admit it! But to what end? I suppose she has a reason for doing it?"

"Family pride, I should think."

"Rot! The old lady warned me I'd find a difference in you. I have. But there's more to it than that." Harvey looked suddenly wise. Then he said angrily, "If you can ignore an honest man's love—and don't forget you were glad of it once, and returned it —then it means that you have met someone else you like better. You are not the kind of girl to run around without a train of admirers. Julie"—and here Harvey's voice was hoarse with consternation and fear—"you haven't fallen for a Frenchman ?"

Julie tried to refute such a fantastic idea, longing to keep her secret to herself, ashamed, too, to confess failure to Harvey in being unable to arouse an answering emotion in Charles.

"I know several Frenchmen," she cried shrilly. "Many of them are my cousins."

"Cousins !" Harvey grimaced. "That heading covers many friendships. What about the Frenchmen who are *not* your cousins ?"

She evaded an answer by saying, "Even if I fell in love with a Frenchman who was reasonably presentable, with charming manners, and who knew how to make divine love——"

"I suppose that is one for me."

"——I could never marry him. All the nice men are already booked by their families to marry suitable girls. I do not come into the picture, for the French are practical; and I have not the first requirement to make a suitable partner in marriage, for I have no *dot*."

"You have your face : isn't that enough ?"

"It goes a long way, and makes friends for me, but it isn't enough for marriage. The *dot* comes first."

"So it has all been discussed ?"

"No, it hasn't ; but I've learned quite a lot about French customs since I've been in Paris."

"A matter of weeks !"

"And in a French family."

"Who discuss whethe a girl has a *dot*, and what size it is. Very funny !"

Julie got up. It was useless prolonging the talk. Her nerves were frayed. It would not be long before Harvey said something outrageous and they began to scrap. It seemed a cheap sort of end to what she had once thought in her ignorance was a beautiful love affair with Harvey. To hide her feelings Julie said something trivial, the first thing that came into her head.

"I think I'll go upstairs and titivate," she said. "I have a French lesson at six."

"Titivate for a French teacher !" Harvey derided. "Is he *the* man ?"

"I am not going to answer such a stupid question."

"Then it is. I shall wait and see this teacher—I suppose it is a man? I shall tell him what I think of him."

"You'll have to work hard because he does not speak a word of English."

"Then if words are no good I shall have to depend upon my fists. *They* are strong, and will need no language to speak for them but their own strength."

"I hope you won't disgrace me by creating a scene," Julie remarked in her coldest tone.

"What do I care? I've got nothing to lose. It may put you in a bad light with him. They may even, as a consequence, tell you to clear out," and he hoped they would.

Julie supposed that *they* meant her family, and she said wearily, "They might." Thinking of Charles had reminded her that everything was at an end between them. After seeing him nearly every day, talking to him on the telephone, or receiving gifts and messages, she had grown to think of him as a part of her daily life. Suddenly this had come to an end. It coincided with his mother's return from the South, and may or may not have had anything to do with it, but the fact remained that she had not seen Charles or received any communication from him for over three days. There was no explanation, just a blank. For a moment Julie was tempted to go back to England with Harvey. That would certainly kill even the faint hopes which she clung to about Charles—that he might fall in love with her so deeply, he would refuse to obey his parents' wishes about the future. It would put an end not only to those hopes, but to the torment and stress to her nerves, a strain which Julie was finding unbearable. It might be the most sensible thing to do. It was her heart which would not allow her to give up that last vestige of hope. Even as Julie stood still, dithering in her mind what to do for the best, Harvey, sensing a certain weakening in her will which brought the bully in him to the surface again, said angrily:

"I might have saved myself the trouble and expense of coming over for all you care. I should have done so if I'd known that my journey was going to be such a washout. You are still furious with me for breaking our engagement. You mean to take it out on me because you didn't get your own way. I always knew you were bad-tempered, but I thought it was soon over. You are sulking, pretending there is some French Johnny who has fallen for you just to make me jealous. I am beginning to doubt your sincerity with anyone. Well, stay here. I'm for England. But when you are sick of it here, don't come whining to me, begging me to make friends, because I won't do it—so there."

Harvey had worked himself into a fine rage. His thick hair seemed to stick up like a mane about his head. Looking at him coldly, Julie thought that with his red hair and red face he had never looked so unattractive. She walked towards the door.

"If this is how you behave when you are abroad, you will soon get yourself disliked," she said quietly. "Now I really must go. Good-bye. I'm sorry about the result of your journey, but nothing could be the same again. If only you had thought to telephone. It would have been cheaper in the long run because I should have told you not to come."

Harvey did not answer.

CHAPTER XI

JULIE had nearly reached the door when there was a quick movement behind her, and Harvey flung himself past her and stood facing her with his back to the door.

"Don't go like this," he cried unevenly. "I didn't mean a word of it. I was afraid of losing you and lost my temper a bit. I won't do it again, I promise you. Come back with me and let's make a fresh start in England, where we belong. How can a man be expected to behave rationally in a foreign city which actually enjoys living on its emotions. I can't go back alone and leave you here, at the mercy of these people."

While speaking he had left the door and stepped towards her, his arms outstretched in a pleading attitude.

Julie adroitly evaded the arms which remained fully extended. Harvey looked like a colossal statue.

Then he said hoarsely, "Julie ! Darling ! You can be so sweet when you like ; be kind to me."

At that moment, the double doors to the library were flung wide open and two men stood on the threshold, their attitudes stiff, arrested by the scene that confronted them.

Julie and Harvey turned their heads.

The tableau remained for one long revealing moment. Charles and the Professor stood side by side in the open doorway. Charles seemed taller, his manner coldly aloof. The Professor stared owlishly. Behind them was Matras, a wooden expression on his face.

Julie saw all three men, but she only observed Charles.

In that moment Julie hated Harvey, who stood towering close to her, looking more like a monster than a man, his hands no longer outstretched towards her but hanging clenched at his sides.

It was Harvey who spoke, his manner overbearing and his voice harsh.

"Who are these men, Julie?" He looked at Julie and saw in her eyes what he had feared to see. He had been right. She had fallen for a Frenchie—one of these men. Harvey thought the Professor appeared too learned and too poor to appeal to her, and his eyes, leaving her face and passing over the Professor, went to Charles—handsome, elegant and proud, with the air of a man who gets what he wants, an air only possible in a man with a well-filled wallet and who has confidence in himself. Intuitively Harvey knew that this was Julie's man—a formidable rival indeed.

The knowledge shook Harvey. It was bad enough to know that another man had stolen Julie from him, but it was worse to think that the victor was better in every way than himself.

'This man has everything that it takes,' Harvey thought bitterly, 'and now he has Julie.'

At the sound of Harvey's hard, penetrating voice, Julie moved. For a moment she remained staring stupidly at Harvey, then in a low voice, nervously, she said, "Mr. Robins—M'sieur Charles Patrice and Professor Gant."

Charles barely inclined his head. He looked like a king taking notice of a miscreant. The Professor held out his hand, and for some unknown reason—unless subconsciously he recognized a fellow-sufferer—Harvey gripped it convulsively.

Charles spoke, his voice thin and distant, "I called to see you, Julie. I did not know you were engaged with your friend." He spoke in French rapidly, and Julie, listening with painful eagerness to the lights and shades in his voice, understood. But Harvey did not.

They all stood in the dim light of the room with its heavy curtains and furniture, and the rows of calf-bound, unread books. A curious happiness had welled up inside Julie at sight of Charles. It was curious because while the happiness at seeing him once more was there, she was suddenly afraid. Charles looked festive, with a pink carnation in his buttonhole, and she guessed instinctively that however censorious his mood was now, he had entered the house in a spirit of gaiety. She had never seen him look so severe as now. It was as though he stood apart from her, like a stranger. Julie knew that he was puzzled and annoyed at Harvey's presence in the room. He might be jealous, too, for Charles had entered the room at that moment when Harvey was behaving ridiculously, and it was easy for Charles to misconstrue his attitude. At that moment Julie loathed Harvey for endangering her happiness.

Answering the look in her expressive face, Harvey nerved himself to step towards Charles and strike a belligerent attitude, hoping to frighten the Frenchman whose build was lighter than his own. "I must ask you to speak in English, sir, the only language I can understand," he declared with pompous dignity. It was the outward expression of an inward fear that Charles would get the better of him in every way, and show him up in a poor light to Julie.

Charles glanced coolly at Harvey. "That is a pity, M'sieur, for I prefer to speak French."

"I take it you can understand my language?"

"English? Oh, yes. Mademoiselle Julie is kind enough to say I speak it very well."

The lingering way in which Charles said the name, Julie, enraged Harvey; but instinct told him that this was not the moment to lose his temper and lay about him with his fists. Losing temper with Harvey usually meant that he said and did violent things he was sorry for afterwards. So Harvey, with obvious effort, tried to remain quiet.

"Then if you won't I shall assume it is because you want to say things to Miss Ryan that you do not wish me to hear," he said hotly, his voice, through sheer frustration, rising in a crescendo of sound so that he appeared to boom instead of speak.

Charles shrugged. "I am not answerable, M'sieur, for what you assume." But he spoke in English.

The shrug said that Charles did not care.

Harvey stood at bay, looking from one to the other, with eyes that were red-rimmed with rage and hate.

Julie spoke. She was full of fear for the reason that she did not want Charles to judge by appearances, to think that she had invited Harvey to the house, or that the meeting was pre-arranged, or even that she wanted to see Harvey—because she did not.

Julie had a longing to stand well in Charles's eyes. She said, and her voice was low but more assured now, "My friend, Mr. Robins, arrived unexpectedly from England to see me."

"Oh!" Charles looked closely at her face for a long moment, as though trying to penetrate its lovely expression, hoping perhaps to read her thoughts. Then he asked abruptly in French,

"May I ask why? You need not answer if you do not choose." His tone was dangerously smooth, and Julie knew that he, too, was trying to put a check on his emotions.

"It is no secret. I do not mind your knowing. Harvey came to ask me to be friends again."

Julie spoke placatingly, hoping that Charles would understand that this unfortunate position had been thrust upon her and was not of her seeking. She had been surprised, too, at Charles's excellent command of English—fluent and accentless. She was unaware that Charles had been spurred to brilliance by a desire to show off before Harvey.

"Ah!" It was a sibilant sound, and Harvey looked from one to the other with suspicious, alert eyes.

He cried, "You are talking about me. Don't dare to deny it. I heard my name."

Charles glanced frigidly at him, then smiled slowly. Watching his face with fascinated eyes, Julie knew that Charles was beginning to enjoy himself in a queer way.

Charles nodded, then ignoring Harvey, spoke rapidly in French to Julie.

"And what was your answer to Mr. Robins? Are you going to make a friend of him again?"

"Never." It was as though they were in a world of their own and everyone else was excluded, a feeling that Harvey recognized and which made him furious.

"Then you do not love him any more?"

Julie drew a deep breath. "I do not think now that it could possibly have been love," she said in a voice scarcely above a whisper.

"Then you will not mind if I send him away?"

"Oh, no. The sooner the better. But please do it quietly. Grandmère will be angry when she knows that Harvey has been here so long."

Charles faced Harvey. He moved like an automaton, as though jerked by strings into position. He spoke in precise English.

"If your business is over, M'sieur, I suggest you leave this house."

Harvey's face lightened. He felt that he had scored a small victory in making the fellow speak English, to him, at any rate.

"Ah, that's better," he said with heavy encouragement. "Now I can understand what you are trying to tell me. My business is *not* over. It could be a pleasure if it were, but you have spoiled that. It will not end until Miss Ryan agrees to return to England with me. I should like to remind you that this is not your home, and I shall certainly not leave it because you ask me—or indeed want me to go."

"Mademoiselle Julie has already given you your answer, and if you have any sense you will accept it. She is not returning to England—not yet, at any rate. She came for a holiday, and it is not yet finished. I beg you to go if only because your presence here is an embarrassment to all of us."

"I like that! It's none of your business, so shut up," cried Harvey rudely. He was at a disadvantage, because if he were to insist on calling Madame Lubin in to arbitrate, the old lady might only confirm Frenchie's request. Yet if he refused to go, then Frenchie himself might send for Madame Lubin. The result would be the same. They were all against him—Julie who might have had the decency to stick up for him, and even that fool of a Professor, who stood goggling at one or another, not speaking, only glancing now and again at the great bronze clock on the marble mantelshelf, as though anxious to assure himself of the time.

"It is my business," said Charles blandly.

"How?" snapped Harvey.

"For several reasons, but chiefly because I am a friend of Mademoiselle Ryan's."

"So am I. She is my countrywoman. I knew her before you did," he cried possessively.

"Ah, but we are in France now."

"That makes no difference. She belongs to England, and so do I."

Charles turned to Julie. She met his look with a smile and a slight shake of her head, as though to say, 'Don't tease Harvey. He can't stand it.'

She noticed that all the pride of possession that had been in Harvey's voice was gone. He knew himself to be beaten, and a sense of pity for him swept through her because now he could never be anything to her or she to him ; and also because in the past she had been quite content with what he had offered, and in spite of stormy scenes occasionally they had had fun together.

She understood clearly what Harvey even now only dimly appreciated.

At the same time her eyes fell on the Professor. He was staring through his thick glasses at Harvey as though he were mesmerized, and there was a queer expression on his face. Then

116

it seemed as though that expression cracked, and he smiled. It sat strangely upon a face which Julie had been accustomed to seeing serious and still. The animation went further, for as the Professor's mouth widened a queer sound issued from his lips. He began to laugh—at first quietly, his shoulders heaving with inward mirth, and then after a series of explosions, he burst into hearty laughter.

Julie was shocked. There could be nothing about Harvey or his position to cause laughter—yet obviously the Professor was amused.

Harvey glowered at the man who dared to laugh while he was wallowing in defeat and misery.

Charles pretended not to notice, but when the Professor showed no signs of stopping, he asked stiffly, "What is so funny ? Perhaps we may share the joke."

Such an invitation should have caused the Professor to pull himself together, but he only shook his head as though it were impossible either for him to share the joke or stop laughing.

Harvey spoke. He shouted to get above the laughter.

"Are you laughing at me ?"

The Professor nodded. He pointed at Harvey. Then he said, almost sobbing with hysteria, "There is a spider on M'sieur's hair. I have watched it travelling on a single thread from the ceiling down—down."

Harvey had no idea what he said, but the other two did. For a moment they looked at Harvey, saw the spider, and for no special reason, unless it was that the Professor's mirth was infectious, began to laugh hysterically.

Harvey began to stamp up and down the room.

"You are all raving mad !" he cried. "Idiots ! Lunatics ! Julie, I will shake you if you don't stop this insane cackle. I know the joke is on me, but at least tell me what it is so that I can laugh, too."

Julie's mouth was wide open. She was laughing heartily, with her head thrown back, and her teeth gleaming, showing the lovely line of her throat.

She cried, between gusts of laughter, "There is a spider nesting in your hair."

Harvey dashed his hand to and fro over his head. "I'm glad you are all so easily amused," he shouted.

But the laughter did them good. It relieved the tension that had been in the room. When at last, dabbing her handkerchief to her eyes, Julie stopped laughing, the atmosphere was lighter and less restrained.

Then Madame Lubin came unannounced into the room.

Matras had heard the noise of quarrelling in the library, and had hurried to tell Madame that the English M'sieur Robins had gone mad.

Madame was dressed for the evening, in trailing draperies of her favourite black. She swept into the library, her long dress touching the carpet.

She was overjoyed to see Charles. In his hurry to tell her about Harvey, Matras had forgotten to acquaint her that Charles had arrived. But she frowned at Harvey as though to say, 'Are you *still* here ; I thought you had gone.'

She held out her hand to Charles Patrice. He took it in his, bowed over it and raised it to his lips.

"Dear Charles !" she said softly. Charles was here in her house, and that pleased her, for at that moment he was the one man she was desirous that this creature, M'sieur Robins, should see. She thought, 'If this friend of Julie's sees what a small chance he has of success with her against a rival such as Charles, he will go away and never come back.'

Unfortunately Harvey did not view himself through Madame Lubin's eyes. He was not that stupid, he did not understand her cold glance and read in it a wish that he should go, but he had no intention of staying away. Obviously Julie was under the influence of these people. But once he could get her away from France, Harvey was sure that she would soon be her old self and turn to him for friendship. They might become engaged again.

Even as Madame entered the room, encompassed the hilarious scene at a glance, and had been greeted by Charles who seemed to be in the best of humours, Julie composed herself quickly. The Professor's face lost the clownish look that unseemly laughter had given it, and was his usual serious self. Harvey alone looked injured.

Madame glanced at the clock and said to the Professor graciously, "It is too late now to give a lesson. Perhaps you will return tomorrow at ten o'clock, Professor Gant."

The Professor bowed. Such was his need of the money that he would have given Julie a lesson at midnight or any hour about dawn if he had been asked. He was keenly disappointed that he had missed today's lesson. There had been some recompense in that burst of unrestrained laughter at the droll Englishman, especially when Julie and M'sieur Patrice had joined in, but laughter did not cost a sou, though a missed lesson meant several francs. His only fear was lest Julie should report his lapse of good manners to Madame Lubin who would probably dismiss him at once. She had impressed upon him at the time of engaging him that the lessons were to be taken seriously on both sides, and that Mademoiselle must be taught quickly.

He bowed himself from the room, his eyes flitting nervously from Madame Lubin to Julie.

Matras, strong disapproval on his face, met him in the hall and saw him out of the house.

As the door closed on the Professor, Madame turned to Harvey.

"Well, M'sieur Robins, have you had a nice talk with Julie?"

"Yes, Madame, we had our talk," agreed Harvey.

"I am so glad." Then she said, "You must come and see her again soon." That was only a polite remark, a feeler put out to learn whether Harvey was returning to London tonight or tomorrow. Madame thought that Julie should have made it plain to her friend that nobody in France wanted him to stay. She was surprised and annoyed to think that Julie had been so careless of Charles's opinion in permitting him to remain to meet Charles. And then she remembered that Charles, too, had not been expected, and his visit was quite as much a surprise for Julie as M'sieur Robins's had been.

To Madame's astonishment, Harvey answered, "Thank you, I will—probably tomorrow, if you don't mind."

"Tomorrow!" Madame wrinkled her brow in thought, well aware of Julie's sudden discomfiture at this announcement and Charles's dismay. She concealed her own thoughts which were rapidly giving her a headache, and said, "We all have a busy day tomorrow."

"I am sorry."

"Oh, you could not know. But come the following day, at nine o'clock in the morning. Will that suit you?"

"That is rather early," objected Harvey.

"But you want to see Julie?"

"I do," and he thought, 'The old witch is making it as difficult as she can.'

"That is her only free time. She has a French lesson at ten o'clock, a fitting at the dressmaker at eleven-thirty, at twelve-thirty the hairdresser is due, at one-thirty, there is a lunch party, at——"

Harvey interrupted the flow of words. He could not bear to listen to any more of these trivial vanities that must cost a packet of money, which took up Julie's day. No wonder the girl was getting spoiled. When he got back to England he would take good care to let Julie's father know about these goings-on.

He would not appeal to her mother because he felt that Mrs. Ryan had too much sympathy with her daughter, and would take her side against him. He said, "I will be here the day after tomorrow, at nine o'clock precisely."

"Then it is arranged. I am so pleased because I know you will be returning to England very soon, and I do so want you to see as much of each other as possible," said Madame graciously, smiling up at Harvey.

But he did not return her smile. He said, "All that is changed, Madame. I do not know *when* I shall go back to London. It depends on Julie."

"But your wardrobe ! You have no baggage, no——"

"I will manage somehow. At a push, I can borrow some clothes."

"You have friends then in Paris ?"

"Several. I did not want to look them up this trip, but I can."

Madame's impulse was to say, 'That is not the truth. You have no friends in France. You are not the sort of man to have many friends anywhere.' But her instinct told her to be careful. Her plans for Julie had not as yet matured, and she did not want to say anything to jeopardize them. So she smiled, saying, "That is very nice." It meant nothing at all.

CHAPTER XII

WHEN Harvey had gone Madame Lubin turned quickly to Charles and said :

"I did not know you would be calling here this evening."

"Neither did I, Madame Lubin, until an hour ago."

"To see me ?" she inquired archly, her wise old eyes fixed on his face.

Charles smiled. There was a dazzling quality in it, the expression of inward joy and happiness which nothing could hide. From his radiant look it was obvious that both spirit and soul were in the throes of a triumphant happiness.

"To talk with Julie," he said simply.

"Oh, then I will go away and leave you two together," she said at once, aware from his jubilant manner, the air of queer elation which made itself felt, as though he were lifted by some great joy out of his ordinary mood, that something unusual had happened. She guessed what it was.

She went to leave the room, aware that he was giving her only half his attention, that his eyes, soft and sweet, were fixed on Julie's face, and that he was emotionally deeply moved.

Charles stopped her. "No, don't go. What I had to say must wait a little longer." He spoke urgently, swiftly and nervously. He added, "I was just leaving, anyway."

"Say it just the same," pleaded Madame prettily. "I do not believe in putting things off."

"No, another time." Charles said to Julie, "*Au revoir*, Julie." His eyes glinted mischievously. "I have not laughed so much for a long time." He had never been in such good humour. His spirits were volatile. There was a tenderness in the way he looked at Julie which made the girl want to cry with joy and delight.

"I shall see you tomorrow," he whispered, squeezing her fingers in his hand, unaware that his hold was hurting her. "It is not very long now." He sighed quickly, as though tomorrow were a thousand years off.

The room seemed strangely quiet without his vivacious presence. A silence fell upon the two women. Neither exerted herself to show animation. There was no need now that the male audience had gone.

Madame looked at Julie, and saw that the girl's face quickly lost its alert look. She looked white, sad and a little chilled, so that her beauty, which depended as much on her colouring as her expression, looked blighted, like a lovely rose that has been caught by frost.

Julie was thinking, 'I am a fool to imagine there is anything in all this. It is just Charles's manner. He must be a born philanderer. Almost I could believe it to be real, that he loves me and wants to tell me so.'

She must wait until tomorrow to know why Charles had come today. Because she wanted Charles to make love to her so much he would probably talk about a new dish that he wanted her to taste, or a new play—things that seemed so unimportant just now, when her whole being yearned for love.

Madame spoke, her voice shattering Julie's dream-world. She said : "It was most unfortunate your friend from London calling at that moment, when Charles visited you."

"Very. I tried to send him away, but he would not go."

"Perhaps you did not try very hard."

"You do not know Harvey. In certain moods he is incapable of taking a hint."

Madame could well believe that.

Harvey's coming had made Julie wretched. She had not wanted to see him, and had no idea how to get rid of him because he was that kind of man who could only accept a fact. Julie could not present him with the fact that she was engaged to Charles. So long as she was free Harvey would continue to force his company upon her, saying, 'You must change your mind. Women do, you know.'

There was only one thing that made her feel a little better tonight, and that was because Charles, alert and impetuous, tender and triumphant, had called to see her, to tell her some news. He had not told her because of Harvey, who had poisoned the atmosphere. Perhaps Charles had been secretly annoyed or jealous at sight of Harvey. Julie could not guess. She had sensed a reserve in Charles's manner when he first came into the room, but that had soon passed when she told Charles that she had never loved Harvey, and would be glad if he were sent away. But the strain of meeting Harvey had spoiled Charles's visit, and he had not felt like telling her his news. Well, she must wait with patience until tomorrow.

There was another setback for Madame Lubin in the morning.

When Julie had finished her French lesson and was in her room, dressing to go out, Madame came in. As usual, she made straight for the windows which were wide open. Closing them with a bang of determination and annoyance, Madame exclaimed:

"One of these days you will catch pneumonia. I could wish that you were not such a demon for fresh air."

Julie knew by her tone that she was put out about something, and waited for the older woman to speak.

Grandmère sat down. "Such a tragedy! One of the guests I had invited to the dinner-party tonight is too ill to come."

"What a shame!" commiserated Julie. "Can't you fill his place?"

"It is a lady. That means that two people will not come."

Julie looked suitably sympathetic. Thanks to grandmère, Harvey would not bother her today; also she would see Charles.

She said, "Your dinners are so famous and you have so many friends, I am sure you will not find it difficult to invite others in their place."

"You do not understand, *chérie*. The dinner was being arranged for these two guests."

"That is a real tragedy."

"I shall have to postpone it." But Madame looked distressed. She gave so many parties that this kind of thing must often have happened before, yet judging by her anxiety this might have been the first time.

Julie was puzzled. She said, "I thought it was to be a dinner *en famille*?"

"It was, but strictly formal, too."

Julie recalled that grandmère wished her to look her best. Madame Lubin said, "My guests were the Patrices."

"The Patrices!" echoed Julie stupidly, turning to face Madame. She did not understand the significance of the visitors, but she knew they were Charles's parents, and wondered why they were dining here. Then she remembered that the two families were old friends.

Madame explained, "Madame Patrice, who has but just returned from the South cured of her illness, has had a relapse. At least, her husband telephoned such news to me five minutes ago, so I suppose it must be true."

"Why should it not be true?" inquired Julie.

"Because——" Grandmère stopped short. Even at this hour so many things might go wrong with her plans. She did not want to take Julie into her confidence until she was quite sure that everything was going right. Up till now everything had been going just right, but there were doubts, what with the Englishman's arrival and Madame Patrice's relapse, that they might not continue to do so.

"You did not tell me the Patrices were coming tonight." Julie said quietly, but her thoughts were busy.

"I never have told you the names of my guests beforehand."

"But this was different, because I am so friendly with their son." Then she asked suddenly, "Does Charles know?"

"I think so. His mother will have mentioned it."

"Perhaps that was why he called to see me yesterday, to tell me?" But Julie was conscious of a feeling of disappointment because this news was unimportant when compared with the news she longed to hear.

Madame shrugged. "Most likely. But the families often dine at each other's houses."

Julie's hopes soared again.

Grandmère said, "That was why I wanted you to look your best. I am proud of you, Julie. I wished Madame Patrice to know that I am as pleased with my granddaughter as she is delighted with her son."

Something happened to Julie. It was as though for a brief

123

moment grandmère had drawn aside a curtain in her mind and Julie saw her own secret wishes fulfilled.

A kind of vertigo and confusion took possession of the girl, and she seemed a little breathless. Suddenly she realized why the Patrices were invited, why grandmère wanted her to wear the best dress, for a purpose she had not seen the reason for until now. It was as though for the first time she glimpsed the plan that had been weaving about her like some glorious tapestry, unknown to her, but approved of for years perhaps by members of her family. It was all too sudden, new and tremendous, for Julie to make much sense of it. The only clear sentence that emerged from the confusion of her mind was 'I am a lucky girl.'

In that moment she was like a person reaching through a mist by instinct towards the only man who could give her that contentment of love her soul yearned for, and which no one but Charles could satisfy. She guessed, too, that Charles had found out the truth, and had come in haste to tell her. He had not done so because it would not have been fitting for him to talk about love in front of her ex-fiancé. Charles was fastidious. In spite of the irrepressible gaiety of his manner, Julie knew instinctively that Charles had been disappointed.

Then, before either of them could speak, the veil descended again, and Julie was not sure whether what had passed was wishful thinking, a figment of her imagination—or even if grandmère had mentioned the Patrices at all.

The whole of the day passed for Julie in the quality of a dream. There was a sense of waiting. It was a strain.

In the early evening Harvey rang up.

Marie knocked on Julie's door, and when Julie opened it, she said that a gentleman wanted Mademoiselle on the telephone. Julie's heart swelled. It was Charles, of course.

For a moment the dizzy feeling that had confused Julie from time to time since this morning, came over her, and she rushed at great speed along the corridor to the boudoir. The air was heavy with the cloying scent of hothouse flowers. Julie had never seen the window open, and the atmosphere was never fresh.

Julie picked up the receiver and listened. What would Charles say? How would she answer?

Instead of Charles's light "'allo, 'allo!" she heard Harvey's deeper tones, saying impatiently, "Hello, hello! Julie?"

She was too disappointed for a moment to speak. But after Harvey had repeated his 'Hello,' in varying pitch and with increasing impatience, she managed to say, "Oh, it's you," in a flat tone.

There was a pause.

"I say, you don't seem too pleased to hear me."

Julie wanted to say, 'Oh, do stop complaining, say what you have to, and go away, I am sick of you.' Instead she said, "Well, I am a bit surprised," and spoke naturally.

"I expect you are after yesterday," Harvey said, quite humbly for him. "I'm sorry I created a scene. I didn't mean a word of it."

"Oh, that's all right," she said, and there was no animation in her tone.

"I was rather upset. The old girl started it, and seeing those other two fellows sticking around made me see red. I get like that where you are concerned. I wouldn't mind if it were any other girl. But you !"

"You made a fool of yourself," she told him resentfully.

"You need not rub it in. I don't know what else to say except I'm sorry, and that it shan't happen again."

Julie was silent, and Harvey said urgently, "Say the word, Julie, and let's get out of this set-up. You are no more at home in it than I am, though you may pretend better than I do."

"Speak for yourself," Julie told him sharply and quickly, anxious to refute such an idea. "I am revelling in this luxury."

"Oh, I don't say it isn't okay for a time. That is why any change is a holiday, but don't wait for it to spoil you so that you will be forever dissatisfied with what life offers you. After all, one must look at it sensibly. You are practical enough to know that it costs a packet of money to be glamorous."

Partly to get rid of him, but also to justify her love of comfort and luxury, Julie said :

"I expect to profit by it."

"But how, Julie ?" Harvey seemed genuinely perplexed. His lack of humour made him take everything she said literally. "It isn't as though you were a star and lived in the public's eye, and your living depended on your looking startling. I don't get you at all."

Julie thought resentfully, 'How stupid he is ; how dull ! It is not his business now. It never will be. I suppose if I loved him I would willingly give up everything to be near him. But I don't. I wish Harvey could be made to understand that it is too late. When we parted in London it was for good. Words seem to have no effect on him. I wish I had never been so friendly with him.'

Her nerves were on edge because waiting to hear from Charles was irksome. It was getting her down ; that and not knowing where she stood with Charles. It was not fair of people to keep her in this suspense.

She went downstairs to the petit salon, where grandmère was giving a cocktail party to some Americans. It was only five o'clock, but Americans like their cocktails early. The hour did not matter much to Julie. She was not old enough to be orthodox about the hour to drink. Any time suited her.

It was while she was there, with only half her mind on what she was saying, that grandmère took her aside, saying casually,

"Charles has but just rung through to ask if you will dine with him informally this evening. He particularly asked that you should not dress. I did not think to disturb you, but said you would go. I hope I did right?"

The relief to the strain of waiting was so great that for a moment a haze swam before Julie's sight-blinding her vision.

Suddenly Julie was happy and excited. She was going out with Charles. Nothing else mattered, no one in the world but Charles. The evening that seemed to spell failure was turning out better than she had expected. Within half an hour she would see him.

CHAPTER XIII

CHARLES arrived in his Patrice, one of the latest sports models turned out by the works of which his father was the owner and managing director. It had all the latest gadgets, and was a show car, having been designed to catch the eyes and empty the purses of South Americans. Charles had demonstrated successfully with the car abroad, and then appropriated it for his own use.

This evening he was dressed in a dark lounge suit, and wore a soft black felt hat. He looked like a business man out for a holiday, though there was nothing of a tired man about him, rather the contrary. He went into the house for a few minutes to greet Madame Lubin and to collect Julie, who was wearing the simple dark dress which had been Madame Lubin's first gift to her.

Charles was in the same exuberant good humour as yesterday,

not so boisterous in expression, if one could use such a term in connection with Charles, but happy in a deep, contented way.

"I am taking Julie out to Versailles, Madame," Charles explained to grandmère. And to Julie, in a softened voice that held a thrilling quality, and which brought a flush to her cheeks, he advised, "Bring a warm wrap with you. The wind is coming from the north-west, and the evening is cold."

There was a short delay while a 'warm wrap' was discussed. The only 'warm' coat that Julie possessed was a Scottish tweed, suitable for country wear, but not for a glamorous evening in Paris with her best beloved. Eventually Nina, who had been more kindly disposed towards Julie lately, offered the loan of her short fur coat, an offer which Julie gratefully accepted, partly because she had never owned a mink coat and it would give her pleasure to wear one, but also because she wanted to look her best for Charles.

She put it on, and felt so happy and gay that she paraded to and fro saying, "How do I look?" She spoke to Nina, but her eyes were on Charles. It was important to know what *he* thought.

"Like a million dollars," said Charles, answering the look.

"That is exactly what I feel in it—rich beyond my dreams," said Julie. She thought, too, 'Oh, dear, how Harvey would disapprove!' But she did not allow her thoughts to dwell on *that* wet-blanket.

How different, too, were Charles's reactions. "You look enchanting," he told her boldly, careless of Madame's presence.

They went off quickly because Charles was anxious to have Julie to himself. Yet they had little to say to each other at first. Julie was shy, and not her usual natural self because there was such a weight of thought on her mind. Since yesterday she had learned so much. Even now she could not make head or tail of what was happening about her. She could only surmise, and that, though it delighted and contented her for a short while, could not satisfy the yearning, longing and aching that went on within her, during the waking hours, for Charles.

"Warm enough?" asked Charles presently. He stretched an arm across her, and without taking his eyes off the road, wound up her window quickly. "You must not catch cold," he added softly, with a fleeting smile.

"I am very cosy in this lovely coat," said Julie, snuggling her chin into the soft brown fur collar.

Paris was noisy. Traffic seemed to rush past them at break-neck speed, careless of everything in its path. Many models of the Patrice car were on the road.

Charles said, "There goes one of our cars." And presently he remarked, "That one was a Lubin. I hear that Lubins are busy turning out some secret models for the Motor Show later in the year."

Julie did not answer because she knew nothing of the Lubin business, and did not know what to say.

So they drove out to Versailles, past shops, cinemas and cafés, all well-lit and doing good business. It was a fine but chilly evening. A lone star shone clearly in the serene sky.

At Versailles Charles drove around the Park. Beyond a yellow sign with black figures, near a village, there was a restaurant, once an old *Manoir*, situated by a lake fed from a stream that twisted like a ribbon over the meadows beyond.

It was dusk then, and the water of the lake shone like a steel mirror between the larches standing in serried ranks, like tall dark sentinels, growing amid an undergrowth of bracken and bramble bushes on the slight rise above the lake. It was tranquil out here, so peaceful that they might have been far from the city, instead of within thirty miles of it.

The fierce new green of Spring had given place to the full and deeper foliage of early Summer, but all this had darkened into colourless beauty with the coming of night.

They had made the journey mostly in silence, content to be with each other. After the strain of the last twenty-four hours Julie had relaxed a little. There was a languid air about her which was the aftermath of that tension which, tautening daily, had sapped her nervous strength lately.

Sometimes, when passing the bright neon lights outside cinemas, Julie had closed her eyes, certain that when she opened them she would find herself in England, and what she thought had happened in France was a dream. She was a little afraid of Charles, too, because she did not know what was in his heart or mind, and had no idea how this evening would end. Would it be 'finis' to their friendship ? She was full of doubt, and things were so uncertain between them that she was afraid to hope. It was no use chiding herself by saying, 'Why worry about anything ? You cannot help what will happen.' She did worry. She could not bear the strain of indecision much longer. It was easier, of course, when Charles was with her, for listening to his soft voice some of her doubts were lulled, though others remained, eating like maggots into her peace of mind.

Charles said briefly, "This is the place. It is run by a couple from Normandy. It may seem rough after Paris, but the food and wine are first rate. I come here sometimes when I wish to be quiet."

It crossed Julie's mind: did Charles ever come here with Lucienne? But she had learned her lesson long ago not to question Charles too closely. Now she respected his wish for privacy of thought and freedom of action.

Charles put the car alongside others in a parking place in the courtyard at the side of the restaurant, and they walked together over the cobblestones towards the entrance, passing a large apple tree, around whose base were pots of brilliantly coloured geraniums glowing in a beam of spotlight trained on to them.

The *Manoir* was a white, oblong building with a mossy-tiled roof that in daylight looked mildewy, but which now looked like dark velvet, cosy and inviting. A large striped awning was stretched along the façade, just above the restaurant windows, on the sills of which were several pairs of newly-made sabots seasoning. Just below, on the irregular pavement and guarded by pots of geraniums and asparagus fern, were numerous little round white marble-topped tables, where people sat, drinking and gossiping, taking more or less interest in all the small happenings around them.

"I wonder if you are going to like this place. It is certainly something different," Charles said. "It is both homely and sophisticated."

"I like the atmosphere," agreed Julie. Her spirits rose at once, for there was a cosy air about the place that appealed to her.

"Shall we go straight in?" Charles asked.

"Yes, unless you think my face needs powdering?"

Charles turned his head to look at her gravely. Then he said in an odd, strained voice, "You have nothing to worry about, Julie. Your face, it is beautiful." He said the last sentence in French.

To reach the restaurant it was necessary to pass through the flag-stoned kitchens, whose oaken beams were grey with age. Shining copper pots and pans hung against blue-washed walls, while scarlet-painted shelves displayed a variety of copper and pewter moulds and platters.

Chefs in tall starched white caps cooked at a great fireplace, while from the dark cavern of the chimney steaming cauldrons hung from hooks. A dozen or more chickens revolved slowly, in golden splendour, on a long spit. A boy stood by with a pastry brush which he dipped in olive oil and expertly 'painted' the carcases. At the side, a shelf of blazing coals heated the grills on which were neat rows of soles. By the side of the fireplace hung several chains of sausages. In an open wooden chest were home-made loaves nearly a yard long and a foot wide, their size alone bespeaking the great hospitality of the *maison.*

Charles and Julie lingered while passing through the warm busy kitchen.

At the restaurant door they were met by the blandly smiling *propriétaire* of the inn. He led them to a table in a corner. The tablecloth was of large check-patterned linen. There was a discreet red-shaded lamp, and a vase of red roses, now in bud, on it. Charles looked at the table critically. He had been at pains to explain the importance of the occasion to the *propriétaire* on the telephone.

The latter inquired anxiously, "Is everything as you could wish, M'sieur ? At this table you will not be disturbed."

"It is all very nice," praised Charles.

The *propriétaire* pulled out Julie's chair and she sat down, then slipped off the mink coat which Charles, eager to forestall her slightest wish, took from her and put on a spare chair beside her, with her bag and gloves. "So that you won't worry and can keep an eye on it."

A wine waiter brought them apéritifs, which had been pre-viously ordered. Presently, leisurely, they examined the menu. Charles chose the meal, but he consulted Julie's tastes before giving the order to the waiter.

Then, peace at last, he put his elbows on the table and clasped his hands. Looking across at Julie who sat opposite to him, he said, "I have so much to say to you this evening, but for the life of me I do not know where to begin. If I make foolish mistakes you must forgive me for I am rather bewildered by the sudden and fantastic turn of events."

Julie very nearly said, 'What events ?' but checked herself in time. Instead she said, "Don't let's worry about anything until after dinner. Let us enjoy our drinks now."

"You are right," Charles agreed. "It is early yet, and we have plenty of time before us."

He picked up his glass, and Julie did the same. They toasted each other silently with their eyes meeting over the upheld glasses. Julie was the first to look away. She said, "This is a lovely spot, but all Paris is lovely."

Charles guessed from the warmth of her voice that she liked Paris.

"I do believe that you would like to live here."

"Oh, yes."

"Yet once you had no desire to stay. Your one idea was how to leave us quickly and decently."

"Did I say that?" Julie asked in some wonderment. Then she added lightly, "Ah, but that was yesterday."

"All right. We shall not look back. I hope if you wish to stay tonight that by tomorrow you will have decided to live here."

Was there a double meaning in what Charles said? The French were adepts at that kind of thing. Julie drained her glass in silence. Presently the tiredness that had clogged her activity all day slipped away from her and she was completely at peace.

Then Charles spoke in a tone that was more like a caress than a voice, "Sleepy, Julie?"

She roused herself from the sweet torpor of her thoughts.

"Not a bit. Have I been rude keeping silence for too long? I didn't mean to be."

"What a question between you and me! If you are tired you must tell me, for there must never be anything but frankness between us."

She looked startled as the true meaning of his words burst upon her. There was no mistaking him that he meant their future to be together.

Julie sat up. "I do seem to have been asleep," she said slowly, answering her own thoughts more than what Charles had said.

The waiter and his *commis* began to bustle around them, and the intimacy of their talk was destroyed.

For dinner they had hors d'oeuvres, some river trout, chicken, with a subtle tasting sauce, and Camembert as the French like it, dry and hard, and a dessert of rosy apples. They drank cider that sparkled and tasted like mild champagne. While they ate Charles told Julie how disappointed his mother was at not being well enough to meet her at Madame Lubin's this evening.

"My mother is not as yet strong, and any excitement it seems can cause a setback."

"There could be no excitement in meeting me. I am harmless enough." In her ignorance Julie even thought, 'Perhaps they want to warn me off. Perhaps they are afraid of my hold over Charles?' The fear of losing Charles had already aroused unexpected resources of strength in her to fight for him, resources which Julie had not known she possessed. She thought again, 'I shall not allow them to interfere with our friendship.' It was a brave thought, but in her heart Julie knew that it was futile. Charles's parents had a great hold on him.

Charles agreed. *"Naturellement!* But I assure you there was great excitement at our house."

Julie laughed lightly, but her heart was heavy, for no matter how much she yearned for Charles's love, the odds seemed against her. This remark was Charles's way of pleasing her by saying something complimentary. She was getting used to Frenchmen's flattery these days. It was very nice, too, for it made her feel pleased with herself.

So she said, "Perhaps I may see her another time." It was a perfunctory expression, for Julie had no wish to put herself out to see Charles's mother.

"You certainly will—and soon," Charles promised, a certain authority in his tone. Then he added confidentially, "If you are good I shall take you to see her tomorrow. She is in bed because the doctor insists that she rests; but I know that you will not mind?"

Julie thought he was making a great fuss about this meeting between her and his parents. Though she could not visualize herself in Charles's house, visiting his mother while she was in bed, she agreed amiably.

"I shall not mind."

"My father, he may be there too. Though he is a keen business man, when my mother is ill nothing will persuade him to leave her side for long."

"Oh, I should think twice before seeing your father."

"But why?"

"I do not know, unless it is that I am afraid of him."

"You must not be afraid of him, or even let him guess that you are. He will spoil you, anyway. Who could help it? But my father has always longed for a daughter. He will be waiting to welcome you into our house with wide-open arms. I think I may be jealous of the privileges he will assume as his right."

As Charles spoke Julie paled. She began to tremble as understanding broke upon her. Obviously there was some definite reason behind Charles's remarks, more than had as yet been admitted between them.

She said faintly and a little testily because she hated being kept in the dark, "You are talking in riddles, Charles."

He laughed, a low happy sound of sheer enjoyment.

"I forget: you do not know." Then he added quickly, "How much do you know about us, Julie?"

That was plain enough. Again a vertigo swept over her so that she felt reality slipping away from her. What was Charles saying? What was she supposed to know?

Julie heard her voice as from a distance, saying, "Not much."

"But you must have guessed." His voice quavered oddly with emotion.

The sound gave Julie strength. Charles was as deeply moved as she was.

"A little," she admitted, her voice faltering with an answering emotion.

"Has Madame Lubin taken you into her confidence?"

Julie roused herself to say, "Only this morning, to tell me that M'sieur and Madame Patrice, who were coming to dinner, had asked to be excused because Madame Patrice was ill. Grand-mère seemed put out."

"It was disappointing for my parents, too. My mother wept, not because of a postponed party, but because it delayed her meeting you. She had set her heart on doing that. It was understandable."

Julie, still seeing Charles' face as through a mist, was staring at him helplessly. 'What is Charles telling me?' she wondered in amazement, less at what he was saying than that she was sitting here listening quietly to—a proposal of marriage.

She asked presently, "When did you know?"

"I knew yesterday evening. I hurried over to tell you. I was beside myself with joy. I could not wait. Matras met me in the hall. Another fellow, the Professor, was there. Matras tried to keep me back, but I refused to wait. When I heard you were in the library I hurried in. And then—I saw you with the fellow, Robins." Charles paused, took a deep breath, and said quickly, "Julie, are you sure that you do not like him any more?"

She nodded, unable to speak, still bewildered by Charles's revelations, not yet able to grasp the full truth.

Charles, too, seemed puzzled at his own stupidity in not guessing it sooner.

"I suppose I should have tumbled to what was happening," he told her, "for everyone in the family has conspired to throw us together. It seems that our families have thought it a good idea for the past year."

Julie did not think to ask why. What she had heard was sudden and confusing, appealing directly to her heart and not her head. She had wanted Charles so much. Now, by a miracle, she knew that it had all been arranged just as she wished.

It was not so strange to Charles. He had been brought up knowing that some day his parents would arrange his future. His only surprise was their choice. It was but lately that Julie had come into his life. He had been at no pains to hide his interest in her from anyone. It was something he could not control, anyhow. Since finding out that it was Julie his parents had in mind for his wife it was conceivable that he may have imagined their choice was made out of love for him, to please him and give him the happiness that by luck had also been theirs.

They sat for a long while over their black coffee and small glasses of Benedictine. Julie smoked several cigarettes. Her nerves, which had been so frayed, were soothed, though her emotions made her excited and happy. The unease of mind and fret had vanished. She was here alone with Charles. Everything was straightforward and simple. She knew exactly where she stood. It only remained for Charles to tell her how much he loved her, and that, intuition told Julie, he would do this evening. Apparently she fascinated him, for his eyes never left her face.

When Julie had taken the first puff at her fifth cigarette, Charles leant across the little table, and stretching out his hand took the cigarette from her lips.

"Pardon," he whispered formally, his smile set and his eyes glassy with pent-up emotion. He stubbed out the cigarette on an ashtray. Then he called for the bill.

When it was paid Charles suggested going for a stroll beside the lake. He pushed back his chair and rose. Coming round to Julie he helped her on with her coat, buttoning it under her throat, his trembling fingers lingering over the task.

"It is chilly outside, and you must not catch cold," he told her.

It was like a dream to Julie, yet somehow it had the foundations of ordinary life.

Outside the *Manoir* it was dark, but there was gaiety and life at the café tables on the pavement, and white-aproned waiters seemed to be doing a brisk trade serving drinks to clients, most of whom had spent the evening there.

Charles turned towards the lake, a tranquil stretch of light haloed by the velvet darkness of the night.

Away from the lights of the *Manoir*, and the high-gabled and well-shuttered houses in the village street, it seemed natural for Charles to put his arm about Julie. For a long time they stood by an ivy-covered old wall, and then, descending some stone steps, walked to and fro on the shore of the lake which was like a vague pastel in the gloaming.

It was not late, but neither of them thought of time. It was as though Nature had blended herself—all sights and sounds— into a perfect whole. If the isolation that encompassed them was unreal, because within a stone's throw behind them were people and gaiety, with someone playing a 'cors de chasse' on a flute, tingeing the night with melancholy, it was also because they moved in that odd world of dreams which all true lovers pass through during the early days of their love.

Julie was happy, dazzled and allured by Charles's personality. She thought, 'There is no one in the world quite like Charles.' And she thought, too, 'This is a dream from which I shall wake at any moment. I am too lucky. It can't last!'

"Sleepy, Julie?"

"No," she whispered, because it seemed a sacrilege to do anything else but whisper on a night like this. "What makes you think I am?"

"You are so quiet."

"Am I? I am enjoying myself."

"Oh, Julie! Dar-r-rling!"

The voice, soft, sweet and compelling, was close to her ear.

The next moment he had twisted her towards him, thrown his arms around her, and was holding her closely, tightly against him. There was firmness and tenderness in his hold, a feeling of safety and security such as Julie had never known.

He pressed her cheek against his heart. She could feel its quick beating.

"I love you!" Then carried away by emotion, Charles broke into French—soft, urgent love-words, each one a caress. "*Je t'adore!* Oh, Mignonne, *je t'adore!*"

Loosening his hand, he put his forefinger under her chin and raised her face.

"Julie! *Chérie!*" How desirable and beautiful she was in the glow of the lakeside lamp, like an angel in his arms.

She breathed his name. "Charles!"

He bent his head and kissed her, gently at first and then with increasing passion.

Julie had never been loved like this before. There had not been anything like this love in her life. It was like being in heaven—blissful, wonderful, exquisite, where time and space had no place.

After a while, a little shy of each other now, they drew apart, and Julie whispered, "What does it all mean?" And she thought, 'It can't end now.' She strove to control her emotions. Such love-making was new to her.

Charles was already master of the situation.

"It means, my love," Charles told her laughingly in a low tone, "that I want to marry you. I have fallen deeply in love with you, and I want to share your life forever. Without you I shall be lost. I shall not wish to live." As he spoke the laughter and joy died out of his voice, and he became vehement and passionate.

Later on, Julie said, "You are quite sure about your family?" It seemed difficult for her to blot out the fear of his family.

"Oh, quite. I admit the position sounds fantastic, that what has happened to us is a chance in a thousand. But it *has* happened. It was not love at first sight. I do not pretend that. But it was close to it. You remember you tried your hardest that first night we met, to put me off? Looking back, my sweet love, I think it drew me on. It created an interest. I have been a spoilt man. People have been too kind to me. Now it is my duty and pleasure to spoil you and love you."

Loverlike, Charles held her hand in his, and exclaimed how cold it was. He raised it, and kissed each finger in turn, hoping to warm them with caresses.

"When did you begin to love me?" he demanded between these light kisses.

Julie laughed, a quavering sound. "I did not love you at first either. You seemed so sure of yourself, so conceited, so——"

"And why not, *chérie*? If I were conceited then, I am doubly so now that I have you. I shall be the envy of all Paris."

"Must Paris know?"

"Why, of course. We are news, dar-r-ling."

There was no room for clear thought in the blurred world of her happiness. Instinct rather than reason ruled, and even that was blunted tonight. In the magic of her enchanted and bemused state, the word 'news' could only affect her if it were connected somehow with hers and Charles's love. Certainly any monetary value would be ruled out. Julie felt protected, cherished and loved. Surely there was never anything so lovely as this love that had drawn them together?

In an aura of happiness, their arms around each other, they went back to the car.

CHAPTER XIV

JULIE's happiness was shadowed by its first cloud that night.

When she and Charles reached home, still in the bemused state of newly-declared lovers, and were saying a lingering 'good night' to each other in the wide hall, Charles accidentally swept a letter lying on the marble-topped console table on to the floor. He picked it up and saw that it was addressed to Julie, delivered by hand, and marked and underlined 'Private.'

"This is a letter for you," he said, and remarked, "It seems urgent."

Julie glanced at it, then seeing that the envelope was in Harvey's writing, she took it quickly and put it in her bag. She did not want to spoil their glorious evening by reminding Charles of Harvey's existence.

"Aren't you going to read it?" Charles inquired curiously.

"It can wait," Julie said with elaborate indifference. She looking lovingly at Charles's handsome face, and forgot all about Harvey.

Charles opened his lips to speak, but quickly closed them again. His expression changed. It was scarcely noticeable in the dim light, and to Julie it seemed that he looked worried for a moment. She knew that Charles did not like Harvey and was suspicious of him, not trusting him as far as she was concerned.

Julie spent the time until dawn lying awake, going over in her mind all the events of the evening, her thoughts circling mostly about those beautiful moments when Charles had taken her in his arms and kissed her, telling her that he loved her. There had been nothing like those glorious and unforgettable moments ever in her life. Charles, in loving her, had brought out subtly all the softness and love in her nature. Surely no man could ever love a girl like Charles. It was a divine gift. . . . Or was it the perfection of experience? That was an unwelcome thought and unworthy of her. Julie felt disloyal in harbouring it. She had a stab of jealousy as it occurred to her that Charles had had much experience with girls, and she thought especially of the actress, Lucienne Jeanson, who was the talk of Paris. She wondered, too, if Charles would end this undesirable friendship, as his family hoped.

Tossing about on the pillow, Julie thought of Harvey, then Charles, of Lucienne and Nina—until she could remember no one's features clearly and became hot and bothered, when her head began to ache and sleep was further away than ever.

In the morning Charles rang up, as he had promised he would. There were loving exchanges and tender inquiries and Charles made arrangements to see Julie in the late afternoon, when he had finished work at the office.

Then, when Julie was feeling her happiest, and the world seemed more beautiful than ever, Charles's voice changed subtly, as he said : "About that letter, Julie, dar-r-rling !"

"Yes ?" Instinctively the smile on Julie's face set. She was on the defensive at once. She might have known that Charles would not forget, that his curiosity once aroused would not rest until he was satisfied. He would ask awkward questions. Julie told herself she should have been prepared for this, but somehow, talking about love with Charles, all memory of Harvey had been obliterated from her mind. His kisses had wiped out the memory of all other kisses she had ever known. His love was all that mattered.

"I would have spoken to you about it last night," Charles added almost apologetically, "but I did not want to spoil our happiness by dragging in Mr. Robins. It *was* from your English friend ?"

There was a pause before Julie said, "Yes, it was from Harvey."

"I suppose I should not say, 'What was he writing to you about ?' "

"No, you shouldn't," Julie replied sharply. Her implied refusal to disclose the contents of the letter was not because Harvey had said anything important (he was only asking her to meet him in the Bois), but from a desire to preserve her own independence of thought and action a little longer.

"You will reply to it ?"

"Oh, yes." Julie tried to speak lightly, but it cost her something to do so. She did not like to be the cause of those oh, so cold tones in Charles's voice.

"And when you have told him about us, you will not be writing to him, or see him again ?"

"I suppose not."

"Julie, please be definite. I am terribly worried. You must not mind my speaking like this. I have the right."

"Why ? Because you are jealous ?" It was the old Julie who spoke, lightly and challengingly.

Charles laughed. "I am an imbecile to be jealous," he told her in the voice she loved to hear, "but it is because I love you. I spent a wakeful night thinking about you. I am still bewildered by the fact that the most beautiful girl in all the world has said she loves me. I am supposed to be adaptable, but it is going to take time for me to get used to the idea. When I think of you, so sweet and good and loving, I am full of doubts. What can such a glorious creature like you see in an ordinary fellow like me? And I am troubled, too, because our nationalities and customs are different, and I do not want you to be unhappy over it. Getting betrothed is a far more serious matter in France than it is in England. In your country an engagement may be broken lightly, and people say, 'What a good thing they found out their true feelings about each other before it was too late.' In France a betrothal is seldom broken. It is a period of waiting until everything is satisfactorily arranged between the two families for the marriage.''

Julie listened in silence. Charles spoke solemnly, and there was no evidence of that sparkling personality which had charmed her so much last night.

She was a little tired, too. There had been so much excitement. She had not slept, and reaction was setting in. The glow that had been over the most trivial thing was missing.

She said, "It all sounds rather solemn. It makes me feel a little afraid."

"Afraid of my love and protection? Oh, *chérie*! Are you not pleased with my love?"

Julie's voice was deep as she cried, "Oh, Charles!" Because there was nothing adequate she could say to agree with him.

"Is it not sweet for us to be together, to know that we shall soon be able to love each other all our lives?"

Charles made the future appear a dazzling prospect, yet solid, secure and enduring as every woman likes her future to be.

Julie thought impatiently, 'This evening cannot come quickly enough for me.'

Madame Lubin was an early visitor to Julie's room. The girl was dressed by then, and sitting at the window writing to her mother and to Harvey, occasionally raising her head to look out of the window from which there was a glimpse of the Bois in which the trees were heavy with foliage. It seemed as though not only in her heart had Spring burst triumphantly, but in Nature, too.

She looked up and smiled when Madame entered the room. There was no need for questions. The girl's face was glowing with happiness and joy. She was preoccupied with love. Grandmère had never seen her like this, and her heart filled with thankfulness.

"Well?" she inquired softly, coming close to Julie, putting

her hands on the girl's shoulders and kissing her warmly first on one cheek and then the other.

Julie nodded. Then as they fell apart, she said reproachfully, "You never even gave me a hint, grandmère."

"If I had it might have spoiled everything. I have had much disappointment with Nina. I did not wish for it again with you." Madame went over to the window and closed it without comment before she sat down.

"You were determined I should marry a Frenchman."

"That is because I am so old. It is natural for me to want my family around me." She had come to find out if Charles had declared himself, and whether Julie had responded, but both query and answer seemed superfluous. So Madame said instead, "Has Charles arranged anything special for today?"

"He is calling here at five-thirty and taking me to see Madame Patrice."

Grandmère exclaimed with annoyance. "He goes too fast, that young man. These things must be done formally. If you go to visit Madame Patrice, then I, too, shall go."

Mentally she reviewed and revised her day's engagements. Then she rose to go to the telephone. She said to Julie, "If you are writing to your mother will you please tell her that I shall be writing to her during today." She kissed the girl again. "You have made us all very happy, *chérie*," she said. "I hope you and Charles will be happy too."

It did not occur to Madame Lubin that Julie was writing to anyone else—for after all, who was there for Julie to write to in Paris?

Julie answered Harvey's letter in which he had said:

It is useless calling at the house, for Madame arranges it cleverly that I shall not see you alone, or at any rate without interruptions. The telephone is out, too. I have tried and usually get the butler-fellow or a maid, each of whom is eager to call Madame first, but never, by any chance, you. So I am writing a note, marking it private, and hope they will have the decency to respect letters to you. I shall be in the Bois, near the ramparts, at five o'clock tonight. Try to meet me there, Julie dear. Yours, as ever, Harvey.

Obviously he would not take no for an answer. He meant to remain in Paris as long as he could. There was no mention of Charles. Perhaps he had been washed from Harvey's mind.

She glanced at the clock. If she posted a letter to Harvey he would get it in time to stop him going to the rendezvous. She could not go. Then she glanced at the little Louis XVI gilt clock standing in the upheld arms of a gilt angel balanced on a green onyx base. There *might* be time to see Harvey if she dressed first before meeting Charles. It would be long enough for her to tell Harvey to go home. It was difficult to put into written words how she and Charles felt about each other. It would be easier to face Harvey, and a way of getting rid of him ? Julie scrunched the sheet of notepaper in her clenched fingers and threw the 'ball' into the fireplace.

At that moment Marie came to the door. She was smiling above a huge sheaf of dark red roses that seemed almost too heavy even for her capable arms.

They were, of course, from Charles.

Julie put them on a table, and undoing the cellophane in which they were packed she picked up a long-stemmed rose and buried her lips in its fragrant petals.

The look of radiance which had been there last night when Charles had told her he loved her, and Julie knew that her longings had come true just like a fairy story, returned, so that for a moment she did not seem like an earthly person, but immortal and glorified like an angel.

Nina came into the room, and Julie, flushing, hastily put down the flowers.

"I knocked but you did not hear me," she said, "and so I came in."

Julie smiled. "It's all right. Aren't these roses lovely ?"

"They are enchanting. Of course Charles sent them ?"

"Yes. You have heard about last night ?"

"Maman has just told me, but I guessed it long ago. It was so right that it had to happen."

She kissed Julie warmly on both cheeks, then she said, "I hope you will be happy, but I know you will."

Julie embraced Nina and clung to her. "Thank you. I am deliriously happy, but it is all new and strange to me, and I have been afraid as well."

"There are bound to be doubts, but they will disappear. Maman is writing to your mother, my sister, to tell her the news, and to ask her to come over to deal with the formalities."

"Formalities ! What are those ?"

Nina laughed. "There is the business side to every French marriage."

"I know, but there can't be much business to do with me. I have no *dot* to worry about."

Nina started. She seemed about to say something but thought better of it and closed her lips. She studied the girl's face, so young and fresh, with clear skin, bright eyes and dewy lips, and the golden halo of the unusual-coloured hair, that was seldom found with those strange grey-blue eyes. The glow of happiness, of being loved, admired and wanted, of entire well-being was there for all to see. Nina noted all these signs, and though a pang of envy darted like a sharp, searing pain through her heart, nothing of this showed on her smooth face. Yet there was a poignant thought in her mind, 'I might have been like this once. But for Maman, I, too, could have found love.' She thought, too, 'But for Maman, Julie would not have met Charles.' But that last thought Nina knew was wrong. It did not require Madame Lubin to let the lovers meet. That had been ordained by Fate. Madame Lubin was simply the instrument of Fate. These two, Charles and Julie, were made for each other.

Nina said, "You are sure to have a big wedding. All Paris will expect to be there."

Julie laughed, "I haven't got to thinking that far. I do not even know whether I shall be married in England or France."

"But Maman knows. She has already decided that you shall be married here in Paris."

Uncle Michel came home to lunch, something he seldom did. Madame had already told him the news on the telephone.

"Charles rang through to me soon after you did," he told his sister. "I immediately got on to the lawyers." Then he said, "It is a great day in our family. Julie must have a trousseau worthy of a Lubin. The Patrices will expect something wonderful, and they shall have it." He was puffed out with importance.

It had been arranged that when Charles called at five-thirty, he would take Madame Lubin and Julie to his parents' house.

Julie dressed early. She knew that grandmère would rest in her room until it was time to dress. She would come down to the salon just before Charles arrived and wait for him there. Julie was expected to join her punctually.

There would be time for Julie to be at the Bois at five o'clock, see Harvey and tell him her news, and get back to the house in time to meet Charles.

Having dressed herself early with care, not for Harvey's benefit, but for Madame Patrice's, Julie ran downstairs and out of the house, hurrying towards the Bois which was at the end of the street, and through an avenue of trees to the old ramparts. It was an untidy part of the city, with children playing about the old walls, and Julie, in her lovely model dress looked rather out of place as she went to her rendezvous with Harvey.

She thought of him impatiently, as a nuisance value in the midst of her happiness. He should not have come over without warning. Indeed, he should not have come at all. He was strange to Paris, and did not seem to fit in with the life. He looked dour and dull, his spirit too heavy for the gaiety, lightness and quick wit that was on every side, a gaiety showing in the people's clothes, the way they walked, seeking pavement admiration, laughing and talking with one another with vivacity and verve, determined to get the best out of each day's life.

Harvey was already there, and Julie thought, 'I shall never think of this spot without dislike,' for it was associated with distaste. He was standing with his back to her, and for a moment there was a critical, appraising and unsympathetic quality in Julie's eyes. She saw his head and the way his hair was cut, his square, aggressive shoulders; and his legs, which seemed too short for his body, and which gave him the impression of strength and the appearance of a gorilla in man's clothing.

Harvey must always have been like this, but Julie had not noticed anything unusual except that he was a man who, in his own way, was very much in love with her, a fact which seemed to count a great deal with her at one time. It did not please her now. She found his expressions, strong and sometimes incoherent and rough, irritating. She could not make out why he did not go away and leave her in peace. On the other hand, Julie was puzzled at herself for ever liking him at all.

Harvey must have sensed her nearness, for he turned suddenly and she was able to see his face and tie, and note that the hands hanging at his sides were clenched. Other men did not clench their hands unless they were angry, but Harvey appeared always to strike a fighting attitude.

Julie waved gaily because she was glad he had not kept her waiting, and also because she was a little ashamed of harbouring such unkind thoughts against him.

Harvey, who was hatless, raised one arm in reply. He came rapidly towards her, smiling because he was so relieved to meet someone he knew in a strange country.

"Hello, Harvey!"

"Hullo! As I didn't hear from you I concluded you'd turn up. I thought you'd be late, having near-past memories, but for once you are punctual."

They met, but did not shake hands. "I'm on time because I happen to have only twenty minutes to spare today——"

"Of your valuable time." Harvey could not resist the sneer.

"Don't let's squabble. Shall we sit down on that seat in the shade—over there. I have so much to tell you."

They went over to the seat placed beneath the grey stone and ivied walls, which was shaded by a lime tree, in full view of the road which was full of passing traffic, and around which some children were playing. Julie settled herself on the edge of the slatted seat, not making herself comfortable as she might have done with someone she liked.

Harvey sat back. He had a good quarter-profile view of Julie's face, and a glimpse of a demure ear lobe which was pink, soft and delicate. It was a new angle for Harvey, and he had the uneasy feeling of looking at a stranger.

The western sun was full on their faces.

Julie's words had aroused an intense curiosity in Harvey, but he waited for her to speak with an air of cold reserve which sat ill upon him. He guessed that she disapproved of his being in Paris, if only because his presence curbed the natural gaiety and exuberance of her style. Julie liked fun. Well, so did he, but fun cost money, and he seldom had enough to spare for his own fun, so how could he find enough for two ?

Harvey saw, with the same critical outlook as Julie had gazed upon him, that she was more smartly dressed than ever. Not that there was more in the dress. It was simple enough, but with a cut and chic that cost money. She was like a fashion-plate. He amended that to 'like a picture.' Why, she might even have been mistaken for a French girl.

He said grudgingly, because he thought it unwise to give too much praise, and Julie was conceited enough already, "You look grand."

"Do I ? I am so glad. I want to look my best this evening."

"I thought you might be dolled up for something special. It can't be for me. What is it ?"

"I am going to a family party."

"Then that excludes me."

"Oh, you could not possibly go."

"Is that why you can spare me only a wretched twenty minutes ?"

Julie nodded. "Grandmère expects me to be back at the house just before half-past five."

It irked Harvey that Julie was so complacent about obeying her grandmother while she treated him cavalierly, and he sneered, "And like a dutiful granddaughter you obey her."

"This is a special occasion."

"Well, let's hear what it is, and I'll tell you if I agree with you."

Julie paused. Harvey was edgy. It meant that if things did not go the way he wished he would fly into a temper. It had

144

happened before, and sometimes she had been at pains to smooth things over ; at others she had not wanted to placate him and they had quarrelled.

Now she hesitated. She was going to hurt Harvey, and though he probably would not feel such a hurt as most men did because his egotism would not allow him to take it from a normal angle, he would have to understand that from now on she would have nothing more to do with him. Julie hated hurting anyone.

"Get on," Harvey said, so roughly that the answer was said quickly almost before Julie was aware of speaking.

"I was glad when your note came last night suggesting seeing me this afternoon. I have some news for you. It is the kind that is better said than written. I am going to see my future mother-in-law presently. Yesterday evening, Charles Patrice asked me to marry him, and I said yes."

Julie's voice was quick and low. She did not look at Harvey as she spoke, but straight in front of her, seeing but not observing, the medley of all makes of cars passing to and fro like shuttles, with rhythmic speed and noise.

There was a long silence during which both sat still as statues. Then Harvey moved convulsively, crying explosively, "I don't believe it. You are only saying this to annoy me."

"No, I'm not, for it is true."

"It can't be. Even you would not really play me false."

"I haven't been false to anyone."

"I hope not. I think we are still engaged. Our quarrel was nothing ; we've had dozens, and when they were over the slate was washed clean. You know perfectly well that our break was only temporary. If you hadn't rushed over here we'd have made it up ages ago. I believe you only came here to give me the trouble and expense of coming over to patch it up."

Julie's temper rose, and with it a kind of despair because she could make no headway with Harvey. If he did not choose to understand, nothing and no one could make him.

She cried now, "What rot ! You know quite well our engagement wore itself out, and we were both relieved when it ended."

"Then why did you turn coward and hurry over here ?"

"I came to Paris because grandmère invited me."

"Because she had her own plans for you ?"

"It seems so, but I wasn't to know that."

"Then if you weren't playing coward, you must have known about the old lady's plans."

Julie shrugged. "If only you would listen to facts, instead of trying to distort them ! I was *not* aware of grandmère's plans for me. It is true I met Charles through her. It is fate that we happen to love each other."

Harvey jeered. "I seem to have heard that before, only I was the fellow then."

"It is true this time ; it wasn't then."

"You haven't changed."

"You said I had the other day."

"Not at heart."

"This is the real thing, anyway."

"That's what you think now. That's your side. Now for the other. It takes two to make a marriage. As for this Mr. Patrice : he is a business man. I've found out quite a bit about him yesterday. He's a great friend of some French actress at the Comédie Française. It's the talk of the town. As if he'd give her up for you ! While if he has transferred his affection to you it is because he is attracted by the size of your *dot*."

Julie had gone white with rage and fear—rage that Harvey should drag Lucienne into the matter and spoil the beauty and freshness of her love, and fear lest there might be some truth in what Harvey said.

For a second she pressed the palm and fingers of her gloved hand tightly across her eyes as though to shut out the picture of Charles and Lucienne in her mind's eye. It could not be as Harvey suggested. It must not.

Then suddenly, aware that her make-up must be perfect to face Madame Patrice, and that she must not play havoc with it, she dropped her hand into her lap, and pulled herself together.

The *dot* part of Harvey's insinuations against Charles's honesty she dismissed quickly.

"I have no *dot*, and you know it. My mother was alienated from her family when she married my father, chiefly I think because he was a poor man. Life has always been a struggle for them. And you are not telling me anything new about Charles's actress-friend. He has told me all about her himself. Their friendship has been open. That is all over now. You can believe me when I tell you that it is me he loves."

"Because he has told you so."

"Of course."

"Judging by the amount of talk that goes on over the slightest thing, words are cheap in France. To me they are so much waste of energy. They don't mean a thing. Patrice probably talks to you with his tongue in his cheek. You are young, Julie, and not experienced with men, whatever you may think. Doesn't it strike even you as odd that a man-about-town like Patrice, the friend of a renowned actress, would find interest in a greenhorn like you ? Be yourself, Julie. If I weren't so fond of you I'd be asking you to tell me when to laugh."

It was depressing talk. Perhaps it was true ? Harvey had the power of destroying happiness. Julie tried not to let him influence her. Why should he ? Whatever had been between them in the past was ended now. She was sick of the sight of him. He brought bad luck to her. Now, feeling frustrated, he was doing his best to ruin her love for Charles.

"I think you are absolutely hateful," she cried between her teeth.

"Because I am showing you a truth ?"

"It is not true what you say."

"You'll live to find out, you silly little thing."

Julie stood up. The talk was developing into recriminations. "I think I'll go now. I've said all I wanted to say to you, that I am engaged to Charles, we shall be married soon, and that I am going to see my mother-in-law today."

Harvey rose, too, and put a detaining hand on her wrist.

"Have you told Patrice about us ?"

"Of course, I have nothing to hide." But Julie spoke defensively because she knew that Charles would be furious if he knew she was talking to Harvey at this minute.

But Harvey was speaking. He said, "Perhaps not, but if ever he should be jealous, and I think he is the sort to be, he'll fix his own angle to our friendship."

"What a nasty mind you have," Julie cried scornfully.

Harvey shrugged. "I feel done—cheated."

"Then you have cheated yourself. The best advice I can give you is to go away and leave me alone. If I parted from Charles tomorrow, and I do not contemplate such a possibility, I should not turn to you for consolation. You are right to call me young. I was when I knew you in London, or I should have realized your true worth. I am older now and able to judge men, and I have learned that you are mean and contemptible. I despise myself for ever being friendly with you. I should have known better. Take your hand off my arm."

"No, because you'll run off before I've finished my say to you."

"I shall not run away. I have never done that in my life. People are staring at us. Two gendarmes over by the walls are watching us. Hurry up and speak because my appointment will not wait."

"What's come over you, Julie? You are absolutely heart-less," complained Harvey, but he took away his hand. It fell clenched to his side.

Julie hunched her shoulder. She thought, 'What a bore he is! How I must have over-estimated him. Surely he will go now.'

Harvey's eyes looked desperate. "You have led me on. Now, because you have met a rich man, with unlimited cash, you want to chuck me aside and forget all about me. Well, you can't do that to me, Julie. I won't let you."

Yet for all his fine words there was despair and defeat in Harvey's heart.

"No?" His talk seemed to amuse Julie, for her lips twisted into the semblance of a grin. "It will be interesting to hear what you are going to do about it."

"I shall see Patrice!" Harvey said boldly, and waited to see the result of this thrust.

This time Julie laughed openly. She wondered what Harvey would say when he met Charles. But she only said, "Do, if you want to, but I shouldn't advise you to go too near. Charles has a reputation for being a wonderful swordsman and a good boxer. I can see that you are the heavier man, but you are out of condition and would be no match for him."

Harvey sulked. She did not seem to mind his threats.

He had no idea that Julie was happy inside because she felt secure in Charles's love, which had been like a protective cloak about her ever since yesterday. But she was afraid, too, not because of what Harvey might say to Charles, but because the actress, Lucienne Jeanson, might still occupy even a corner of Charles's heart.

Harvey, still sulky, said, "You don't know when you're well off, and I don't mean cash when I say that. Marrying a French-man is very different from marrying an Englishman. Over here, you marry the whole family."

"I don't understand you," Julie told him patiently. She was anxious to leave him, but thought it wiser to make a good ending of their friendship now, rather than let it drag on into another meeting. "I am well off, and I know it, and I am not talking about cash either. I have met Charles, who loves me. I am happy with him as I never was with you. We were always quarrelling, mostly over trivial things, but they did show clearly how we felt about each other in our hearts. I never want to quarrel with Charles."

"Of course you don't. There is nothing to pick a quarrel over. He is rich and can give you everything you unreasonably want."

"That's a hateful thing to say."

"What is ? Telling you you only want him for his money ? Well, don't you ? Would you want him so badly, I wonder, if he were poor ? I doubt it. There's nothing hateful in telling you what you are going to get out of this."

Julie hid her dislike for Harvey, and said, "You have no right to be impertinent, and I am not interested in your thoughts about anyone, least of all Charles. He can look after himself, and me as well. As for Charles's money—if he were poor it would make no difference. But I don't follow your reasoning. One minute you suggest that Charles wants me only for my *dot*, something you know very well that I do not possess, and inferring that he is poor and in need of it ; the next you accuse me of marrying Charles because he is rich and can give poor me all that I can unreasonably want. What do you really mean ?"

Harvey shook his head. "I'm stumped, kind of muddled. Perhaps I am right and wrong. It is a puzzle in which the pieces seem all mixed up, so that I do not quite know who's who and what's what. What I thought was simple is now complicated ; and those I thought were my friends seem complete strangers to me. But until I get it all straightened out to my own satisfaction I mean to hang on in Paris. I can't go to Madame Lubin's house. She doesn't like me, and makes it difficult for me to see you alone. It is a bother to telephone, partly because I don't know the lingo, but also because you never answer it. So we must meet occasionally and you must keep me posted how things are going . . ."

"What for ?" demanded Julie, aghast at Harvey's suggestion. "I think you are crazy." She felt uneasy and afraid of some disaster happening between Charles and herself, with Harvey as its cause. Now that all bonds between Harvey and herself were severed he had turned hostile and suspicious. She never knew at what angle Harvey would try to attack her happiness with Charles. Love had come easily to her and Charles ; it would, if she continued to see Harvey, go as quickly, for Charles was a proud man and would brook no interference from an ex-fiancé. Julie wished with all her heart that she had never met Harvey.

She spoke quickly, "I do not want to see you again, Harvey. We have nothing in common. Can't you understand that I have outgrown any need I ever had of you ?"

"As I see it," Harvey told her slowly, "you are afraid I shall make scenes and spoil things for you."

Was that in his mind ? Alertly, Julie said, "I have outgrown even that fear. I feel nothing for you at all. If you made an unpleasant scene I should know how to deal with you, as I would a stranger who pestered me with his attentions."

"I mean to see you, Julie," said Harvey doggedly.

"What do you suppose Charles would say to that ? Would you like it, if your fiancée went out with her former friend ?"

Harvey shook his head slowly from side to side. "If he is as quick-witted and intelligent as you say all the French are, then he will understand that I have a prior right to you. Personally, I think all Frenchies are conceited. I am sure he despises us. Look at the way he baited me the other evening, his malicious laugh when he thought he was top-dog. You all joined in. That hurt, and I shan't forget it in a hurry. I don't intend to sit down under it. I won't give up until I see that laugh wiped off his face."

"You'll have to wait a long time. If Charles were going to the guillotine he would mask his deepest feelings with a gay laugh. He is like that. It is his way. I have no intention of asking Charles to understand you. I mean to be loyal to him, and so shall not be seeing you again. If you continue to bother me——"

"Bother you ! I won't do that, I promise you. As for being loyal to the Frenchman, that is up to you. They are brave words, anyhow. But neither you nor anyone can shift me from Paris because you do not want me here, or are sick of me. I'll go when I am ready and not before. In the meantime, I shall stick around at my present address. If you should ever want me you will know where to find me."

"I shall not want you," Julie said deliberately. She glanced furtively at her wristwatch.

"Perhaps no—possibly yes. Time will show." He had seen her impatience, and added quickly, "I take it you don't wish me to see you home. . . ."

"No, or ever to see you again," cried Julie passionately.

Harvey had spoilt her day. The memory of this half-hour would ruin her evening. She felt wretched, drab and ashamed. She wished Harvey had never sent that note or that she had not come out to meet him. What a mess she had made of everything. The happiness that had been about her like a cloak all day seemed to have disappeared so that she felt cold.

She must hurry back now. It was late. Grandmère would scold for being kept waiting. Charles would be there—worried at her absence, perhaps puzzled, but certainly angry.

Without looking in Harvey's direction, Julie turned sharply away and began to run back to the house.

CHAPTER XV

MATRAS was on the look-out for Julie. As she entered the house sedately and carefully, the old butler held the door open for her, saying nothing, but his eyes cautioned her. She crossed the hall apprehensively, not thinking of Harvey any more, her thoughts going forward into the salon where grandmère and Charles would be waiting for her. She entered a silent room. Charles and grandmère were sitting stiffly on gilt-framed fauteuils opposite to each other. They were not speaking. Charles looked pale and ill at ease. His clothes appeared gayer than his expression.

At sight of Julie, grandmère's anxiety found vent in annoyance. "At last, Julie! Where have you been? We have been waiting for you a quarter of an hour. Why did you not say you were going out?"

"I did not think it was necessary to tell you, grandmère, because I thought I should be back in good time." Julie spoke composedly enough, but her eyes wavered as they met Charles's steady gaze.

He had risen when Julie came into the salon and now hurried forward to greet her. He smiled, but it was chilly and the smile did not reach his eyes. He came to a stop in front of Julie, took her hand in his and bowed low. Everything was so correct. In vain Julie told herself that this correct attitude was a pretence because grandmère was in the room, looking on, and that Charles was one of those men who hate showing their softer feelings in public. She chanced to meet his eyes. They did not crinkle at the corners in an answering smile, and Julie looked away troubled.

Instinctively Julie guessed that Charles had seen her with Harvey. *He knew.* Well, that was her bad luck. Now she would have to explain her meeting with Harvey before the ground was prepared. While searching in her mind how best to approach this new problem, Julie said quietly, "Are you ready to go now, grandmère?"

"What a foolish question! *Certainement*, I am ready. I have been waiting here in the salon for a long time, and so has Charles. He came early, but of what use when you were not here?"

"I am so sorry." Julie spoke with humility.

"Perhaps you did not notice the time," suggested Charles.

Julie did not answer. Charles spoke as a jealous man. Jealous of Harvey! If he only knew! But realizing Charles's mood gave Julie a clue how to appeal to him.

Grandmère led the way from the room.

Julie hung back a little, pretending to take her powder compact from her handbag, to renew her make-up before starting out. She looked over her shoulder at Charles—a languishing, pleading expression in her lovely eyes.

"Charles!" There was nothing to hide. Charles knew, anyhow. But Julie wanted his sympathy and understanding.

"Yes, Julie!" His voice was flat, the beautiful fluty tones absent.

Julie felt suddenly sick. She said in a hurried whisper, "You are angry with me?"

"Not angry, *chérie*, but hurt." His voice was as toneless, but the eyes that were fixed on hers were softer and more kindly.

"Because of Harvey?"

"Yes."

"You saw us?"

Charles nodded.

"Please trust me, Charles dear."

"That is difficult."

"Not if you knew all. You would then. I will explain later, I promise. Just trust me."

"Can you ever explain? That, too, will be difficult for you."

"No, it won't. If you love me as you say you do, you *will* trust me."

Charles was silent for a few seconds.

Madame was talking to Matras in the hall. The butler was making a long-winded complaint to his mistress about the weakness of the lock on the front door.

Charles's hand sought Julie's. His fingers entwined themselves in hers.

"Julie! Dar-r-rling."

The relief was so great that before she could stop them tears spurted from Julie's eyes.

"Darling you, too, Charles," she whispered, swallowing hard in an effort to conquer her emotion, in fear of spoiling her make-up.

Impulsively, Julie raised his hand with hers to her lips, and pressed her mouth convulsively on the back of Charles's hand.

152

"I knew I was right and that you would understand," she said confidently.

"Julie!"

They started forward. "Coming, grandmère!" she cried gaily.

The Patrices' house was quite different from the Lubins'. It was an important moment to Julie when she crossed the threshold and entered what was, to her, a sumptuous palace. There was a marble staircase with a delicate wrought-iron balustrade, statuary and painted ceilings which made an impressive and glittering entrance to a rich home furnished with care and taste in antiques of a bygone, gay age.

Julie would have been more impressed by her surroundings had she not been governed by the fear of meeting her future in-laws, worrying in case Madame Patrice took a dislike to her, not liking her looks or her taste in clothes. Charles doted on his mother and was much influenced by her. Supposing Madame Patrice's first feeling was one of dislike, then Charles would be unhappy.

The fear increased as they were taken up the shallow marble stairs to the first floor to a thickly-carpeted corridor towards the double doors of Madame Patrice's bedroom.

Grandmère entered the room first. She looked pale and dignified, and carried herself erect as though she were conducting a mission into an important person's office. This was partly true, and probably explained her attitude.

Julie followed her, and Charles, restless and excited, brought up the rear.

In one swift, comprehensive and startled glance, a picture of the great room and its furnishings was impressed, like a photograph, on Julie's mind. It was not until later, when going over the events of the day, that Julie recalled in detail all that she had seen, and was able to appreciate the taste and luxury of the room.

The bedroom was light, airy and spacious. There was none of the heaviness and airlessness that pervaded the Lubins' house. A large Aubusson carpet with a cream and mushroom coloured ground, with blue true-lover's knots and flowers in old-world pastel colourings in the corners, was spread in glorious richness on the honey-coloured parquet. It matched the lambrequins framing the tall narrow windows. The domed, painted ceiling bore fleecy clouds which in turn supported fat cherubs with wings, who disported themselves to soundless music played by nymphs on strange-looking flutes, harps and horns.

Most of the furniture in the Lubin home was of the Empire period, solid and unimaginative. Gabrielle Patrice had beautiful tapestry and gilt chairs of the Louis XV and XVI periods. There were Kingwood and marqueterie commodes with ornate handles and keys—cupboards and door panels were painted in the Watteau and Fragonard manner, brilliant, gay and romantic.

It was a magnificent bedroom such as Julie, who was a great film fan in England, had never seen either on the films, or in real life.

The great bed stood on a daïs approached by two shallow carpeted steps. The coverlet was of the soft breast feathers of the eider-duck, a mixture of white and fawn, like velvet to see and to touch. The painting in the gilt-framed bed-head was a pastoral scene of gaily-dressed people dancing in a forest glade, with lovely children on floral-roped swings, a profusion of flowers spilling from a curved vase on a gate-post, and small dogs playing with doves.

Julie saw all this in a fleeting moment, not taking in each article of furniture, or the detail in the composition of a painting, but as in a photographic flash.

She felt someone take her hand. It was a warm, comforting hold. Charles was giving her comfort, but she was not conscious of this.

Her eyes had moved from her surroundings and were fixed in wide astonishment on her future mother-in-law, Gabrielle Patrice, who was sitting in the centre of the great bed.

Julie stopped.

Gabrielle, looking absurdly young to be the mother of a grown-up son, looked at Julie across the room.

She sat between silk sheets and surrounded by fat pillows, and looked calm and beautiful as a great picture, with a heart-shaped face, a wide mouth and large expressive dark eyes. She wore a little lace confection at a rakish angle on her dark hair which enhanced her beauty and made her appear younger than ever.

She looked expectant. She greeted grandmère with a smile, spoke a few words of welcome, and exchanged kisses with the older woman, then turned all her attention to the slight figure standing just inside the door.

In that look Julie not only saw with admiration the expressive loveliness of Gabrielle Patrice's face, but also that she was the feminine counterpart of Charles. The knowledge calmed her fears and comforted her. Intuitively, too, because of the sumptuous but gay note of everything about her, Julie guessed that Charles's light-hearted spirit was inherited from his mother. Her's was a youthful face, with no wrinkles, one that laughed easily as though she found life good. Though just now the effects of a long illness had refined the delicate features, they were of a remarkable beauty.

There were several vases of flowers in the room, lovely in their austerity, but no sign that this was an invalid's bedroom.

Seeing such beauty in these perfect surroundings made Julie feel gauche, unfinished in some odd way and lacking in poise.

She smiled uncertainly at the melting large eyes, which were staring frankly at her, appraising her, probably wondering if she were the right girl for Charles and would make him happy. In her youth Gabrielle Patrice had been acclaimed for her beauty, grace and wit. She had been a gay, restless, lovely creature, and might have been forgiven for not wanting a rival to her son's affections.

Suddenly Gabrielle held out pretty dimpled hands with pointed fingertips. She smiled and her whole face lit up.

"Why, she is enchanting, this child," she cried in a musical voice. "So sweet, so young, so fresh ! Charles, *quel bonheur !* I am so happy. Julie ! *Chérie !*"

Someone pushed Julie forward. It could only have been Charles.

After the first hesitating steps Julie went quickly over to the bed. She put her hands in Madame Patrice's, and was pulled gently forward and kissed warmly on both cheeks.

Julie, embarrassed, laughing and happy suddenly, sat down on the side of the bed, her hands still imprisoned in Madame's, a slight burning sensation behind her eyes.

"I am so glad," she said in a low voice. "I was so afraid you would not like me." She freed her hands gently.

"Afraid ! Of me ? But no, it is I who have had a fear of you who might take away my Charles. Now that I have seen you I am afraid no more, for I know you will make him so happy."

She spoke quickly in French, with pretty gestures of her hands. She was using a scent—or a powder—that had an intoxicating and subtle allure. Julie could not give it a name. Possibly it was one of those individual creations especially made for Madame Patrice. Julie was to associate that particular heavenly perfume with her all their lives.

M'sieur Patrice, bullet-headed, partly bald and wearing glasses, came into the room. He, too, was full of admiration for

Julie. He spoke in English with studied slowness, enunciating carefully, because it was a strange tongue to him. He said laughingly to his son, "You told us that Julie was marvellous, but you did not say half enough. She is like a girl who comes to life only in a dream." He turned to his wife. "Do you not agree with me, Gabrielle?" And in case she did not understand he repeated what he had said in French.

She nodded vehemently. "But yes, she is charming. I am so proud of her and Charles—all of us."

Everyone was happy. Charles beamed with pleasure. There had been some doubt in Charles's mind how his mother would react to Julie. She had reigned for so long in his and his father's hearts, she might have been forgiven for feeling sore at being deposed. She was behaving magnificently, and Charles loved her more than ever.

Champagne was brought, and with it the black French poodle, Mitzi, who wore several tartan ribbon bows, and looked so wise and human and clownish all at the same time. They all drank to Charles and Julie.

By that time Madame Patrice looked tired. Charles showed his mother every consideration. He slipped an arm under a pillow and told her to rest against it. With his free hand he lifted her hair from her forehead and stroked it gently.

M'sieur Patrice rang the bell, and a white-capped nurse appeared at once and suggested that Madame should rest. Julie realized for the first time that Madame Patrice was a sick woman. She was full of remorse.

"We have tired you," she said. "It is time for us to go."

The nurse nodded discreetly, and Julie rose from the side of the bed.

Madame replied, "Just a little perhaps, but I am so happy. Tonight I shall sleep content, and tomorrow I shall get up for a while. I want to talk to you so much, Julie—much, much, all about yourself from the time when you were a baby. When I am better we shall have fun together, the four of us."

Grandmère, who had effaced herself with rare tact throughout the visit, sprang a surprise.

"Julie's mother and father will be over here by the weekend," she said.

Julie was overjoyed. It meant that she would see her mother soon, when they could talk about this great adventure that had happened to her; it meant, too, the reconciliation of grandmère and her mother. It accounted perhaps for that queer tremor in grandmère's voice just now, when she said, 'Julie's mother and

156

father . . .' Possibly grandmère had felt the separation more than anyone guessed. Julie bent to say *'au revoir.'*

Gabrielle Patrice cried, "*Bien*, then I shall see them soon."

She put her arms around Julie, and hugged her, kissing her again with fervour, repeating how delighted and happy she was, saying to Julie, "Come soon, if you can spare the time."

"Oh, I will."

"You understand me very well?"

"Perfectly."

"I am so glad you speak French. I congratulate you on your accent. In no time you will look and speak like a Frenchwoman. It is good."

Outside the room, Charles's father said to Julie, "I have a very beautiful wife. You think so, too? She has always been my consolation and inspiration. I am forever grateful for that."

"I never expected to see anyone so lovely," Julie cried fervently.

"She loves you already because she knows you will make our boy a wonderful wife."

"Shall I?"

"We think so. Charles has changed much since he has known you. I make no attempt to hide it that he was a little wild, but now he is steady and anxious to settle."

Julie felt happy. 'A little wild'! What did that matter? A man had to learn by experience. She thought no more about it.

Then Charles's father added, "But we love you, too, because you look good. We have to thank Madame Lubin for telling us about you. Also, it is a great help to married people if they love each other. So many things go to make a perfect marriage."

Charles and his father embraced warmly.

"Will you be at home for dinner this evening, Charles?"

"Not tonight, it is a club dinner."

"I forgot that. Perhaps tomorrow then—or the next day?"

"Possibly. I will let you know when I ring through in the morning; but it will not be Friday, for I have another engagement then." Charles spoke definitely.

"Then I shall wait until you telephone me tomorrow."

Charles took Julie and grandmère home. The lovers held hands all the way.

Julie said, "André and Hubert are giving a party for us tomorrow. You won't forget?"

"No. What time is it?"

"Not until after ten o'clock. You could dine at home if you wished and then come on. Tante Nina will be with me."

Charles nodded. From now on, until they were married, Julie would be chaperoned. Some time this week he would buy the engagement ring, a narrow platinum band which Julie would wear on the third finger of her right hand. He had also decided to buy Julie a diamond ring to wear, English fashion, and for the benefit of her English friends, on the ring finger of her left hand. That, thought Charles, would make Mr. Robins understand that the engagement was a *fait accompli*, and there was now no further chance for him. He could return to England.

He said, "I might do that. It sounds exciting. They usually give good parties, with lots of amusing people in the stage and film world. In the meantime you must lunch with me tomorrow, Julie, as we have arranged. Nina may come, and I will find a partner for her." He smiled. "Do you remember our misunderstanding over that."

They laughed, and Charles squeezed Julie's fingers, conscious that her exciting freshness was making his pulses race a little faster. He said to grandmère, who was pretending not to notice anything unusual about the behaviour of the two people sitting beside her on the broad back seat of the car, and who was taking a passionate interest in everyday objects in the street,

"I do not think, Madame Lubin, that I can wait long for Julie."

Grandmère was not surprised at the remark. She replied soothingly, "It all depends on the lawyers. Often these settlements take time."

Julie was sitting in a bemused state, one half of her mind with Charles, and the other half remembering all that had happened at the Patrices' home. Grandmère's remarks hardly registered.

Charles's decisive answer, "Then I must hurry them up," was meaningless because Julie did not know its context.

Madame Lubin shrugged. It was up to Charles to get the business side of the contract through without delay.

Julie and Madame Lubin sat talking in the latter's boudoir after Charles had gone. Grandmère was well pleased with Julie's instantaneous success with the Patrices, and was most affable, and willing to discuss future plans.

They spoke firstly of Gabrielle Patrice, and Madame Lubin said, "I have told Charles's parents more about you than you know about them. Gabrielle Patrice was married out of the schoolroom, you understand. Her parents' choice of a husband for her was lucky, as they in turn seem to be for you. One can choose a sound partner for one's son or daughter, but one is not able to direct love. M'sieur Patrice put a large sum into the marriage settlement, and Gabrielle brought her name and the furnishings of an old castle which escaped vandalism at the time of the Revolution. She is of the family of De Locco, which once owned much land near the Italian border in the South. She is of better birth than her husband, but they love each other and love forgives so much, especially," added grandmère with a touch of cynicism, "when it is helped by a limitless purse."

Then she spoke of Julie's trousseau which would be occupying all their minds and time in the coming weeks. She discussed this exhaustively with a Frenchwoman's intelligence about clothes.

When the lovers met for lunch next day, Julie, wearing flowers that Charles had sent to her earlier in the morning, was accompanied by Nina. Charles had brought along a business friend. The quartette went to a restaurant where Charles had booked an oblong table set parallel to the wall. Charles with a grin of understanding at the other two, took Julie's arm and drew her to sit beside him on the wall-side seats. The table bore a high decoration of flowers. Nina and Charles's friend, Henri de Betancor, sat opposite. They might have been at another table, for they could neither see the opposite couple, nor hear what they said—unless Charles and Julie stretched their necks to speak to them.

Charles said once, "You will pardon the arrangement?"

"We understand," they smiled, speaking in unison. It was obvious that Charles was a hopeless companion to them, being completely absorbed in Julie to the exclusion of everyone else.

Having ordered the lunch, Charles turned to Julie again, and sliding his arm along the back of her chair, said in her ear, "You are looking most beautiful this morning, *mignonne*, so beautiful that in spite of all these people staring at us, I am tempted to take you in my arms and kiss you."

"Oh, don't do that," Julie cried in mock alarm, obviously pleased with the compliment, "you will disturb my make-up."

"What does that matter when you look so ravishing, anyhow. Do not pout or I shall kiss you not once but a thousand times." He glanced at her dress and the red roses on her shoulder. "I wish I were a rose." Then he laughed. "I have seen this dress. It is a part of you, but there is something fresh about it today. You seem good enough to eat."

"It must be your flowers. Thank you for them, Charles; they are glorious."

"No, thank you for wearing them. They are the lucky ones, those flowers."

Charles sat back in his chair while the waiters served the first course. He spoke to the others, but presently turned again to Julie, saying,

"I do not wish for a long engagement. How soon can we be married?"

Julie had not yet thought of a date. "I am still in a dream about our engagement. But grandmère is giving me my trousseau. It is to be a wonderful one. She wants you to choose some of the designs for my dresses."

"How kind of her! Of course I will. Madame Lubin is most generous to you, and I am grateful. But how long will this trousseau take to make?"

"I do not know. There is to be a conference at Madame le Gère's this afternoon."

"Excited?" Charles inquired softly.

"Tremendously."

"So am I. It is quite a business getting engaged and married; and it is not only the clothes, but we must make a home, find and furnish an *appartement* before the wedding day."

Julie had few ideas on a French home. She suggested, "Couldn't we stay in your rooms until we find exactly what we want? I mean, there is no hurry."

Charles shook his head decidedly. "Mine is a bachelor *appartement*, and ladies are not permitted—well, you certainly would not be." Then he added quickly, "When I was twenty-one and left home to set up my own establishment, I joined in with two of my university friends from Grenoble. But first one was married and then the other. Now I am living alone."

"Aren't you lonely?"

"Not often. I have many friends."

"But you just said that ladies weren't allowed in your *appartement*?"

Charles glanced at Julie sharply as though he suspected that she was trying to catch him, but he saw that it was only mild curiosity which prompted the remark.

"Not girls like you, *chérie*," he told her drily.

There was a short silence, during which Julie's face was

160

shadowed. Then she said, "Oh, dear, I hope you are not going to have secrets from me, Charles."

He was quiet for a while, then he said, "That goes for you, too, Julie. What about Mr. Robins yesterday ?"

Her face cleared. "I didn't think you'd mind. It was only Harvey."

"Then why did you not tell me when you received his letter the night before ?"

"Oh, I couldn't spoil our lovely evening talking about Harvey," she cried. "Besides, I meant to tell you."

"But you did not ?"

"I forgot. Anyhow, you did not give me the chance."

"Do you feel like telling me now ?"

Julie shrugged. "There isn't much to tell. Harvey wanted me to go back to England with him."

Charles's jaws set firm. "You refused."

"Of course."

"What did Mr. Robins say to that ?"

Julie smiled. "Quite a lot. Harvey is going to stick around in case I change my mind."

"But you will not, Julie ?" How anxious Charles sounded ! She looked at him tenderly. "No."

"Women do sometimes."

"Not this one. Besides, I was never in love with Harvey, and I am with you."

Her mind harked back to Charles and the visitors who went to his *appartement*. She sighed because there were women in Charles's life, friends of his that she had not met. There was a side of his life in which she had no part, and never could have, if only because she was the girl who would be his wife, cherished, protected and loved, but on a pedestal, where she must remain.

Her mind flew to Lucienne Jeanson. It was a name that often occurred in Julie's thoughts, and lately, like an evil genius, in her dreams. Resolutely she pushed it aside as she had often done before, for it invariably caused her a fierce pang of jealousy that seared her like a pain and spoiled the rest of her day.

Charles was not content. He said urgently, "Promise me, Julie, that you will not see this Mr. Robins again ?"

"I won't promise, but I do not wish to see Harvey ever again."

"That is not satisfactory. It is not being fair to me."

"For that matter you were not fair to me. You must not have girl-friends in your *appartement*."

Charles looked haughty suddenly. "You deny me any parties ?"

"Not parties, only girl-friends." For a moment it looked as though they might squabble, but a moment later the cloud passed and they were laughing, and Julie said, "One of these days I shall ring you up and see who answers the phone."

Charles mocked, "You do not know my address : or do you ?"

"No, but I can look it up in a telephone book."

"You must be quick then, because only this morning I gave my landlord notice to quit."

"Why didn't you say so before ?" said Julie, conscious of a feeling of relief ; and also a little ashamed of herself for not being more trustful.

But later in the meal, over cigarettes and coffee, and breaking a long, satisfactory silence that had fallen between them while they held hands tightly under cover of the tablecloth, Charles returned to the subject of a home.

"Have you any ideas on what district we shall choose for our home, Julie ?" he asked.

"I don't know Paris very well."

"I would suggest Neuilly, but both your people and mine live there. If you were a French girl it would be ideal. You would be expected to pop in and out of either house daily, or whenever you should want advice—a communal way of life which would not appeal to you. Being English, and oh, so independent, you will probably never ask an 'in-law' for advice ; you would call that interference. Why are you wrinkling that little nose of yours ? Am I not right ?"

"What would you like, Charles ?" asked Julie, in an any-where-with-you mood.

"I have long thought that the ideal is a small *appartement* in Paris, and a seaside villa on the Normandy coast for *vacances*." He shrugged. "So long as we are together does it matter much where we are. I like Normandy because I was born at Avranches. But if you would not like the idea we will not go."

"I am content with your choice, Charles," said Julie. She thought, 'Anywhere with Charles.' And she wished passionately, 'If only we could be married today !'

Suddenly Julie became emotional and shy, which was so unlike the Julie she knew that she flushed, and began quickly talking about something else, because her shyness made her want to keep all her emotion to herself, while she was afraid that if the others knew they would laugh at her.

Charles said, "Then I will ring up an agent this afternoon

and get him to send a list of suitable *appartements* round to my office. I can bring them with me to André's party tonight."

Then, when Julie was at her happiest, and the quartette were laughing and talking gaily, all in the best of spirits, on their way out of the restaurant, they were jostled by a small crowd of people struggling to get in. In that crowd were Lucienne Jeanson and a friend of Charles.

"'Allo, Charles ! This is a surprise !" Lucienne said laughingly, her eyes flickering with some emotion as they rested lightly on Julie's face.

Julie had grown pale. She strained her ears to hear what Charles said in answer, and found it easy to pick out his mellow tones from the babel of sound around her.

"Lucienne !"

'Lucienne !' thought Julie in sudden misery. To her jealous ears the lovely syllables sounded in glad surprise. She was deaf to the cry of dismay in Charles's voice.

He said to the others in a hurried tone, unlike his usual one, "Go on. I will join you in a few moments."

The crush was so great, the crowd milling around them, that Nina, who was broader than Julie, and was trying to force a passage, stood still daunted, and Julie heard a part of what Lucienne replied to Charles.

". . . I am going to André's party tonight . . . I must be there to drink my felicitations to you and . . ."

Julie knew instinctively that there were no felicitous thoughts in Lucienne's mind for either Charles or herself. She had quickly looked away from Julie, but she acted as though conscious of her audience, using her flexible intonation to reach every ear.

Julie's heart sank. Suddenly she did not want to go to the party tonight. The thought of meeting the redoubtable actress struck terror to her heart. There was an easy familiarity, even proprietary manner, towards Charles which caused Julie to wonder how friendly the two were. They were still friends. Why had not Charles given up Lucienne as she, Julie, had rejected Harvey ? Something must be done about it. She could not permit his friendship to continue with the actress, especially on the old terms. It was not fair of him to expect her to allow it. She would speak to Charles about it this evening. There was no time now for he would put her with Nina into a taxi and return at once to his office. The word 'insist' occurred to Julie. But in her heart she knew that if she persisted in demanding that this friendship must cease she would only succeed in driving it underground. Suddenly she despaired of ever winning and holding Charles's love in its entirety.

Julie remembered now what had hitherto seemed of no importance, that Charles's father had spoken of his son's wildness. Were his words a hint or a caution or what? Was he referring in an oblique way to Lucienne Jeanson's friendship with Charles? Why mention the fact at all? Why, indeed?

The three reached the pavement outside the restaurant, and stood still rather meaninglessly waiting for Charles to join them. On either side of the doorway were several rows of small marble-topped tables, most of which were empty, as the afternoon rush for coffee had not yet begun. Waiters with folded arms waited for new customers.

The lunch had been such a success, and now this!

Charles joined them within the promised moments.

He cupped Julie's elbow in his palm.

"You are quiet, dar-r-rling?" he bent to whisper.

"Am I? I don't think so." But Julie was not even aware of answering, her heart was tortured with the unrest of wild, unreasoning jealousy.

"It is getting late, and I have a conference at three, so I will put you in a taxi to go home," said Charles.

"Do not bother," said Nina, who was still in the gayest of spirits, for Henri de Betancor had made friends with her over lunch, and she who had been neglected and unwanted for years found herself admired and wanted. Her blighted looks freshened under the shower of compliments that fell from Henri's lips. "We are not going home, but to the Rue St. Honoré, to see designs for Julie's wedding clothes." She smiled at Julie as she spoke, but there was no answering smile on Julie's lips. Nina thought, '*Now* what has happened? Oh, these lovers, blowing hot and cold at the slightest adverse wind in their own particular world! We might be going to discuss a funeral and not a wedding from the look on Julie's face.'

Julie nodded mutinously, not because she agreed with Nina that they were going to talk about wedding clothes. Indeed, if Charles could not behave decently, Julie was determined there would be no wedding, and therefore no discussion on the necessary clothes. She would have no compunction in being unorthodox and hurting French feelings in breaking the engagement. Not that it would help if she did. She would still be unhappy without Charles. She would be unhappy either way while Lucienne

Jeanson were alive, and the actress was too strong and healthy to be killed off by jealous wishful thinking.

There was an edge to Julie's voice as she said *"Au revoir"* to Charles. It was Lucienne who had put it there. Charles appeared not to notice it.

Nina advised him, "Come early tonight."

Charles nodded. "I will try," he said, "but I am dining at home and I cannot count on my father, for when he begins to talk about business problems, as he will, he forgets the time."

Charles held Julie's cold hand between both of his warm ones. *"Au'voir*, dar-r-rling," he said gaily, but it was a forced gaiety and he looked long and uncertainly at her. "Julie !"

She was looking away from him, taking an interest in the passers-by. "Please, Julie ! Just a little smile." But Julie turned a deaf ear to his pleading. Her heart and mind were full of jealous hatred for Lucienne.

Charles looked down at her hand lying passively in his. "You are cold. Put on your gloves."

Julie did as he bade her, giving all her attention to fitting on her gloves, seeing that the seams were straight.

Then Charles was gone, and Julie felt cold, wishing she had not been such a fool, wishing . . . She pulled herself up sharply. She had always despised people who lived their lives in wishing.

Nina asked perfunctorily, "What is the matter, Julie ?"

"That woman !" cried Julie stormily. "You saw her—heard her. She is my enemy. What am I to do about her ?"

"I thought that was it," replied Nina, with an irritating placidity. "But why do you worry ? You will be Charles's wife. His heart is yours. But it is a mistake to show your feelings so plainly. Just because you are engaged to Charles it does not mean that you must possess him body and soul. If that should be your aim and desire then do not let him know it, for that is the surest way to lose him to Lucienne Jeanson for ever. It shows how young, inexperienced and unsophisticated you are that you reveal your emotions so unashamedly. That way, you hurt yourself in the end."

Julie listened to Nina's advice. Her mood lightened as she realized Nina had spoken a truth in saying that she, Julie, would be Charles's wife, and some of the irritation went. "I mustn't let that sort of thing break me down," she said. She thought, too, 'I behaved stupidly to Charles. I should not have kept silence weighing heavily in the air. I should have pretended—acted, as *she* did.'

But the incident in the restaurant was only in the nature of a preliminary skirmish. The battle royal would be this evening when they all met at André's party, for then everyone would have the leisure to fight.

CHAPTER XVI

JULIE bathed, powdered and dressed that evening with care. She chose one of her smartest dresses to wear, sure that Charles would suggest going, after the party, to dance and have supper at a night club. Her nerves were tensed, and her eyes hot and dark whenever she thought of the evening. She must look sensational, and be a popular success. She over-emphasized her good points, sure that she would be noticed. Nina shook her head disapprovingly at sight of Julie, but said nothing. When Julie went in to see grandmère before going to the party, the old lady was not so reticent as her daughter. She was startled by Julie's beauty, which seemed mature and enchanting in this golden dress, and said frankly, "You are overdressed, Julie. What would le Gère say if she could see you now ?"

"Madame le Gère made the dress !" said Julie lightly.

"It is not necessary that you wear such a dress at one of André's parties."

"Oh yes, I must look as nice as the other girls. You have never been to one of André's parties or you would know that all the big names of the stage and screen are there."

"It is one of the latest models in Paris, I might almost say in the world. Such a waste ! It is too classic, elegant and exquisite. You are naughty to wear it."

"That depends on who is there," persisted Julie, and her pulses throbbed feverishly.

"All sorts of people, and few that I would care to meet."

"And one in particular, grandmère," said Julie boldly.

"Charles ?"

"No. Try again."

"Not Lucienne Jeanson ? So, she is going to be there." Grandmère spoke with some asperity. Then she said simply, "Rub off that rouge, child. It does not become you to look like *her*. You appear to be suffering from a feverish disease."

Julie stiffened. "I do not use rouge, grandmère."

"Oh ! So !" The old lady snorted. She had spent a tiring day with her lawyers, and signed her name to some large cheques.

She was not at her best, and testy because she was worried, not so much about this marriage now, but how deeply Charles cared for Julie. A few weeks ago grandmère would not have worried about Julie's happiness so long as her own pet scheme was successful. Now the plan was a success, but it seemed unimportant when set against Julie's happiness. She decided, 'Michel must speak to Charles who must understand that he is marrying a girl with English ideas on marriage, one who expects all of her husband's heart and not a portion of it.' She wished that Julie's mother could fly over at once. She understood Julie and would know how to deal with this tricky situation, something which grandmère, with her French outlook, felt incapable of handling.

She said grudgingly, because she did not want to spoil Julie with too much praise, "I see by your clothes that you have considered the position from a feminine angle. I think, when she sees you, that Lucienne Jeanson will be unpleasantly surprised. She may well be frightened."

"I am the scared one."

"That is natural, for she has all the arts of charming men at her fingertips. All the same I back you to win." Then grandmère gave some parting advice, "Do not show undue pride in possession. Remember who you are, and who this woman is. Do not forget *what* you are—the fiancée to Charles. Above all, do not embarrass Charles. He would never forgive you that."

Julie smiled. So many do's and don'ts ; she had forgotten them already. "I will try to remember, grandmère."

"It is of no use *trying* ; you must."

Charles had not arrived when Julie, in her golden dress, shimmering with every movement, joined André's party. Both hosts, André and Hubert, embraced Julie warmly, kissing her on both cheeks, congratulating her on her engagement, and frankly envious of Charles. Then they stood back and admired her, for the reflexions from the dress threw out a halo of light, so that she appeared bathed in a lambent glow. Everyone in the room knew who Julie was and clamoured to know her. She was quickly popular and was at once the toast of the party.

"Where is Charles ?" was on everybody's lips.

Julie could not concentrate on her new friends. When her eyes were not searching the room for Charles they were looking for Lucienne Jeanson. As time wore on, and Julie sipped her third drink, which was more potent than she knew, her eyes were beginning to look anxious.

Once Nina asked her, "Do you know where Charles is?"

"He is certainly not here."

"I could tell that by your face." Then Nina added, "Can't you hide your feelings a little, Julie?"

The plaintive suggestion caused Julie to mask her emotions. To conceal her anxiety she began to talk and laugh to those around her. In her own ears her voice was a babble of sound, but the men who were gathered about her evidently found what she said funny for they roared with laughter at her quips. Julie's French was now in the 'good' stage, but she still uttered words without knowing their true meaning, with a comic result.

The champagne cup was in jugs set in a huge cooler filled with a mixture of ice and saltpetre, but the ice was already melting when the jugs were empty. They were refilled and put back in the cooler.

It was late when Lucienne arrived. She had come on after the theatre, and still wore the magnificent picture gown encrusted lavishly with semi-precious stones that she had worn in the last act of the play. It suited her to perfection. It had been designed for her by a theatrical dressmaker who was a showman and artist. Of course Lucienne made an entrance.

At sight of the actress, who was never known to arrive anywhere 'in time,' because an effective entrance was such a help to success, Julie's heart sank and she felt depressed. There was a time, not so long ago when she first came to Paris, that Julie had stood in a queue with Nina to see Lucienne. That was before she had grown jealous of Charles's friendship with the actress. But before they reached the box-office a notice was put up that the house was full, and she and Nina had turned away, promising each other to book seats at the first free afternoon available. Now, since jealousy had ruled Julie's heart and mind, she had come to look upon Lucienne as something hateful and repulsive.

Even to Julie's critical gaze Lucienne was fascinating. She had no idea that Lucienne was wearing the dress and the heavy theatrical make-up as a kind of armour against this meeting with Julie and Charles.

To Julie's relief few people had been introduced to one another. Those who were not already friends were expected by their youthful hosts to make friends. But neither Julie nor Lucienne showed any inclination to join up. Each was surrounded by her own admirers, those who liked the fresh colouring and immature charm of the one woman, and those who preferred the mature enchantment of the older woman. It was as sunlight is to moonlight. Yet for the next two hours, in the constant change of the pattern of the crowd, Lucienne contrived never to be far from Julie.

Once the two women touched each other accidentally, when Julie trembled so much from the contact that she had to sit down to recover. Sulka Knizburg, the band leader, happened to be talking to Julie at the time, and when he saw her descend from his eye level, he looked down to find the reason.

"Not faint, Mademoiselle?" he enquired anxiously.

"No, but it is a little hot."

"Hot! It is suffocating. I shall myself open all the vindows at once." He suited his words to action, and immediately there were cries of protest from everyone in the room.

Lucienne's voice, scornful and denunciating, was heard above all the others, saying in English, "What do you expect this eefening when you mix the French and Eenglish togethair? The Eenglish like fresh air so much, it is a gale. You must put up with it. I 'ave brought my ermine to wear. I knew 'ow it would be."

Lucienne ostentatiously put on the wrap she was carrying. Mirth crept into her voice as she said, "Now I do not care eef it snows." But she would not have said this if Charles were there.

Still Charles had not come, but people spoke about him, and it seemed to Julie as though the essence of his personality was in the room. As the evening dragged on for her, Julie's insensate jealousy deepened. She had been able to govern it earlier, especially when Nina had warned her not to show her feelings too openly; but now, after several glasses of champagne cup, it mastered her. Her eyes kept wandering to Lucienne—brilliant, voluptuous, her fingers no less than her gown sparkling with jewels. There were clips in her rich dark hair and diamonds dangling from her pale ears. 'Did Charles give her those?' wondered Julie, and she thought, too, 'How much does Charles care for her?' Sometimes, when Lucienne seemed aware that she was being watched, and acted with more abandon accordingly, Julie did not look straight at her, but stared obliquely through a wall mirror, wondering sullenly why Lucienne was the best-looking, best-dressed and most evil woman in the room. Her large eyes spelled mystery, her magnolia skin was alluring, and her gestures, frequent and pretty, were enchanting. There was the recklessness of despair, an impertinence bordering on rudeness, in her manner towards Julie, but the latter could say nothing.

Julie glanced at the open doorway which led into an ante-room. There was no sign of Charles, and Julie was glad. Almost at once Julie was sorry not to have him standing loyally beside her, for Charles had a sense of the fitness of things. He had a duty towards his womenfolk, and would not allow Lucienne to poke fun at them.

André came up to Julie. "I have phoned Charles's *appartement* several times and can get no reply," he said. "Do you know where he may be?"

"Of course I do. Charles is at home with his parents."

"I'll try there. I had not thought of anything so simple. There must be so much business for him to discuss this week. Perhaps I was a little premature in throwing this engagement party. I should have waited, but I wanted to get in first."

André went away happily. The party was at its height. There were no more people to come, and guests had not yet begun to go. The chattering was like the buzz of a swarm of bees. Someone broke a glass. The brittle splintering sound caused people to turn their heads.

Sulka whispered to Julie, "I have written a new song. May I dedicate it to you?" he asked gallantly.

"How very kind of you! Yes, I shall love that. No one has ever thought of doing that before. It makes me feel proud. I do hope it is a success." She spoke breathlessly. She was pleased, but she could not give him her undivided attention.

"But of course—I—Sulka—have written it. I shall play my song next week. You vill come to hear her, yes?"

"Yes."

"And you vill vear this so beautiful dress?"

"If you wish."

"I do vish. You look like a princess out of a fairy tale, only much much intelligent."

Then André returned, and Julie was glad because Sulka, though kind, tired her.

She looked at him eagerly, with what he thought a pathetic expectancy in her large blue-grey eyes. He said at once, "I can get no answer." He spread out his hands and hunched his shoulders, thrusting out his underlip. "Someone has taken off the receiver."

Julie's eyes questioned André, and he shook his head slowly. They both knew that Charles had no intention of coming to the party. André knew nothing of the incident after lunch, when Charles had learned that Lucienne was going to the party.

It was that knowledge which had caused Charles to change his mind. He had known for a long while that Lucienne thought she had a right to his companionship and consideration. He had learned, too, that she would be a bad loser and a vindictive enemy to any woman rival. Charles had not minded. It did not seem to matter. But since he had known Julie it had come to count very much.

As Charles did not wish to expose Julie to Lucienne's hate, which would be much more active if she were to see him with Julie, he thought it wiser to stay away from the party. It had been difficult to decide what it was best to do, and he had sought Nina's help in protecting Julie during his absence. But when he telephoned Nina she had already left the house.

Not having the gift of second sight, Julie could only think that Charles had stayed away because he was afraid to face Lucienne, and not for the first time she wondered what degree of friendship there was between them.

Julie was disappointed not to see Charles this evening, yet she was conscious of relief, too. She would not have to watch them together, as she had sat entranced looking at them that evening at the night club when André had told her that the actress was Charles's girl-friend.

André had spoken loudly. He had been sipping champagne-cup all the evening, not realizing what an insidious drink it was. His voice attracted Lucienne's attention and she stared at Julie with interest.

Julie was aware of Lucienne's presence. She said suddenly, with almost vehement gaiety, "Never mind about Charles. I am enjoying myself so much, and intend staying until the end." She accepted another drink and drank it straight off. Then she smiled at Sulka, who was greatly attracted to her, partly because he was swarthy and a fair skin fascinated him, but also because Julie was English, and he had a great respect and liking for the race. He knew exactly how Julie was feeling because he had watched from his band-leader's daïs, the friendship between Charles and Lucienne grow, flourish and dim. He had seen one star wane and another brighter one appear on the horizon. He knew, too, why Charles had tactfully stayed away tonight, and what it had cost him to do so. In his own funny way, Sulka constituted himself Julie's guardian. So when he saw her make a great effort to act, not knowing even the rudiments of acting, he responded to her pretence of gaiety with a gallantry equal to that of a great courtier. If he was a trifle heavy it was because he knew Julie was whole-heartedly in love with another man, a fact which somewhat cramped Sulka's style.

To Julie the evening wore on in a dreary farce of gaiety,

though judging by the laughter and the curious humming noise in the room she appeared to be the only one who thought so.

She drank many glasses of tepid champagne-cup. The earlier cold and stinging drink had gone because the ice had melted, but no one seemed to mind.

Sulka never left her side. Julie was like a magnet to him. He sunned himself in her golden presence. But he made things possible for Julie. No one was critical of her any longer, and her pretence of gaiety passed for the real thing.

Once Julie's eyes strayed to a small clock on the marble mantelpiece. How slow time passed! Then from behind her she heard a challenging flexible voice, and though she did not turn, Julie was aware that Lucienne was behind her. Even if she had not heard the voice Julie would have guessed at Lucienne's nearness, for the actress used a heavy scent which Julie had noticed earlier in the evening. It was individual, like most scents that Frenchwomen use.

She was talking to Hubert, for she named him, and spoke rapidly.

But Julie had been taught the French language by a master who spoke fluently and rapidly always. They were now reading French plays, for Julie was anxious to speak Charles's tongue so well that she would find herself thinking in French.

Julie understood what Lucienne said.

It was : "So the great Charles has been caught at last." The laugh that accompanied the words was falsetto.

"Caught by my fair cousin," replied Hubert with satisfaction. He looked oddly at Lucienne who, as deposed love, was behaving quite nicely. He had not wanted to invite Lucienne, but André, who loved intrigue, had insisted. "We are very pleased."

"But Charles! I wonder how he likes it? I should have thought he would be attracted by someone older, more sophisticated, not just a little English miss—so sweet and simple—but the jam is sweet, too."

"You must not forget this is Madame Lubin's work. She wants it. As it happens Julie has fallen for Charles. That is understandable, for Charles is an attractive man and irresistible to some women. Many men model themselves upon him. He is popular with all sorts of people."

"I know all that. But—what does our Charles see in her? It is a puzzle."

Hubert laughed as at a joke. "Not to the rest of the family."

"How is that?"

"Rather sordid, my friend. I do not know the amount of

Julie's *dot*, but as Uncle Michel and old Patrice are still rubbing their hands and chuckling since it was arranged, I can guess it is a large one. But apart from that, or should I say, in spite of it . . ."

Julie did not wait to hear anything more. She had heard enough, and moved out of earshot. Her one desire was to run away, to be alone, and see no one.

If only she had waited, Julie would have heard Hubert say words that would have mitigated everything. Hubert's sentence continued : ". . . Charles is a rich man and so would not be influenced by money. He loves Julie. I have never seen a man change so much. He was a man-about-town. That is dropped. He is content to be with Julie. He adores the ground her little feet walk upon. He cannot keep away from her. They say he is in touch with her, in some form or other, every day, by phone, with flowers or chocolates, letters, taking her here, there and everywhere, showing her off to his friends at the races, the theatre, and loving her as only Charles, I am sure, knows how to love. That is sufficient to sweep any girl off her feet."

Julie did not hear any of that.

After the first shock had worn off, Julie went to find André. He took her hand in his and clasped it tightly and carried it to his lips.

"You are wonderful, Julie. Everybody is in love with you. They say you are so unspoilt."

"Do they ?" she smiled. "I am so glad." But her heart was like lead in her breast. "I think it is time to go home. Will you find Nina for me ? This has been such a lovely party. I shall never forget it."

"But we have not yet drunk your health—yours and Charles's. Do wait a little longer. He is bound to turn up."

"I think not. In any case, I shall not wait. You must not blame Charles. It is M'sieur Patrice's fault. I know Charles is with him. I was afraid it might happen. We shall both come to see you another evening soon."

"That is a promise ?"

Julie nodded.

She waited with Sulka while André went to find Nina. By that time Sulka was humming over the air of his song. "The vords are taken from an old Viennese song. I haf adapted them to suit you," he told her. "Now please to listen. If you do not like them you tell me, yes ?"

So Julie, who felt that the life blood was slowly oozing out of her heart, had to rouse herself to listen to Sulka.

She sat very still in the taxi on the way home, and Nina, who had enjoyed herself, asked,

"Why are you so silent, Julie?"

"I am rather tired."

"Did you not like the party?"

"It was a good one, but I am not used to so much champagne cup, and now I have a wretched headache."

"Poor child! Are you disappointed about Charles not turning up?"

"Not much. I think he was wise."

"So do I. Lucienne Jeanson can be a miserable wretch."

"She is very beautiful."

"In a sultry sort of way."

"I admired her."

Nina did not reply.

Julie sat back in her dark corner of the taxi. Her plea of a headache had stopped Nina talking about the party. Her thoughts were lively, however, about that *dot* business. She recalled many odd phrases that one or another had let fall lately and which were obviously pointers to the truth, and which, if she, Julie, had had all her wits about her, might have been understood. She was English and believed in her country's views on marriage. Now it seemed as though everything had been arranged, French fashion, between the families. No doubt Madame Patrice's kind thoughts about her had been gilded by the fact that a big *dot* would accompany her proposed entry into the Patrice family. Uncle Michel had been anxious about her friendship with Charles. He and grandmère had used every bait to make Charles like her: wonderful clothes, parties, and money. But Julie felt now that no amount of goodwill and help from them would have been of much avail without the added promise of that big *dot* behind her.

She had no idea what they hoped to gain by it, but she would find out.

And Charles—that was the humiliation which bit deep into Julie's soul. Charles must have known about the *dot*. Their love was bought. It was a question of francs.

'That is not love at all,' she thought rebelliously, her heart swelling.

If it had not been for that *dot*, there would have been no welcome for her from Charles's family, no wedding at all, certainly no Charles.

She thought dully, 'If I had not gone to the party I should not have known this now—before it is too late.'

Through her thoughts there emerged a dislike of her grand-mother who had tried to wreck her daughters' lives by this method of marrying them, and succeeded with one of them. Grandmère was trying to arrange her, Julie's, life, and interfere with her happiness. She must be stopped.

The taxi came to a stop in the street outside the great doors of the Lubin mansion. One half was open, and there was a dim light in the courtyard beyond. Somewhere a clock struck four.

'It will soon be another day,' thought Julie tiredly.

Nina asked, "Do you feel better? Can I get you anything when we get in?"

"No, thank you. My head is worse and I feel sick."

"I will sit with you a little while."

"No, please don't. I want to be alone."

Nina waited to pay the taxi, and Julie went in ahead of her. There was a message from grandmère on the hall table. It read: *Charles has phoned three times. The first time he asked for Nina. He sent his love to you, Julie. G.*

The note left Julie unmoved. She was still holding it in her hand when Nina came in, locking and bolting the door after her. She passed the note to Nina to read in silence.

"Poor Charles!" Nina exclaimed as she gave it back to Julie.

Julie swung round angrily, "You mean, rich Charles! He appears to have everything a man can want."

"You are not so poor yourself," retorted Nina unsympatheti-cally, "some people might say you were spoilt. But you are not well. Go to bed, *chérie*. The best thing you can do for yourself and everybody is to forget this evening."

"I wish I could." Julie had felt humiliated and angry, and now she was lonely and lost. For it was impossible to tell Charles what was in her heart. What could he say? Though he might sympathize he could not understand, because this *dot* business was a part of French life.

Nina left her at the end of the corridor, kissing and embracing Julie, telling her not to worry because everything always worked out in the end—somehow.

Julie went along to her room. As she passed the boudoir she could hear the faint insistent ringing of the telephone. Almost without hesitation, automatically, Julie went into the boudoir, which smelled of stale air and the dying scent of sweet-smelling flowers, and switched on the heavily shaded lights. Nervously she picked up the receiver.

"'Allo! Julie?"

"Yes, it's me," she replied, a little shaken by the sweet tone in Charles's voice when he said her name. Invariably Charles's voice had the power to rouse her emotions, even when Julie was angry with him, as she was now.

"*Bien*. I have spoken to André, who said that you had just left. I have been trying to get on to you here on and off all the evening."

"You should have tried André's *appartement* earlier. You knew where I was."

"Oh, yes, but I did not wish to do that. It was such a long party."

"What do you want?" Julie's tone was uncompromising.

"What do I want? What a question! Why you, of course. I should like to see you, to hold you in my arms, to kiss you a thousand times—and then to begin all over again—and so on ... and on. And next to that I have a longing to hear your voice —not that little clipped, crystal tone you reserve especially to hurt, but soft and whispering, with that cute little quaver in it, which makes me want to take care of you forever. I have missed you so this evening, dar-r-rling. It has been a horrible time for me wondering what you were doing and if you were missing me, and even worrying whether you still love me as truly as I love you."

Julie shook off the effect of the sweet words. It was all talk. Words of love came easily to Charles. Men were always pleased with successful money dealings. Love was never so important as money.

She said, "You would have quickly known if you had come to the party."

"I know, but that did not make me feel any the better. André said that you stole the show. You wore a wonderful dress that put every other woman's in the shade. You were sparkling and gay. I can see you, Julie, with your head thrown back, revealing the lovely long line of your throat, your eyes narrowed with laughter, and your teeth gleaming. What I missed! How I should have loved to see you."

"Why did you stay away?"

There was a long pause, then Charles said slowly, "I think by your so cold and aloof voice, which hurts me so much, that you have guessed."

"It was an easy guess. You were afraid to face your actress-friend." Julie's tone was harsh.

"Not *afraid* as you are counting it, but in fear lest she should come between us," Charles said quickly.

"What is there between *you* ?" The question was sharp and crisp.

"Nothing. Please believe me, dar-r-rling. It is a long tale and I will tell you all about it soon."

"When ?"

"On Saturday."

"We are supposed to be lunching together tomorrow."

"Not 'supposed' ; we are. But Saturday I shall take the whole day off. First we will look at some *appartements* the agents have sent to me. Then we will drive into the country and be together all day. Nina is a good sort and we can shake her off easily."

"And you will tell me everything ?"

"If you wish." Then Charles added, "Say you will like that, my little dove ?"

But Julie only said, "We shall see."

"I will fix up a wonderful time for you, Julie. Now you are tired, my dar-r-rling, all the colour is drained from your voice. Go to bed and have a good sleep. You will feel better for it. Forgive my ringing you up at this hour, but I had to hear from your own lips that you were safe or I could not go to bed myself."

"I am all right," Julie assured him, making an effort to speak naturally.

Dissatisfied, Charles rang off saying in an emotional voice, "I love you, Julie. God bless you, my little dove !"

As she replaced the receiver Julie's nerve broke and she began to sob helplessly. Everything was in such a mess, and there seemed no way out of the muddle unless she could bring herself to hate Charles, and that she could not do.

She got into bed quickly and wept luxuriously because she was without an idea how to meet the situation, until, exhausted, she fell asleep.

CHAPTER XVII

LATER in the morning there was no question of Julie getting up from bed, much less lunching out. Instead of the headache losing itself while she slept it was worse when she awoke, the pain at the back of her neck having such a paralysing effect that Julie could not raise her head from the pillow. She refused to eat any *petit-déjeuner*, and Marie reported this to grandmère, who slipped on a wrap and went to see what was wrong.

As soon as Madame Lubin looked at Julie's face she said severely, "It is what they call a—hangover. You drank too many cocktails last night."

Julie knew that this was not true, but she could not collect her disconnected thoughts sufficiently to speak. They seemed to be floating about, with gossamer lightness, somewhere in her weary brain, having no beginning or end, and entirely without direction. It was a curious sensation. Even those bits of thoughts were blurred by the severity of the pain, and once, in a crescendo of agonizing pain Julie thought wildly, 'Perhaps I shall die.' And after the pain had diminished a little it came to her, 'It might be the best thing for me.' Yet she never remembered thinking such things.

"You must have aspirin and strong black coffee at once," decided grandmère.

The suggestion nauseated Julie. She tried to shake her head in refusal, but could only groan.

"It will make me sick."

"At least you will be sick with something." She insisted on Julie taking the aspirin. "It will send you to sleep. You will wake up at noon feeling well enough to go out to lunch with Charles as arranged."

Though grandmère spoke cheerfully she was worried because she thought that Julie would not recover until later in the day. As she told Nina soon afterwards, "I know those migraines. They are due to nerves. Julie has had an exciting week, and has been too gay for a girl who is not used to much excitement. I must warn Charles to look after Julie better."

Nina was not deceived. She looked squarely at her mother.

"Julie's migraine is not due to being in love and parties. She thrives on gaiety. Lucienne Jeanson was at the party last night. Charles, as you know, was not there. One can believe that Lucienne, angry and disappointed at losing Charles to a little English girl, would go out of her way to hurt Julie and try to ruin the child's happiness. Both love Charles."

"But it is Julie that Charles is marrying." Then grandmère asked, "Did Mademoiselle Jeanson speak to Julie?"

"No, for I would have known."

"Then I do not see how she could have hurt Julie."

"Neither do I, but she did, for Julie was wretched when we left André's."

"She was nervy before you went. Julie told me that Mademoiselle Jeanson would be at the party, that was why she wore her new dress, much to my annoyance. Fancy dressing up for a boy like André."

Nina smiled wryly. "Julie was worse when we came home," she persisted.

"It is inconceivable, because Julie has much just now to make her happy. I will talk to her later. It may be but some small thing has upset her, and I shall be able to explain it away." Somewhat disconsolately Madame said, "I must ring up Charles and tell him not to expect Julie for lunch." She thought crossly, too, 'I have never been able to talk to Nina. Always I have the feeling that she is blaming me for something I have done—but what?'

These thoughts remained with her all the morning, even while she personally arranged the glorious flowers sent to Julie by Charles with his love.

In the late afternoon, when Julie was feeling better, and eating *oeufs pochés*, Madame Lubin visited her again. She sat down opposite the bed and fixed her dark eyes on Julie. Grandmère thought the girl looked pale and listless. In a remote way it angered her, because she was as strong as a horse herself and so did not understand pain in others, least of all in Julie, who should be happy and yet was not happy.

She said, "How is your migraine, Julie?"

Julie sensed the lack of sympathy in the formal inquiry, and she said quickly, "I am much better thank you, grandmère."

"It was a bad attack."

"Yes, I felt like dying."

"Nonsense! If you had been that ill I should have sent for a doctor. It is not so easy to die."

"I have found that out."

"A girl of your age should not dream of dying, when you have everything to live for."

Julie said quietly, "I am sorry to have been such a bother."

"It was no trouble, and anyhow it has not lasted long. Are you often ill like this?"

"I am never ill."

"*Bien!* What brought on this attack?" asked Madame relentlessly.

"I was upset at hearing Mademoiselle Jeanson discussing me last night."

"Yes?" Grandmère took out her cigarette case. It had a picture of Marie Antoinette on the cover. In the Queen's day, the picture had been surrounded by diamonds, but during the Revolution some vandal had taken out the diamonds and hammered the setting flat. She selected a cigarette with care, and presently flicked to life her pencil-lighter and held the flame to the tip. Then she sat back in her chair and puffed contentedly.

The little act relieved a tension that had sprung up at the mention of Mademoiselle Jeanson's name, and the atmosphere seemed a little more human, grandmère showing more sympathy than she had yet done. She said perfunctorily, "You do not want to smoke?"

"No, thank you."

Grandmère did not speak but sat comfortably in her chair and continued to watch Julie solemnly.

It was Julie who spoke, saying quickly and nervously, "Grandmère, why did you not tell me that you were offering Charles a big *dot* to marry me?"

"That is a crude question, and I am surprised you ask me in such a bold manner. I certainly did not offer Charles a *dot* to marry you. It is the custom in France, when a girl marries, for her to have a *dot*. The custom has lapsed somewhat after two wars, but it still exists. It makes for a woman's independence. She takes her proper place in the marriage as an equal. It is good, for, having her own dowry a wife does not have to beg, plead, cajole or threaten her husband for money, as she has to do in England, especially if he happens to be mean or close. That kind of inferior treatment gives her the status of a slave. In France it is different. *You* are marrying a Frenchman. He expects to make your future secure, but your family should help bear the responsibility, too. Charles has offered generous settlements to you. When he dies, according to our laws, he is bound to leave you a certain portion of his money. All this is arranged by the lawyers of both sides. What have you to grumble about?"

"I am not grumbling, but I do not understand these 'arranged' marriages. I do not understand why Charles, who you say is rich, needs to marry a wife with a *dot*."

"It is the custom. Without a *dot* a girl could not expect to make a good marriage. To some extent your social status is determined by the size of your *dot*."

"Mademoiselle Jeanson suggested that had it not been for the size of my *dot*, Charles would never have looked at me," Julie said. There were twin spots of colour in her cheeks, and she looked like a beautiful tragic doll.

"It would not be human to expect a defeated rival to praise her victor. If I were Lucienne Jeanson I should feel like scratching your eyes out. Not that it really matters to us what she feels. I doubt if she knows the truth about you and Charles."

"She must have known that their friendship had to come to an end some day, when Charles married."

Grandmère shrugged. "Nothing is impossible to a woman in love. Perhaps she thought their friendship could go on for ever, or that there was not a girl available in Paris just now whose family could put up a large *dot*. I do not pretend to guess. She has had a terrible shock over you. Charles has not only found a wife, but she is young, fresh and beautiful, and moreover, it so happens, that he is in love with her as well. I do not suppose that Charles himself, being rich and generous, has ever given a second thought to your *dot*. His one impatience is to get the law part settled quickly because until this is done we shall not permit the marriage to take place."

"You are terribly businesslike, grandmère," sighed Julie, looking happier now that she understood some of the ramifications and complications of French family life, especially where marriage was concerned. She did not feel humiliated any more, but it had certainly puzzled Julie why a rich man should wish for more money from his wife.

"I am practical, *chérie*. These things are new to you, but I grew up with all these ideas and they are good. Also I have tried to see this marriage from the English point of view because, though I wished very much that you should marry Charles, I also wanted much for you to be happy. If I had warned you beforehand, 'This is the man you shall marry,' you would never have loved Charles. So I arranged for you to meet at one of my *recherché* dinners. I realized directly I saw you that you would be something new for Charles, and that he would be attracted to you, and I was right. It could not have happened better."

Julie smiled. The happiness that a short while ago had seemed gone for good, now returned to her, so that she thought, 'Dear, dear Charles!' There was something new, too, in her happiness which had not been there yesterday. She thought, 'I love him more today than I did then.' Some of her old confidence returned and she said in a different voice, "Did Charles send those lovely flowers?" But she knew he had. No one else would think of sending such fragile blooms.

When grandmère had gone Julie lay back among the pillows. Though tired, she was feeling well again. She had nothing to do but rest and think of Charles. When she had done this for a while her mind flitted to what was close to Charles—his home. She contrasted the Lubin and Patrice houses, the austere solidity of one, and the sumptuous luxury of an earlier, grander and exquisite age. She recalled now what she had scarcely realized noticing at the time, the great light blue and gilt Sèvres vases, standing on onyx and gilt pillars in the Patrices' hall, the pictures which were after the manner of Boucher, with dancing shepherds and shepherdesses, rich waving corn, a woodland glade, and merry blue and white skies, reminiscent of the blithe spirit in the gay, frivolous age of the kings of France, when from Court to peasant there was a reckless display of the whole gamut of the emotions, when life appeared to sparkle with wit, beauty and dancing, and the world seemed such a lovely place.

The Lubin house also boasted its Sèvres vases. Julie had examined them many times with interest. They were of a later age, when the kings were gone and the first Emperor reigned. The vases were of the same height and voluptuous curves as the earlier ones, but these were of royal blue, with a large gilt N enshrined in a chaplet of gilt laurel leaves on the neck of the vase, and another at the base. The scenes on the porcelain vases, though rich and important, and not gay and flamboyant, were warlike, depicting the clash of armies, of blood, wounds and death ; and great victories—Napoleon crossing the Alps, 1800, Napoleon at the Battle of Austerlitz, dated 1805, and on both, in the foreground was a painting of the military despot in characteristic pose. These vases were on black marble pedestals.

Julie's thoughts went to the Patrices' home. She had more in common with them. Her spirit was akin to theirs. That is why she loved Charles. They both liked the same things. There was where her happiness lay.

She thought, 'And now I must forget this foolish jealousy, and try never to think of Lucienne Jeanson again. I have been all mixed up, but gradually I shall get it sorted out. Perhaps I have been in too great a hurry.'

Julie rested in bed all Thursday, gazing for long minutes at Charles's flowers, matchless in their white purity in a big cut-glass vase. Next day she felt well again, with the right perspective on life, blooming as a woman who is loved and cared for blooms.

There was the usual French lesson in the morning. Julie was enjoying the reading of the French plays. Since Professor Gant had found that Julie did not tell Madame Lubin about the disgraceful fit of laughter in which he had indulged in the library, at Harvey's expense, there was an air of understanding between them. The Professor was more human, or the mask of the dignity of his profession had slipped and the man beneath was revealed. Instead of greeting Julie's mistakes, which were often funny with an owl-like stare, he laughed at her. As Julie did not mind his enjoyment at her expense, she laughed with him.

Grandmère had caught them and threatened to dismiss the Professor. She told him icily, "I do not expect you to come here to laugh. You must never forget that you are giving Mademoiselle Ryan a French lesson."

When grandmère had left the room, Julie said, "I am so sorry. It is all my fault." Then she added kindly, "I have still so much to learn. When I am married and have my own *appartement* you must continue to teach me. Then we can laugh as much as we like."

His expression brightened. She had been an apt pupil—too quick, for the lessons he had been at such pains to give, and which she had eagerly assimilated might, for that very reason, end soon. Now Julie meant to carry on with them, and he was pleased.

Later, Julie told Nina that she was going for a walk as far as the Porte Neuilly.

Nina went away, and Julie dressed to go out. The morning sun was behind her and cast a long pencil shadow ahead of her on the pavement. Julie felt happy and peaceful, with the terrible fret to her nerves of yesterday all gone. She was rested, and now that grandmère had made everything clear and feasible she no longer felt humiliated by this *dot* business which was a part of the marriage system over here, and life seemed simple once more.

She had spoken to Charles on the phone this morning for a long time. He could not have been nicer about her migraine, worrying about her health as no one had ever done before. He was sorry about their lunch yesterday, and said they would make up for everything tomorrow. Today, unfortunately, he had a long-standing engagement at his *appartement*, and when Julie laughingly teased him, saying that he was probably throwing a wild party, Charles answered lightly that he was entertaining in his *appartement* but that it was not a party.

They had parted on a gay note.

She became aware that someone was behind her . . . He kept pace. . . .

Suddenly Julie stood still, and a flash of anger came into her blue-grey eyes. She drew a quick breath as Harvey came up beside her. He was the last person she expected or wanted to see, but she said casually enough,

"Oh, hello, Harvey !"

"Hello, yourself. I watched for you yesterday and you did not leave the house."

"Since when have you turned detective ?"

"Only the last few days."

"I didn't know you expected to see me," Julie said coldly.

"I didn't really, but I thought I'd take a chance."

"Well, if you must know, I was ill in bed."

"Oh, that was it. I'm not surprised—you've been on the gad ever since you came over."

Julie did not reply.

"Better now ?"

"Yes, thank you."

"Prim, aren't you ?"

Julie was silent for a while, then she burst out, "You should know better than to force yourself upon me."

"I must. I can't phone or write. All I can do is to stick around and hope for a sight of you."

Julie was tired of arguing with Harvey. You could never make anything clear to him if he did not wish to understand, and in the end you only wearied yourself, felt beaten and lost confidence. Words made no impression on him, so she stamped her foot at him in sudden anger. "You are impossible !"

Harvey grinned suddenly. "That heel of yours has quite a martial sound."

"Oh, be quiet !" Then she asked, "Where are you getting the money to stay on here, Harvey ?"

"I like that ! What do you care ? As a matter of fact I have enough to last me a week. I can't make money stretch for ever, even though yours seems to be elastic," he said nastily. "As I remember you in London, and that must seem a long way off to you now, you always had an empty purse."

"Don't be rude. Grandmère gives me all I want."

"All ! When you have everything ! One's values get mixed over here. A roll of thousands of francs bulging out of one's pockets boils down to a few English pounds."

"Well, you are wasting both your time and money here. Everything is fixed up between Charles and myself. I am very happy about it. Everybody is. My parents are coming over this week-end. Perhaps you had better have a talk with Father—if you are still here. He may be able to make you see sense, for I can't."

Harvey replied somewhat unexpectedly, "I do see sense—even your sort—but I can't accept it. I know you better than

184

you do yourself, and I am sure that it is only a question of time before you come round to my way of thinking."

Julie knew that Harvey was putting a strain on himself, trying to be fair, and working himself up into a temper, when they would spar with each other like two strangers. Julie guessed, too, that any moment now the mutual recriminations would begin, when an awful quarrel would develop. That in itself might be a good thing if it meant a permanent parting, but it was a tiring means to a desirable end. The break came abruptly, and without any recriminations.

Harvey went on, "You must not marry this Charles," he told Julie earnestly. "He isn't the fellow for you. He is the one who has come between you and me. It is only a temporary break. You'll get him taped soon. Of course I see how it is done. He makes pretty love to you. All Frenchmen seem to have that knack. It is a means of getting their way with women. It has gone to your head, and you probably believe all the nice things he says. Flattery is like champagne to some girls. But what's the betting that when he isn't with you he is entertaining Mademoiselle What's-her-name, the actress, in his apartment? They probably have a good laugh together over the little English miss, who wears her heart on her sleeve for all to see—that is, in between their embracings, of course—I say, Julie!"

Harvey got no further, for he was left gaping, his eyes bulging, staring at Julie's receding back. His head buzzed and he wondered what on earth he had just been saying to cause such a show of temper.

Julie was running away from him as swiftly as though he were some evil thing.

There was no point in pursuing her. In England, when they had competed for fun in races, it was Julie who proved to be the swifter and always won.

Harvey might have felt happier had he known what Julie was thinking as she ran down the street.

Harvey's carelessly uttered words had aroused that demon of jealousy which Julie had thought yesterday was gone for ever. But it had only been sleeping, waiting for some such malicious suggestion to bring it to active life again.

Long before Julie reached the end of the street where she lived, the most incredible imaginings had gained possession of her mind.

She went on running, her heels making occasional little pings of sound on the pavement. As she ran Julie was working herself up into a terrible state about Charles and Lucienne.

She recalled how definite Charles had been when telling his father that he would not be at their home for dinner on Friday night. Apparently a long-standing date kept him away.

Charles had never wanted her to visit his *appartement*, but he had admitted that other women went. What other women? She, Julie, had a right to know. Why did he not name them? Now she came to think of it, those two knew each other very well—how well?

Charles had not denied that he was entertaining someone in his *appartement* tonight. He had laughingly told her that it was not a party. If only one woman—Lucienne perhaps—were there, it could not truthfully be called a party.

Might not Charles have stayed away from André's party, not for fear of embarrassing her, Julie, but because he was afraid of what Mademoiselle Lucienne would say to make him lose face. Julie saw herself as a laughing-stock. How easy it had been to fob her off with facile explanations! But she knew better now.

Not that she minded causing a laugh occasionally; only it meant that Charles must have thought her a fool. As Harvey had so brutally reminded her—Charles and Lucienne must have had a good laugh at her simplicity.

That brought another thought in its train. What right had Charles to call her to order about Harvey, when he himself was playing around, like a good-time-Johnny, with his actress-friend? No wonder that Lucienne Jeanson could afford to stare at her with such triumph in her eyes the other night—triumph and proud proprietorship. Knowing that she still held Charles, Lucienne could afford to laugh at her rival's poor efforts to hold him.

Then Julie knew why she had never been completely happy with Charles. There had always been a shadow between them, an indefinite something, the fear that she did not possess Charles wholly, and dared not face him with it.

"I love him," she gasped feverishly as she ran. "He means everything to me; what I've always wanted in a lover." Then she thought wildly, 'I never want to possess him body and soul, as Nina suggested. I only ever wanted whatever Charles had to give to be mine and not shared by another woman. It will be awful if I lose him to her, for I can't live without him.'

But if a part of Charles's heart were reserved for another woman whom he had known for years, then why did not he say so? He was frank about most things; why not this? Julie knew that there are some secrets of the heart which men do not share even with the person they love most in the world.

She had reached the house by now, the tall, secretive, net-curtained windows, like eyes in the flat façade, and the great doors through which in former days coaches were driven, seemed like a prison to her. She paused, and the welter of imaginings which had increased as she ran, milling about in her brain, grew thicker and more sinister.

The small door let into a panel of one half of the big doors was ajar. Rushing across the courtyard Julie had to wait again at the polished mahogany doors of the house, with their orna-mental bronze knockers and knobs, until Matras let her in.

Without glancing at him she said "Thank you" mechanically, and went up to her room, thankful not to see anyone on the way. Her movements were slower now—not so rushed. In seconds Julie was behind the closed door of her room : she tore off her hat, and threw it, with her handbag, aside, and sat down on the bed to regain her breath. Gradually her pulse rate became slower. She sat with her hands clasped on her lap, staring in front of her, trying to find an answer to her imaginings. Everything about her appeared to droop, her mouth, her neck, her spirits. Julie's suspicions against Charles increased so that it was easy to believe of him everything her tortured mind could think of. One jealous thought fed upon another until the case against Charles and Lucienne Jeanson appeared one of cast-iron. Julie was able to recall many long-forgotten incidents, which had seemed harmless enough at the time, but which, seen now through eyes filled with jealousy, built up a mountain of guilt against Charles.

The finished picture, a tortuous muddle of suspicion, was incredible and fantastic. But Julie thought it was true. She did not deny that a small part of Charles was attracted to herself. She was new, and as a mixture of French and English, probably appealed to that in Charles which liked something different. But a larger part of Charles's heart was undoubtedly in possession of Mademoiselle Jeanson.

If only she knew for certain ! If only these tortuous doubts which made her head ache would go forever, and she could have some peace !

It was then that a flash of light illumined Julie's tired brain. How easy it would be to find out if Charles were deceiving her. It could be done. Why not ? It would prove Charles's guilt or innocence at once. Perhaps Harvey was right about him after all. Poor Harvey ! He had been badly treated lately because he was so devotedly in love with her. She had slighted him as un-wanted and a nuisance. Though she did not love Harvey, Julie was sure that all his love was hers. That was one good point about

Harvey, a girl could be sure that no other woman was in his life.

Perhaps that was her destiny, to go home to England and, in time, marry Harvey who would make, Julie supposed, an average husband. It would be dull living with Harvey ; but he could be trusted. It seemed that if a man had a dazzling personality, like Charles, he was not a constant lover.

Julie rose restlessly and began to pace the room, her excitement increasing as her plan took shape. It was that she would go to Charles's flat this evening, catch him with Lucienne, who was of course his visitor, and tax them both. What she would do when Charles was proved to be a gay deceiver Julie did not know.

Everything fell in to make for the success of Julie's plan. Grandmère had announced that she and Nina would be out this evening. She had advised Julie to go to bed early and Julie had seemed to agree. When they were gone, Julie decided that she would take a taxi to Charles's *appartement*.

It was not a difficult matter to find Charles's address in the telephone directory. She made a copy of the address and slipped it into her bag. The feverishness had gone now. Julie's mind was clear and calm. 'Grandmère will never prove this for me and so I must do it myself. Even if grandmère did know something against Charles she would never admit it. Either she would say, "It is not etiquette," or she might question the wisdom of disturbing me by repeating the truth. This is something I must know,' she decided, not as an excuse for what she meant to do, but in an effort to placate her conscience which was troubling her faintly, because she was not suspicious of her friends as a rule, and had never done, or wanted to do, such a thing as this in her life.

The day seemed interminable.

In the evening grandmère came in to say *Bon nuit* and *Dieu vous bénisse*. "Have a good rest, *chérie*. You still look strained. There are shadows under your eyes. I want you to look well for Charles tomorrow. If you should be dull go upstairs to Uncle Michel's *appartement*. He will probably be playing chess with himself. He will be delighted to see you."

When they had gone the house was quiet. The servants had relaxed when the mistress was out and withdrawn, *en masse*, to the staff quarters behind the double baize-lined doors at the back of the hall.

Still wearing her dark day dress, which would be inconspicuous in the street, Julie dined alone at a small table in the boudoir. The room was fresher because she pulled back the heavy curtains and opened the windows to the warm Spring night, something she dared not have done if grandmère had been at home.

On the tray was an egg dish, and covered, to keep it warm, an *entrecôte* with some shredded potatoes and a mushroom sauce, and a dish of fruits. Julie ate little, but it had to be sufficient to satisfy Marie, for what was left on her tray would be reported to grandmère who would scold and threaten to call in a doctor.

But Julie's thoughts were not on Marie. She kept thinking, 'What is Charles doing?' She visualized him with Lucienne in his *appartement*. What were they eating and drinking for dinner? Would Charles see that the actress had the best tit-bits on her plate, as he did with her, Julie? Would he peel her a peach, or pile her plate with grapes whose skins in their velvet bloom looked as though they were wrapped in chiffon? Would they toast each other, look deeply into each other's eyes? Oh, why go on with this special kind of torture? Of course Charles would.

Julie tried to tear her thoughts from Charles by reading a book, then found after some minutes she was holding it upside down and still thinking furiously of him. She watched the clock. She picked up a newspaper and looked down the advertisements of new plays. Three were due to open this week. But Charles's face came between her eyes and the print. She could not keep her mind on anything. Nothing was interesting. Her thoughts kept milling around between Charles, Lucienne and Harvey.

Julie thought of ringing up Harvey and asking him to go with her. He would have jumped at the chance of 'having a go' at Charles, as he called it. But that would make him think that she was frightened. She was, but not in the cowardly way Harvey would imagine. Julie was only afraid of what she would find.

She felt slightly bewildered that a girl called Julie Ryan of whom, until lately, she had thought a great deal, could stoop to trick any man; but quickly Julie repressed the feeling, in case she stopped to think too hard and shied away from her plan to trap Charles. She chain-smoked furiously for a long time.

At nine o'clock Julie jumped up from her chair and put on her coat. She wore no hat. Her face was pale with strain and there were deep rings under her eyes; but nothing could dim her wonderful colouring—the golden hair and the porcelain quality of her skin. Her beauty would always be there, whatever her age, for she was born with that peculiar haunting look in her grey-blue eyes which gave character and drama to her face; and the lovely high flat cheek bones which were limned under her white skin; and the sensitive curl to her generous mouth.

Picking up her bag, Julie crept downstairs, ready to put a

189

bold face on her adventure should she meet one of the staff. No one was about.

By that time, too, Julie's headache had come back. She felt reckless, but worried, too, and she thought, 'In an hour's time I shall know the worst.' Then it struck her as strange that not once had she considered knowing the best. She was *so sure*. That was what made her reckless, the sureness of finding Charles out. Her mind was full of him, so that even if she had been met by one of the servants, or Matras had tried to prevent her going out, or the porter at the gatehouse had stopped her, it is doubtful if she would have taken any notice of them. Matras, anyway, was probably in the kitchen regions—in his pantry—perhaps having his supper.

The gatekeeper, who lived in a funny little *appartement* next to the outer doors, which was a part of the ground floor of a block of flats next door, and who was also a watchman and janitor, *was* having his supper.

Julie breathed deeply when she was safely outside the small door. She had found it ajar, and left it the same. Then she sped along the street to the main road where there was more chance of picking up a taxi. She stood in a halo of light beneath a street lamp and hoped that an alert taxi driver would see her quickly.

CHAPTER XVIII

IT was not easy to get a taxi. It was the time of day when most of them had taken fares to the theatres and restaurants, and the drivers were either eating in cafés or waiting about until the theatres debouched the home-going crowds and there was a rush outwards.

Julie was just thinking of walking to the Métro when a taxi passed, and at her signal the driver drew up at the kerb. At first the driver was unwilling to take her. He explained, with the usual wealth of gesture, in the clipped *patois* of the French gamin, that he had had a long day and was going home. Julie promised him a big *pourboire*, and they bargained good-humouredly. The driver had already made up his mind to take the English Miss where she wanted to go. But Julie, not knowing this, and feeling desperate, meant to offer him treble fare rather than be left behind. She sighed with relief when the matter was settled, and jumped in quickly in case the man changed his mind.

Julie sat forward in the taxi, her hands gripping her bag in her lap, her nerves taut. She tried to keep calm. 'Relax,' she told herself. 'I must relax.'

She gazed out of the window at the dark streets whose shadows made them seem unfamiliar, the pavements of which were lit up at regular intervals by pools of light below the lamp standards.

Julie's heart beat so fast it threatened to suffocate her. She swallowed hard, trying to get rid of a constriction in her throat. It would not move. There was a queer and unusual pricking sensation behind her eyes. Nervously she unclasped her hands, and raising an arm with effort, smoothed back a wave of hair that seemed to make her forehead hot.

The boulevards were crowded with people. They looked so happy. The cafés were full of evening customers. It was a fine evening.

Suddenly the taxi swerved around a corner on two wheels and came to a standstill behind what Julie saw at once was Charles's auto. It was unexpected but not surprising, because it had not occurred to Julie that Charles might be out. She had often sat by Charles's side in that gleaming car.

Julie found herself powerless to move until the taxi driver shouted, asking if she were asleep. She stirred, and stumbled out. She did not bother to say, 'How much do I owe you?' but took a large roll of notes from her purse, not knowing what they were worth, and handed it to the man without comment.

Julie knew by the man's fulsome thanks that she had overpaid him. She did not hear him say, "Ah! *Qu'elle est belle,*" but turned swiftly towards an open door which was sandwiched in between two outfitting shops.

Julie walked in and was confronted by a glass-panelled door behind which and to the side was a tiny cubby-hole, obviously the concierge's office, for it had a shelf and a high stool. A newspaper was on the shelf, and a pair of glasses was on the newspaper. The stool was empty.

There was a baize-covered board on the wall and mahogany plaque with keys on hooks neatly labelled with the owners' names and the numbers of the *appartements*. There was Charles's name; his *appartement* was on the first floor. Again a queer thrill shot through Julie and she felt faint.

After a little while she walked quietly up a well-lighted,

carpeted staircase, and now her pulses were drumming and there was a horrible buzzing in her ears. The house, too, seemed restless and noisy, as though great activity prevailed, but the sounds were muffled and seemed to blend in with the drumming in her ears. Anyway, they did not concern her.

She stood outside the first door which had a card in a metal frame in the centre of the upper part, and saw as through a mist Charles's familiar name.

There had been times when she had taken up a pencil and written her future name on paper. Julie Patrice. Lately it had looked more fitting than Julie Ryan. It seemed a long while ago now.

She was conscious of a fresh rush of emotion, and a sinking feeling of apprehension which turned her legs to jelly so that she sank back to sit on the stairs which led to the next storey. But even as she did so, breathing hard, trying for self-control, she heard voices, a man's and a woman's, coming from inside the closed door.

Instantly Julie rose to her feet, all *malaise* gone. She had no headache, no weak legs, no fluttering sensations of fear—only the courage and dignity of a gladiator.

Julie knocked peremptorily on the door.

There was a sudden silence within the room. Julie could well imagine the consternation born of guilt. She rang the bell with angry vehemence. It was as well to let them know that they were caught.

Then Charles's voice cracked the silence, melodious as always, but edged with faint annoyance. *"Entrez!"*

Julie was conscious of a sharp pang of agony. It would always be like that until she died. Charles had that power over her emotions. She could have run away then, and he need never have been the wiser that she had called.

Instead she turned the handle and opened the door, but her movements were slower, the impetuosity gone. Her action was unwilling, with no eagerness or vehemence in her manner.

Her guess had been right. Charles *was* entertaining Lucienne.

She had not noticed if there were other noises in the room— a party in progress—or people quarrelling. All that Julie could distinguish in the din and buzz within her brain were two voices —Charles's and Lucienne's.

In a tense silence, slowly, Julie, her fingers gripping the knob of the door, went into the room. Then she stopped, her eyes strained, flickering like steely-blue lamps, at Charles.

He was standing in front of the mantelpiece, his hands thrust into the pockets of a wonderfully coloured silk dressing-gown, his neat hair dark and shining, brushed close to his well-shaped head, and—*he wore no collar.*

Julie's eyes flickered momentarily at his companion.

Lucienne, feminine, scented and alluring, sat on the fat arm of a huge easy chair. Her long slim legs were displayed to advantage. Oh, surely she had everything to tempt a man, to arouse his emotions, and to make him forget his fiancée and family?

Julie's eyes went back to Charles. Her face was colourless, and the skin stretched over the high flat cheekbones glistened a little.

At sight of Julie, in one quick movement Charles took his hands from his pockets and sprang forward towards her, his eyes widening with surprise and annoyance.

He exclaimed, his beautiful voice harsh, *"Bon Dieu,* Julie! What are you doing here at this hour?"

She drew herself stiffly away from him.

She spoke, almost without volition, and there was a piercing clarity in the words, "To see you."

"What for? What has happened? Julie?" Charles sounded agitated.

"To find out if what I have suspected about you is true."

She glanced coldly at Lucienne, whose alert mind had quickly taken in the situation and the implications that anyone might draw from finding her alone with Charles. She smiled with satisfaction and ironic amusement, her mobile mouth twisted satanically.

Julie took no notice of her.

There was a deep silence in the room. A rose among those in a bowl on a side table spilled its overblown petals on to the table and then to the floor, as though touched by an unseen hand. Julie stared stupidly at the fluttering petals. She saw without observing, but to be remembered later, that the carpet had been rolled back, and there was a stout red cord threaded through metal stanchions, encircling the centre of the large room.

Behind Lucienne, heaped on the floor, was a heap of strange objects which Julie could not place—not that she tried to do so. But Julie *did* notice that no food or drinks were spread for a party.

It was Charles who cracked the silence. He asked in a hard voice, such as Julie had never heard him use to her before, "What is it that you have suspected?" he demanded.

"Your friendship with—that woman," Julie told him between clenched teeth.

Charles's dark eyes glowed. He did not pretend to misunderstand. "You are wrong."

"Am I? Shall I ask her?"

Charles looked at Lucienne. He saw the strange triumph on her face. He exclaimed loudly, "You are crazy, Julie."

"I expected you to say that. Do you suppose I have been blind?"

Charles glared, but when he spoke his voice was coldly reserved. "How dare you come here and talk to me like this."

"I expected you to say that, too," Julie repeated, aware that Lucienne was laughing at her, and also of the intense curiosity in the actress's eyes. "You don't like being found out."

Charles went back to his original position in front of the mantelpiece. "All right. Let it go at that. You have found me out. I am here, with Lucienne Jeanson." He laughed mirthlessly. "I am even wearing a dressing-gown and no collar. So what about it?"

Julie repeated the words stupidly.

"Aren't you ashamed of yourself?"

"No, I am ashamed of you for forcing your way into my *appartement*. *That* is inexcusable. You should know better than to do that; or"—and here Charles's voice was raised in anger— "is it a habit of yours to do this in England?"

He was turning the tables upon her. That was not fair because he was in the wrong. Julie was furious.

"How dare you suggest such a thing to me!"

"Why not? You do not mind coming here. It makes me wonder if you have had such experiences before."

"We are not talking about me—but you."

"Well?" His voice tantalized her.

"You are impossible! Now I know what to do."

"I wonder. Do not be too clever doing it." Charles looked long at her. Then suddenly he pushed forward a chair. "Suppose you sit down and explain what it is all about," he said in a kinder, more persuasive tone, as though speaking to an irresponsible child.

Julie, conscious now of an insupportable depression, a leaden weight of exhaustion in her mind and limbs, sat down. She was still angry.

Charles's mood had deepened to one of cold fury. He was angry with himself, Julie, Lucienne, everybody—even the janitor who should have stopped Julie from coming up and making the silly child the butt of Lucienne's bad humour. Of course, tomorrow, Lucienne would tell the story. All his friends would hear about it. By tomorrow evening a fantastic tale would be gossiped about with malicious pleasure by his intimates.

Lucienne had said nothing so far. She had laughed cruelly, and was watching the scene with a lazy kind of joy. It appealed to her dramatic sense to be acting in this scene.

"There is nothing to explain. It is obvious to me that you have thought me an ignorant fool, and have tricked me like one."

"You are behaving childishly, Julie."

Julie shrugged. It was difficult to make any headway with Charles.

Lucienne spoke in her rich, flexible voice. She said to Julie, "You must not be angry with me. Charles and I are old friends. I called tonight to felicitate him on his engagement to you."

That was untrue. Lucienne had come in anger, not to felicitate Charles, but to upbraid him on his neglect. There had been a scene. Charles was in a bad mood. She had disturbed his evening. He had refused to listen—and now, here was Mademoiselle Ryan, upset because of Charles's neglect, on fire with jealousy, ready to end everything that there was between Charles and herself. Well, there might be a chance for her, Lucienne, yet.

Julie saw through the smooth pretext. She cried, "You may be Charles's friend, but you are my enemy." And to Charles, "I have nothing more to say to you now—or ever."

"Julie!" There was consternation in Charles's voice.

She had spoken rashly, not meaning to sound so final, trying only to frighten Charles, to hurt him as she was hurt. The cry in his voice made Julie realize that Charles was taking her literally. The truth was that Julie did not know how to handle a situation she had so deliberately created. Her French vocabulary was sufficient for all ordinary purposes ; it was growing daily ; but it was inadequate for an emotional argument. Dimly Julie realized that she had been impatient through jealousy, and forced an untimely issue of what, if left alone, might have worked itself out in her favour, with no loss of prestige to herself. Beforehand, when going over the scene, she had been the heroine, dictating what she would say, and how they would answer ; but in practice it had been different. She had not counted on the strength of her own emotions or, indeed, the human element that opposed her. It occurred to Julie that she had angered and alienated Charles, irritated Lucienne, and hurt herself. She had satisfied her jealous curiosity, but she was no better for it. Indeed, the physical ache was too much for her.

Julie did a silly thing. She rose abruptly to her feet. And as she did so, something cracked within her, the something unnameable that she had built up between Charles and herself.

She gazed across at him, her mouth quivering, and her lovely eyes, blue now as gentians, with the grey and steel gone out of them, full of tears.

Then unaccountably, because Julie wanted to run away but could not, she sat down in her chair, and leant forward, hiding her face in her hands, and wept bitterly.

Lucienne looked on impassively at this waste of emotion.

Charles did not move. His features were a mask, but his hands were shaking badly.

Presently he went to the telephone and called up a garage which often served him.

"Send two cars around immediately," he ordered, giving his name and address, and added, "Tell the chauffeurs to ring the bell." Then he replaced the receiver, and said to Julie and Lucienne,

"Cars will be here at once to take you home." Then he added to Julie in a colourless tone, "I think perhaps we had better postpone our date for tomorrow."

She nodded, trying to regain control of herself.

"Perhaps you will write to me over the week-end and confirm what you have just said, 'that you have nothing more to say to me—ever'?" Carefully he looked anywhere but at Julie.

"Yes," she said in a thick muffled voice. "I will."

"Now please, dry your tears. It would be unwise to let the chauffeur see that you have been crying when he arrives. There is nothing for you to cry about."

Julie thought dully, 'Charles is right. There is nothing for me to cry about, unless it is my own foolishness.'

It was only afterwards, on the way home in the hired car, that the scene she had so eagerly created took on a sense of reality.

Thinking only of herself, her suspicions, and humiliating Charles, Julie had done something she had never before done in her life. She had gone alone to Charles's *appartement*. It was bad enough to do that in England, but it was worse in France, and even sillier to do so before her enemy.

In trying to insult Charles she had only succeeded in humiliating herself. She had done her worst, rushing headlong to her own doom, unthinkingly harming herself—for what was existence worth in the future without Charles to give it life?

There was nothing more left for her, only a blank.

As if that was not enough to depress her, there was, too, the memory of those last minutes in the *appartement*, when Charles, bowing stiffly and distantly, had left the room, and gone into another, where he was greeted by strange and youthful voices. That was a mystery to Julie, and must, she thought wearily, remain so. She did not recall hearing anyone talking while she was in the *appartement*, but then she had been preoccupied with her own business and unaware of anything outside it. Alone together, Lucienne Jeanson had screamed abuse at her in temper, calling her a fool and other epithets, all of which Julie hated hearing because she knew them to be true. Only a fool would have behaved as she had done. She had been terrified lest Lucienne should attack her. That might have happened only there had come a timely ring of the bell, and someone had knocked loudly on the door.

The best thing she could do now was to get home quickly and quietly and try to think things out. She had made a nice mess of everything.

There was still the necessity to creep into grandmère's house.

Happily no one was about. The house was warm, dark and secretive.

Once in her own room, with the door safely locked against intrusion, Julie switched off the lights, and flung herself face downwards on the bed and began to cry, not quietly and luxuriously, but loudly and tempestuously. She cried for a long time, until out of sheer weariness she could cry no more.

Then once again she was aware that her head was aching badly, and prohibitive of clear thought.

Long afterwards, Julie heard a hesitant knock on the door, and someone tried the handle.

The door did not give, and Nina's voice said urgently, "Are you all right, Julie?"

She kept still, afraid that if she opened the door and Nina came in, the latter would see her swollen eyes and question closely, when the truth would be bound to come out.

Presently Nina went away.

Julie spent the night in wakeful thought. 'Now it is all over. Even if I apologized, and Charles were to find it in his heart to forgive me, which he won't, nothing can ever be the same again. Our engagement is over. Today everybody will hear about it.'

Occasionally her spirit rose, and she thought fiercely, 'Why should I be expected to sit down quietly under such treatment? Charles is in the wrong, and he knows it. If I had not confronted him he would have continued to deceive me. I should be living in a fool's paradise.'

But above and behind all the pros and cons that fought with each other throughout the night, there remained the bald fact —that she had lost Charles. She had given him up. He had acquiesced, and made no fight to keep her. Perhaps he was glad secretly, as Harvey had once been. It was true that Harvey had quickly repented, something Julie was sure that Charles would never do. Possibly there was something about her nature that men tired of easily. It looked like that. Yet Charles had said many times that he loved her truly. His behaviour now did not make sense with those protestations.

Then Julie thought in a kind of panic, 'I've got to get away from Paris—away from Charles, and from grandmère's anger when she hears what has happened, away from all my relations, and Charles's people. I shall have to go home.'

It was the best thing to do. That way she might be able to forget Charles a little—and to forget was of paramount importance to Julie.

It would have to be done secretly, for grandmère, with her love of intrigue, and her hope of bringing her and Charles together again, never acknowledging defeat, would keep her in Paris if she knew. There were plans to make. Julie, who had never before run away from anything, was going to do so now.

Julie thought of sending a cable to her parents telling them not to come over today on a useless journey, but she had to abandon the idea because the flat in London was shut up, and she did not know where her parents would be staying for the night.

It was natural that Julie should think of Harvey. He was in Paris solely on her account. Considering that he had come over expressly to take her home, Julie knew that she could count on his help. With little money to spend he must have had a thin time. She would ring him up a little later in the morning.

To that end Julie got out of bed and looked in her bag for Harvey's telephone number which he had pressed upon her in case she should want him, and which she had noted partly to keep him quiet, but also because in some odd way it pleased him and seemed a little thing to do to make him happy.

Want of money would not be a stumbling block. Grandmère had been generous, trying to inculcate within her a sense of money values.

"It is more important to know how to spend than to save," she had said.

CHAPTER XIX

It was still early morning when Julie, depressed in spirit, but eager to get away from the two families, put on a wrap, and unlocking her door, went along to the boudoir. She telephoned to Harvey.

He was a long time coming to the telephone and his voice sounded sleepy.

"Hullo there!"

"Harvey?"

"Julie!" His voice quickened with interest and surprise. "Anything the matter?" he asked.

"Nothing, only if your offer to take me home still holds, I shall be ready to start tomorrow morning." She spoke in a businesslike tone.

"Julie! Why, of course! I always told you I'd come from the ends of the earth to help you if you needed me." He spoke excitedly, and Julie knew that he was putting his own meaning to her readiness to go with him and it was not true.

She said slowly, "The reason I am asking you is because you are *not* at the ends of the earth, but in Paris, and can help me quickly and quietly." She stressed the last word.

"Oh! Well! I get you. But what does it mean, Julie?"

"It is a long story. I can't tell you now, but I've had enough of Paris and want to go home."

"Atta girl!" cried Harvey. "You can't think how glad I am. I told you you'd change some day, but I never thought it would come quite so quickly as this."

"It isn't I who have changed, but circumstances."

"I see." Harvey spoke so dubiously that Julie guessed he did not see at all.

"I am only going with you if you promise to behave properly."

"Okay." Harvey was willing to agree to anything. "I give you my word. I am to help you, but there are no strings attached."

"That's right."

"Making use of me, aren't you?"

"Only because I look upon you as a friend." But Julie only *said* this because, if crossed, Harvey could be difficult, and by keeping in with him he would be easier to manage.

"I am your best friend," Harvey assured her. Then he said diffidently, "About cash? One can't get out of France without a ticket."

"I know. I was just going to tell you that I am putting some money in an envelope. I shall leave it for you at the gatehouse."

"When?"

"Within an hour. I must do it before grandmère leaves her room."

"I understand. 'Mum' is the word!"

"Don't forget that."

"Sure you can trust the chap at the gatehouse to hand it over?"

"I shall give him a *pourboire*."

Harvey laughed. "I see. You've taken care of everything."

"I've had all night to do it."

"Awake?"

"'Um!"

"Poor little Julie!"

"Don't pity me."

"But I do."

"Then I shall cry."

So it was like that! Harvey pursed his lips.

"Then everything will be okay for tomorrow?" Julie asked.

"Tickets bought, seats reserved—the Calais route, of course? I could manage for tonight if you like?"

"No, I can't do it." Julie shrank away from hours of wakeful darkness, when all the ghosts of her thoughts would be clamouring to keep her company. She said briskly, afraid of self-pity, "Let me know when the train leaves, and where we shall meet. Perhaps we'd better decide now on the Gare du Nord. The man at the gatehouse will take a message or note."

"Are you bringing much luggage?"

"None at all, only my handbag."

There was such a forlorn note in Julie's voice that Harvey said, "You don't sound too bright about saying 'good-bye' to gay Paree. You are going to be happy again, Julie."

"I hope so." But Julie sighed tiredly, for she never expected to be happy again.

Harvey did not like the sound of that sigh. It was like a regret, and he asked anxiously, "You won't change your mind, Julie?"

"Oh, no. It is too late for that."

Harvey had to be content. Obviously at this moment Julie meant what she said, but it was impossible to be sure with a woman. No one could be surprised when they changed their minds.

This little intrigue with Julie, directed, so it seemed, against the interfering Madame Lubin, pleased Harvey.

But Julie was sorry about the deception. There would be trouble for everybody when grandmère found out. She herself would be placed 'outside' the family for ever. So much the better. She would never have the chance of seeing or hearing about Charles and being extra wretched. For the moment, too, any kind of deception did not matter so long as she was able to get away quietly, without any fuss.

When Julie was dressed, and had paid her visit to the gatehouse, bribing the keeper to deliver her note to Harvey and to hand over surreptitiously any letter that he might want given to her, she felt better.

Matras had seen her go out. He would have taken the letter she carried and put it in the post-box for her, but there was that in Julie's face this morning which kept him quiet. He stayed in the background until Julie came back and had gone up to her room.

Marie brought in Julie's *petit-déjeuner*. Usually they had a little chat, but this morning Julie did not smile so generously. There was a chilled air about her pale face which made Marie think, 'They have quarrelled.' She felt miserable, too, because Charles was Marie's idea of a Prince Charming, while Julie was her ideal for loveliness and charm. Somehow, even the room had a desolate air, and, puzzled, Marie looked about her furtively as though expecting to find labelled luggage ready for departure. But the room was as tidy as usual.

She left the room in silence, and such was Julie's inward despondency that she did not notice the maid's going. She drank scalding hot coffee, and ate some croissant which tasted like straw in her mouth, and presently sat down and smoked a couple of cigarettes nervously.

Soon afterwards, grandmère paid her usual morning visit. She saw the half-eaten croissant on Julie's tray.

"Not hungry, *chérie*?" she asked, kissing the girl lightly on both cheeks.

"Not this morning, grandmère."

"But you must eat. One cannot live on love."

Julie thought desolately, 'One can die of it ; I know.'

Grandmère saw the heap of cigarette ash in the onyx tray,

but made no remark. She knew that Julie had arranged to go out with Charles today and might have commented upon it, suggesting what dress Julie should wear, but there was something else on her mind which worried her.

Without preamble she said, "I have a disappointment for you. I am a little put out about it myself, but it is just one of those things that are beyond our control. Your mother has written that owing to a strike in Cork the boat in which she and your father had reserved berths is not running. They have made reservations on the mailboat from Rosslare. That means they will not be over until the middle of next week."

"Does it matter?" Julie asked a little wearily. But almost at once she felt a relief. 'It will save them a fruitless journey,' she thought, 'and they will not have to listen to what grandmère has to say about me—for by then, everybody will know that Charles's engagement to me is at an end.'

"Of course it matters. You are not of age, Julie, and until your parents have signed the contract you are not officially engaged to Charles."

Julie simulated an interest. It cost her a great deal to do this, for she was not a secretive girl. It was her nature to be frank. She thought, 'It doesn't matter for the moment, and what has happened will be public property in a few days.' She thought too, 'But I've got to get away. I can't stand it much longer.'

She only said, "It is only a postponement."

"But I want everything settled," complained grandmère fretfully. "I have always been impatient with delay." They spoke in French nowadays because grandmère found it easier, though Julie did not always understand the idioms.

Julie went over to the window, and stood for a moment looking out over the roofs of Paris. She saw nothing, for she was thinking, 'I shall be back in London before they start.'

The prospect brought her no pleasure.

There was a silence, and presently grandmère said, "I do not understand you, Julie." She looked annoyed.

"I don't understand myself," she retorted.

"When I was a girl——" grandmère began, but Julie swung round, crying out:

"That was a long time ago, grandmère. Things have changed since then. There seems to be a new fashion even in love."

"I will not believe that. Anything to do with human nature does not change. Its expression may, but fundamentally love is unalterable. One can love or hate by expression, but basically both feelings are one and the same. That sounds cynical, but it is true."

She saw that Julie was not listening, or did not understand what she said, and continued in an altered tone:

"Now I shall go. Charles is sure to ring through presently, so listen for the telephone bell. *Au'voir, chérie.*"

They kissed each other, and Julie, in a rush of emotion, wished with all her heart that she could have thanked grandmère for the many kindnesses she had bestowed upon her since coming to Paris, but she did not dare.

For a moment, however, she clung to the old woman, saying brokenly, "You are always so good to me—so kind, and I can never hope to repay you."

Madame Lubin was strangely moved, and to hide her feelings she spoke testily.

"It is as nothing, child. The day you marry Charles Patrice you will have paid me a hundredfold."

Julie did not answer. Indeed, she looked paler than usual, and there were deep bags under her eyes, a proof of the strain she was going through. But what strain? Love such as Charles delighted in showering upon his beloved carried no strain with it.

Madame thought, 'The child needs a tonic. She cries.' Madame could not recall that falling in love in her youth undermined her emotionally. 'I shall be glad when Julie is married,' she thought again.

It was annoying that Julie's parents were not here. Their absence was slowing things up. Madame blamed the dockers for their silly, inopportune strike which deprived a girl of her guardians at such a crisis in her life.

Her hunched shoulders were eloquent as she left the room.

About eleven o'clock Matras knocked on Julie's door.

For one wild moment Julie thought that it was Marie bringing in a peace-offering from Charles. But could she accept it? Would she? Behind the thoughts Julie knew instinctively that she would seize it and hug it. She could not refuse. It was like that with her. She loved Charles, not a good man or a bad man, but one man, the one named Charles.

So strong were her feelings that she felt on the point of collapse. It was a dreadful sensation and lasted for some moments, and when it passed Julie was exhausted. She was about to call *'Entrez,'* when Matras opened the door, expecting, after Julie's strange behaviour earlier in the day, to find her gone. His face expressed surprise at seeing her.

He apologized for the intrusion, saying, "Pardon, Mademoiselle . . ."

She could not speak, but stared at him in silence, and the revulsion of feeling nauseated her. Julie did not want to see Matras or anyone.

He said, still with the apologetic manner which sat so well on him, "It is M'sieur Patrice——"

Again there was an agonizing moment when Julie thought Matras meant that Charles was *here.* Her face lit up with an unearthly light, while her hand flew to her heart to still its beating.

"M'sieur Patrice ?" she gasped.

"Not M'sieur Charles, Mademoiselle, but his father."

"Oh !" Julie tried hard to hide the disappointment which filled her at this news. She heard herself ask, "What does he want ?" Then she panicked. "No matter. I can't see him. Did you not tell him so ? Madame Lubin will talk to him. . . ." So Charles had told his parents ! *They knew.*

Matras shook his head. "M'sieur Patrice is in the library, Mademoiselle. He asked to see you in particular."

Julie stared wide-eyed at the servant's parchment-coloured face.

"Send him away," she cried harshly. "I won't see him."

Matras looked at her with gentleness. "That is not possible, Mademoiselle. It is important, I think, or he would not have come." He understood the poignancy of the situation. It was obvious that the lovers, so passionately in love with each other, had quarrelled.

Julie was silent, aware that Matras was waiting for her 'Yes' with an adamantine patience that would not take 'No !' She said then, "All right. I will come. You can go, Matras." Her voice was hard and cold, for his persistence annoyed her.

When Matras had withdrawn, Julie went over to the dressing-table, and taking out her powder-box, swiftly dabbed her face with the swansdown puff, trying to hide the dark circles under her eyes which misery and wakeful nights had caused.

Then, holding her head high, she went downstairs, and outside the door pressed her hands tightly together in a prayerful attitude, striving for control. *How much did he know ?*

She went in so quietly that M'sieur Patrice did not hear her enter.

He was standing at the window, looking out through the

pleated net curtains, into the street. His hands were in his trouser pockets, and Julie heard the faint chink of keys or coins being played with by restless fingers. He looked a successful business man in his dark suit, but the poise of his head was the same as Charles's though his figure was more mature and thicker set. Julie had the impression of an ebullient personality, of a happy man brimming over with verve and vitality, a man of great strength, physically and morally.

Oddly, just looking at his back, gave Julie comfort. She knew intuitively that Charles had *not* confided in his parents. Suddenly M'sieur Patrice turned quickly, and saw her watching him with her lovely, wistful eyes.

Julie said nothing.

Charles's father took his hands from his pockets and hurried towards her, his manner gay, even boisterous, because there was that about this quiet-looking girl which made him nervous, and think that perhaps his wife was right that morning when she told him her fear that something was wrong between the lovers.

He cried, "Julie, *chérie*!" and placing his hands on her shoulders, bent to kiss her first on one cheek and then on the other, aware as he did so of her youth, freshness and softness, all of which made a pathetic appeal to his big heart.

She was unresponsive, submitting almost passively to his embrace, and he thought uneasily, 'Something is wrong.' He let her go abruptly. He said nothing because his wife had given him advice before leaving his house. She had counselled him not to question, for this might well be one of those delicate situations which required a woman's tact to handle. But he had to say something to justify his visit. Without preamble, because of his nervousness, he said, "Forgive my calling at this early hour, but I wanted to see *you*, and not Madame Lubin. For that reason, too, I did not telephone. My wife, as you know, is not well. She has this morning expressed the fancy that you should spend the day with her."

"I could not possibly go," Julie replied in a whisper. With matters as they were between Charles and herself she could not accept his mother's hospitality.

"May I ask why?"

"I—have another appointment," she said in a low voice.

"But you were going out with Charles," said his father in a puzzled tone.

Julie looked at him sharply, wondering what he knew—or guessed.

"I was."

"Charles telephoned his mother as usual this morning. We were surprised when he said he was playing golf all day. It was that which gave my wife the idea of having you at the house and getting to know you."

Julie listened to all this. She was quiet for a while, then she said, "It is very kind of her to invite me, but I cannot go."

"Not even to please a sick woman?"

She made no answer. Charles's father did not understand, and she could not bring herself to explain.

"Is not that being cruel, Julie?" he asked after a pause, when her silence could only mean denial.

"Perhaps—a little." Her mouth was firmly set. "I told you I had a date."

This time it was M'sieur Patrice who did not reply; and Julie, tortured, cried defensively:

"You don't believe me."

"Frankly, no. But——" He broke off and shrugged. He had to accept Julie's word. He was sure now that there was something seriously wrong between his son and this beautiful girl. He thought that perhaps she did not wish to meet Charles. It might be so. A certain light came to him, and he said, "I assure you that you will be quite alone with my wife. Charles will not be back until this evening, and I have a conference. I am sure that you would do my wife so much of good. She is inclined to mope when alone, for there is so much of importance to the family going on just now which concerns her, and in which, because of her illness, she can take no part."

Julie glanced up at him, and their eyes met in a long straight look.

Julie had the feeling again that here was a strong man, a pillar of strength. She felt how useless it was to pit her strength against the obduracy of his willpower.

M'sieur Patrice smiled suddenly. It was a heart-warming smile, and Julie was conscious of that queer pricking sensation behind her eyes that had been her undoing in Charles's *appartement* last night, when she had made such a fool of herself. Suddenly she was tired of fighting people, afraid of that confusion in her mind which led her to say and do the wrong thing, harming everyone, but herself most of all. She was sick of trying to forget Charles when everybody and everything seemed to combine to make her remember him.

She tore her eyes from Charles's father, and turned away, childishly pressing her fingers for a moment on her closed eyelids, over her aching eyeballs.

"All right," she whispered. "I will come."

"Now?"

"At once." And to herself Julie said, 'Before I realize what I have said, and must change my mind.'

"Do not bother to put on a hat," M'sieur Patrice said hastily. "Come as you are. I have an auto outside."

"I must let grandmère know where I am."

"It will not be necessary, for she will think you have gone with Charles. I do not see that it matters, but if you wish we can leave a message with the butler."

Julie shook her head. "No, as you say, it does not really matter."

They left the room together, Julie dimly aware that this new turn of events was fantastic, one especially designed by Fate to cause her extra misery, for what torture could be worse than listening to Charles's mother talking about her son, as she was bound to do; and sitting in his home, amidst furniture that he had lived with all his life?

The two sat side by side in the car which was a limousine and driven by a chauffeur.

Charles's father took Julie's limp hand. "You are cold," he said, and chafed first one hand and then the other in his own strong fingers, and pulled the rug higher over her knees.

It was much as Charles used to do—attentive to her creature comforts—and at the remembrance Julie nearly broke down, and only saved herself added humiliation by staring hard out of the window by her side.

CHAPTER XX

DIRECTLY Julie entered the Patrice home she was caught up by the light atmosphere that pervaded it like sunshine, even when no sun was shining. It was what she had remarked on her former visit, as though invisible hands wrapped her in a comfortable cloak. No one could be wretched, dour or sombre in that home. Julie even smiled when M'sieur Patrice said that he would take her up at once to his wife, who was expecting her.

Julie said, "You were so sure I would come."

He laughed. "We know you have a marvellous good nature. You do not know my wife very well. She is a woman not only of intelligence but purpose. I am sure that you will not have to wait one minute for some hot, refreshing coffee."

He paused outside the bedroom doors and faced Julie, who had also stopped. He put two fingers under her chin and raised it so that he could look down into her face.

"Such a lovely little girl!" he told her gently. "Do not look so sad, though. All shadows pass in time, my dear."

Julie smiled because she had never seen such kindness and sympathy in a man's face.

Almost at once, as she looked down again, a bitter thought came to her that if M'sieur Patrice knew that she and his son had parted for ever there would be neither kindness nor sympathy for her.

Within seconds Julie was inside the doors, and M'sieur Patrice was saying across the big room to his wife, "I have brought Julie to you, Gabrielle."

He did not remain in the room but left quietly at once, closing the doors after him.

Conscious of a long wave of fright, Julie took a few steps forward.

To her surprise, Gabrielle Patrice was not in bed. She did not even look an invalid, but was fully-dressed in a slim-fitting black house dress with touches of white at the collar and piping following the fold of the bodice and down the skirt.

Before Julie came she had been sitting at an ornate desk standing against the silk-panelled wall. There were large medallions on the panels of the cupboards, of nymphs against the Sèvres blue background. There was a large china inkstand with pretty, coloured china roses.

As Julie entered, Gabrielle rose quickly and hurried towards her guest. She seemed taller and thinner than when she was in bed. The black poodle with the tartan bows barked and pranced about Julie.

Gabrielle put her arms around Julie and kissed her warmly. "I am enchanted that you could come," she smiled. "We shall have a lovely day together." Then she rang the bell, and within seconds a tray of coffee was brought in.

Julie had time to remark the innate goodness of the Frenchwoman's face, the tranquil look of a woman who has known pain and suffering and learned how to bear it without making a fuss.

Julie said, and it was from the heart, "I am so glad you are better. I thought you were still in bed. That was where I looked first when I came into the room."

Gabrielle laughed. "I was in bed too long. It does not do to be too obedient. I have lost so much time. Now, today, I am trying to catch up with letters and household accounts, and many other occupations which I have neglected of late."

"Can I help you in any way?" Julie asked, but she meant today, because tomorrow she would be far away. It hurt to have to deceive this kindly woman, but it was impossible now to tell the truth. Almost passionately Julie wished she had been strong and refused to come.

"Indeed you can, *chérie*. It will be so pleasant to work together. There are things I can tell you that I cannot easily say to others." That was an oblique reference to Julie's future relationship with the family. It meant that Gabrielle Patrice welcomed and accepted her.

She seemed, however, in no hurry to begin, for they sat for half an hour over the hot coffee, smoking and chatting. That is to say, Gabrielle did most of the talking. Julie sat quietly listening, admiring the older woman's sincerity and simplicity, her tolerance with and consideration for others. Whether by accident or design, Charles's name was not mentioned, though it was something which Julie waited for with dread, for she had no idea how she would react.

Then for an hour they opened the pile of letters which had accumulated in a wire basket since Madame Patrice went away. Julie learned that Gabrielle Patrice, for all her apparent fondness for clothes and as leader of a gay society, had a serious side, too. She was an active worker on the board of many charitable societies, and headed the list of generous donors to the poor and sick. She was especially interested in an orphanage, and ran a home at the seaside, on the Brittany coast, for convalescent children. She was kind, too, to the aged and infirm. Julie looked at her with new eyes and a growing respect. She saw behind the lovely laughing face the courage of a woman who knew what pain and sickness meant, and the warm heart of one who loved being kind to those of her fellow creatures who happened to be poorer than herself, or who were in need of care and comfort.

Gabrielle was full of a plan she wanted to launch in the autumn to help lonely old people, the unwanteds whom age had pushed out of the activity of life.

"I do hope you will want to help me, Julie. Together we could do so much."

Julie did not speak. How could she ? What could she say ? So she took refuge in quietness, hoping that it would not be noticed. In her heart she would have loved to help this woman, partly because she was quickly growing to love and admire her, but also because Gabrielle had the talent for inspiring her, and probably others, to *want* to help.

Once Julie burst out passionately, saying, "Why do you do so much for others ? You will only make yourself ill again by doing too much."

Gabrielle said, "So many people need help of some sort, and even at my best I can do so little."

They had a cosy lunch together in a little room off the great dining-room. It was a light, enjoyable meal, beautifully cooked, and when it was over, the nurse who was still in the house came to see that Gabrielle rested.

By that time it seemed as though Julie had thawed a little, for she talked freely about her childhood and friends. Even Harvey's name was mentioned. It sounded like a comic interlude in Julie's life, and Gabrielle asked, "Where is this young man now ?"

"He is in Paris," Julie replied, much to her hostess's surprise. "He came over to see me."

"Do you mean he is living here ?" She wondered if this Harvey was at the root of Julie's trouble with Charles.

"No, only staying." Then Julie admitted slowly, "I believe he is returning to London tomorrow morning, by the boat-train."

Gabrielle looked at Julie's face closely. While she was doing this, the white-dressed nurse came into the room. It was an inopportune moment for Madame Patrice, and she said decidedly, "I shall not rest today, I think."

The nurse looked at Julie for help, then protested.

Julie had just realized that she was talking too much about her own affairs. She said, "But you must rest or you will never get well."

Gabrielle was willing to obey her doctor's orders, but she dared not permit Julie to return to that shell of reserve which had encrusted her heart and mind throughout the morning.

"I will if you come and sit beside me for a while," she said.

"Of course."

So the two women were left together in a darkened room,

Madame Patrice lying on the bed under her magnificent fawn down-quilt, and Julie sitting in a gilt and tapestried fauteuil beside her, with Julie's fingers playing absently among the thick black curls on the poodle's head, and gradually loosening his absurd tartan bows.

Gabrielle said, "Your grandmother phoned me this morning that your parents are forced to postpone their visit. It is disappointing for all of us, but it cannot be helped. I know you are feeling the strain, too. I think you will be glad to see them next week."

Julie could reply truthfully to the last sentence. "I shall be very glad," she said fervently, knowing that her mother's angle on the tragic situation would agree with hers. In her mind she visualized seeing her parents in England, but she knew that Madame Patrice saw them against a background of France.

But Gabrielle Patrice was not deceived. This very day, under her eyes, she saw that Julie's wretchedness had deepened, though as the hours flew by among many interests she noticed that the girl hid it deeper behind a façade of pretence, gaiety and trivialities which fooled no one but herself.

Gabrielle knew, too, what was causing this change. Julie's mind had made a decision that was not agreeable to her heart. The older woman guessed by her long silences to leading questions, and the complete absence of any talk about Charles and the future, that Julie had not changed her mind, though she could not help a certain softening of the heart.

'Poor little one,' thought Gabrielle, looking at the quiet face in the half-tones of the room. 'What a torment she is enduring.'

She would not force Julie's confidence.

When her husband came in at six o'clock and said he was ready to take Julie home, Gabrielle did not suggest that the girl should prolong her visit and meet Charles. It was obvious to her that the two had quarrelled, but how seriously Charles's mother was not prepared to say.

Julie loved Charles. Madame Patrice was convinced of that. To want only one thing in the world, yet to have the strength of mind to renounce it took a rare courage. She was aware that something fundamental and terrible must have taken place between the two to make Julie do this. It perturbed her deeply. She did not know how to tackle the problem because she was in the dark about it, but she was sure that the longer it was left unsolved the more difficult it would be to reach a solution.

Gabrielle clung to Julie when she went. "It has been so lovely.

211

I hate that you should go. Do come again, but not when I send my husband for you, but because you want to come."

Julie, as Gabrielle expected, answered evasively. She even cried a little.

Scarcely had Julie gone than Charles came home. He went straight to his mother's room, kissed her warmly, and asked how she was. "You look brighter and younger today, Maman," he told her, aware that there was a subtle change in the atmosphere of the house, but unable to place it.

"I feel both. I have had a new tonic which has done me much good."

"What is it?" Charles glanced about him vaguely as though looking for the tonic.

"An English one." She was watching him, smilingly.

Charles frowned. "English!" he repeated, and sat down beside her, giving her his full attention.

"You will never guess."

"Then tell me," he coaxed, his mind lazy because he was pleasantly tired, having spent the whole day in the open air.

"Julie!"

Charles sat up alertly and looked at his mother. She saw then, with a pang, that his eyes were bright with strain, and his face drawn. He contemplated her with silent inquiry. "What was *she* doing here?" he asked harshly, and his mother knew that he was not only tired through playing golf, but weary mentally.

She shrugged eloquently. Then she said clearly, "It is simple. When your date with Julie fell through——"

"Who told you I had a date with her?"

"Why, you did; don't you remember?"

He shook his head, saying, "If you say so, then I did, but I do not recall doing so."

"Let me finish, Charles. I did so because you decided that golf was more important than taking Julie to look over some *appartements*. So—I asked her to come here to me instead."

"What for?"

"I longed to see her. I wanted to get to know my new daughter-to-be."

Charles digested this in silence. He looked away, saying moodily and evasively, "Plenty of time for that."

"Is there? I do not think so. I do not care to feel that Julie is neglected by my son. It is not good for her. She is so lovely. You know it. Other men see it."

"Who is in your mind?" Charles inquired sharply.

"Charles! I do not permit you to speak to me like that."

"Pardon."

Appeased, his mother went on, "What about the Englishman —M'sieur Harvey something . . . ?"

"What of him?" Charles sounded angry.

"I think you should know that Julie has been in touch with him lately."

Charles exclaimed, and his mother hastened to say, "Do not worry yourself, for he is returning to England tomorrow by the morning boat train."

"Who said so?"

"Why, Julie—how else could I know?"

Charles caught his lip in his teeth. "That is good news," he said at length.

"Yes, it is good—if he goes alone."

"Now what do you mean?" Charles made an effort to regain his temper. This news frightened him as he had never been before.

"I do not know, Charles. As I told you, Julie was here today. She was sweet and lovely—but pale and detached. Already I love her so dearly. But there was something—I do not know what— I could not reach the real girl. There was a barrier between us. I questioned adroitly, but she made evasive answers, or was silent. She said little, but her manner told me so much. Charles, if you have quarrelled, for whatever reason, I beg of you to make it up before it is too late. Charles . . ."

While she was speaking Charles rose from the seat in some agitation and walked restlessly about the room.

"The quarrel is not mine," he said stiffly. "I can do nothing to mend it. I am waiting anxiously for a letter from Julie. She will tell me how she feels about—everything."

Madame Patrice gasped. "You are waiting! Charles, what has happened to you that you are content to wait upon love? It is not like you." Then she added, "Why did you not tell me this before?"

"I did not want to worry you."

"But I knew something was wrong. It was in your voice when we spoke on the telephone this morning. You do love her, Charles?"

He was silent, as though going through some inward struggle. Then he burst out, saying, "Life will hold no more meaning for me if she goes out of it."

"Then," said his mother briskly, "you must make the effort to hold her."

"She wishes me to wait."

"I repeat that is unlike my son."

"That is true. I do not seem to feel like myself these days. My behaviour is strange, so is my manner. I cannot think calmly. I am confused. Two persons are within me, the one warring against the other. I cannot shrug it off as I should wish to do."

Madame smiled softly to herself. "It is love," she told him gently.

"I can only repeat that the quarrel is not my doing."

Gabrielle Patrice shook her head in bewilderment. "But you must have done something to upset Julie?"

"It lies in Julie's imagination. She does not trust me. How can we hope to be happy until she learns to trust me?"

"That is selfish. Think of Julie's point of view."

"Even you are against me," Charles said sorrowfully.

"I do not blame you, but Julie may also be right. She would expect love to make you kind and gentle, forgiving and loving."

"Love!" Charles's lips twisted cynically. "It upsets my nerves, creates jealousy, and generally throws me into a raging temper when my sole desire is to hurt Julie, hoping that she will be as wretched as I am."

His mother threw up her hands in despair. "The sooner you get married the better."

"That should go for Julie, too."

"Certainly it goes for Julie, too. See her at once and make friends."

"If I do not hear from her by Monday I promise to see her."

"Why not tomorrow?"

"Tomorrow I am playing golf at Chantilly." He laughed hollowly. "I went by train today. For once I could look out of a train window and see the countryside, instead of having to keep my eyes on the road as in an auto."

Gabrielle smiled. The remark eased the tension that had sprung up between them. "Yet you are a most envied man, for you have a fleet of cars at your disposal."

"I prefer the train."

His mother would not let him digress. She sighed, saying, "Golf versus love."

"I played a brilliant game today; I could do nothing wrong." Only Charles knew how hollow was the pretence.

"And you forgot Julie."

"You mistake, my mother. I thought of Julie all day."

"Not with love."

"No, with hate, and I was wretched."

"There, you see, Charles, you are unhappy, and content to remain so. I beg of you do not waste a moment of time."

"What can it matter before Monday ?" he asked stubbornly.

"Really, Charles !" Then she said cryptically, "That is what *you* think." She continued sharply, "You will speak to your father tonight, Charles."

"About Julie ?"

"Yes, after dinner. I shall arrange it. This engagement must not break down. Things have already gone too far. Two people in love and yet as far apart as the poles. It is fantastic, absurd and childish. I shall not permit my son to be the laughing stock of Paris."

Charles burst into laughter, but it was only an armour to hide his misery.

As in Julie's case, such odd behaviour did not deceive his mother.

Meanwhile, Charles's father dropped Julie, at her own request, outside the big doors of the Lubin house, facing on to the street. They were closed, but the small door was wide open. M'sieur Patrice waited for her to pass through before he waved a final farewell and drove away.

Julie paused for a moment at the lodge door. She did not ask if there was a letter for her. The gatekeeper was on the look-out. He handed her a letter silently. It was in Harvey's writing.

Julie said, "*Je vous remercie*," in a low voice, and put the envelope up the sleeve of her dress.

Then swiftly she crossed the courtyard and went into the house.

While Julie was changing for dinner Nina came into her room. She looked much brighter lately, for there had come into her life a man who showed some interest in her, who appeared to need her as Nina had sometimes dreamed she would like to be needed. She was carrying a newspaper, and seeing this, for a moment, Julie panicked. She had been afraid that Lucienne would advertise her break with Charles. It had happened. It was the last thing required to write 'finis' to all that was between Charles and herself ; and now it was too late Julie felt that she would have given anything on earth to prevent its happening.

That the families would be furious and blame her went without saying. Not that anything they might say or do was of much importance now. She waited, a curious expression on her face, for Nina to speak.

Then it occurred to Julie that Nina's face was not expressive of disgust or dislike. Nina was smiling in a subtle sort of way.

"What do you want, Tante Nina?"

"I thought we had dropped that ageing 'Tante'," objected Nina. She saw that Julie was standing in her thin petticoat, and she said, "Put on a wrap or you will catch cold, when Charles will be angry with us for not taking more care of you."

When Julie pulled on a wrap, saying impatiently, "What is it?" Nina handed her the newspaper.

"Only this. You remember we have been wondering all the week what Charles's important engagement was last night. Here it is in the paper. See."

With a trembling hand Julie took it from her, and looked at the spot where Nina's finger pointed.

For a moment the print was a blur and unreadable.

When the mists cleared Julie read: 'Charles Patrice, the middleweight amateur boxing champion, gave a brilliant display before twenty boy boxers in his *appartement* in the Rue Stephan last night, beating de Sutro, le Canard and Syd Marcha in two, three and four rounds respectively, his hard punches driven in with telling effect. The referee was M'sieur Henri de Betancor. The boys were visitors from the Meaux region, and competed afterwards for a cup given by Charles Patrice, who was also the referee.'

For a while Julie sat still, her mind busy with hurried, acute and vivid flashes of the truth. At first her fingers held the paper firmly, then they relaxed, and the paper fell with a rustle to the carpet. The room was suddenly filled with Charles's presence. She stared unseeingly at the wall opposite her, visualizing Charles's *appartement* as she had seen it last night, recalling what she had forgotten—the absence of all those small objects which make a home of a room, the red rope enclosing a square space, the far-off din coming from another room—Charles's dressing-gown—the heap of boxing-gloves. She must have been asleep. She did not recall noticing most of those things at the time. They had had no meaning for her—only Charles, in a wonderful dressing-gown, entertaining the voluptuous beauty, Lucienne Jeanson. Yet now, in retrospect, Julie could see the room plainly in detail. Each item had its meaning now—the boxing ring and boxing-gloves. All unnecessary ornaments had been put away as out of harmony with the business of the evening. Charles, under his gown, was prepared for boxing. The din in the next room was the boys, talking and eating, banished temporarily because Lucienne had come. She must have been blind not to have tumbled to it all then. What a fool she had been ! What an utter fool !

It did not explain Lucienne's presence there—but knowing about the other matters did mitigate the actress's being there. If she had given Charles time he might have explained. She had not given him a chance. She had contrived clumsily to hurt his pride so that he had been too angry to care much what he said or did. Obviously by his manner, and that terrible remark, 'What are you doing here ? You are crazy, Julie !' he had been disgusted at the way she had forced herself into his *appartement*. Lucienne had not made matters better. She knew well as an actress the effect of the calculated timed laugh, the gentle aside, the easy explanation, the sneer—oh, the whole gamut of human expressions that were available to her because of her training and experience, weapons used by an artist against a hated rival.

"Well," Nina exclaimed, a little puzzled at Julie's prolonged silence. "Now we know. I often used to wonder at these important engagements of Charles's which could never by any chance be postponed, but I see now why. Charles is like his mother. They say she devotes more than half her day to charities ; and he imitates her. I wonder if he will expect you to do the same when you are married ? You do not help because you must or it is your duty, but because you wish to help others. Why are you so quiet ?"

Julie stirred. "I was thinking."

"Are you glad to know ?"

"Oh yes, very."

"Don't you believe it ?"

"Of course, though a boxing-match in an *appartement* sounds incredible."

"It must have happened or the newspapers would not say so."

Julie moved then. She sat down on a stool at the dressing-table and began to make up her face, but she was thinking of tomorrow.

She had read Harvey's note. It was brief and enclosed her ticket for London, and some notes which were her change. He wrote : *The train leaves the Gare du Nord at eight-fifteen. Be at the station half-an-hour before the train starts. Take your seat, don't wait for me. I'll find you. Love, Harvey.*

"You look depressed," said Nina.

"Do I ? That is because I am tired. I have got what I wanted, so I should be happy."

"You should indeed."

Then Nina went away, closing the door after her, and in an agony of remorse and self-pity, Julie, realizing the mess she had made of everything, and thinking of her wrecked life, began to sob.

CHAPTER XXI

MONSIEUR PATRICE was a man devoted to his son, and utterly sincere with him. He believed that a parent's responsibility never ends, though he tried not to be guilty of that over-devotion to duty which often ends in separating a son from his father.

As Madame Patrice had insisted, he had a frank talk with his son about Julie. Charles knew that to have such a talk his father must be perturbed and worried about him.

The two men sat in the Patrice library, a little table with drinks on it placed conveniently near. Both men smoked cigars.

The father spoke without preamble and quietly. "I understand, Charles, that you have seriously quarrelled with Julie, or I should not dream of interfering."

Charles nodded to show that he understood, and replied moodily, "It is not an ordinary quarrel."

"If you would care to give me a few details I will do my best to give you some good advice."

"It is no secret. I do not mind your knowing. Indeed, I shall be glad to get the matter off my chest," said Charles, and told him how Julie had come to his *appartement* last night and found Lucienne there—and the rest of the wretched tale.

"What if she did go ?" asked his father truculently. "One must be broadminded about certain things. It was foolish, but understandable, for the poor child was probably tortured with jealousy. Julie is deeply in love with you, Charles. She must often have seen you with Mademoiselle Jeanson. She would certainly have heard gossip. We have all listened to it these last two years. For Julie to find Mademoiselle Jeanson in your *appartement* would be the confirmation of her worst fears. It would seem proof that the gossip was true. No wonder she is upset."

"She could have given me a chance to explain."

"It is a position that would take some explanation," was the grim retort.

"I could only say the truth."

"Did you try?"

"Well, I was angry with Julie for coming and creating a difficult situation."

"You showed anger?"

Charles let that pass.

"It was not that I minded her coming so much, for I knew she was safe with me; but because of the interpretation that Lucienne would put on the visit, for she has an unkind tongue these days—acrid and loud. She is in with the Press and could do much harm to Julie's name."

"Not with you to protect her. Did you invite Mademoiselle Jeanson to your *appartement*?"

"*Bon dieu*, no! She arrived but a few minutes before Julie. She said she had come to talk seriously to me. The boys were having supper. I had just changed, ready for the first bout, when Lucienne walked in. I told her I was busy entertaining friends. I did not even offer her a drink. She was cross, but quite ready to go. Then Julie burst in. She spotted Lucienne, and I was in my dressing-gown. I regret I lost my temper. I rang for two taxis and sent them both away. It was an abrupt dismissal."

"Did you not explain the position to Julie as soon as possible?"

"How could I? The boys did not leave until after midnight. I have not seen Julie since. I left early this morning to play golf, and I hear that Julie has spent the day here with Maman."

His father exclaimed with annoyance. "You should have made a chance, son, abandoned the golf, and spent your day with Julie as arranged."

"I know that now; but neither of us was in the right mood to view *appartements*. As a matter of fact, I ordered Julie to write to me over the week-end. I expected an apology."

"You *ordered* her? You must be crazy, Charles."

"Well, I was angry, and full of apprehension for her because of Lucienne."

"Have you not already told Julie about this friendship?"

"No. I meant to, of course, some day. It was practically ended when I first met Julie, who, being English, may misunderstand that I liked Lucienne because she was older and flattered me, or that I once thought of marrying her, but did not; or indeed that I have long grown tired of her companionship. It would sound priggish and conceited to her."

"You will have to tell her just the same—that is, if Julie is to trust you, and you want your marriage to start right."

"Well, I do. I love Julie and want to make her happy."

"Then you are going the wrong way about it by leaving her alone, with Mademoiselle Jeanson sitting pretty in between you. That way the barrier grows apace."

"I seem to have been a fool."

"Your mother thinks that Julie is planning to leave Paris secretly."

Charles refused to believe this. "Impossible ! Julie loves me."

"That may be true, but for that very reason, because she cannot trust you, she may prefer to break with you by going home. It would be the best way to forget you."

"Julie would not know how to set about going."

"You must think her a fool, Charles. Julie has been with your mother all day. Not once has she mentioned your name. She has evaded any settled talk of the future. That is unnatural. The normal talk of a girl soon to be married would be to discuss her wedding and all the details connected with it, her future home, and certainly her fiancé. Julie carefully avoided such talk."

Charles looked serious.

"Your mother thinks, too, that Julie may be arranging to leave Paris on the Calais boat-train in the morning. It would be easy for Julie, through servants, or her English friend who I understand is staying in Paris solely on her account, to get her a ticket and tell her the time of departure."

"Julie is not a coward. She would not run away from me."

"She has been living under a great strain. Your mother says she is pale and miserable. She is unhappy."

"But that is absurd. We love each other."

"I should not talk too much about love, son. My experience," his father said diffidently, "is that women are not content for long with abstract love. They like the concrete expression."

They had parted amicably, his father's parting words, *"Bonne chance*, Charles," said feelingly, with a comforting slap on his shoulders.

As a result of this talk Charles spent a wakeful night in a torment of uneasiness. He was much disturbed by his father's talk.

In the morning Charles dressed with extra care because he knew that this was going to be one of the most important days in his life. Wearing an immaculate dark lounge suit he took his car out of the garage and drove to the Gare du Nord.

Approaching the station, Charles felt foolish because he was partly convinced that he had embarked on a fool's errand. Julie would not be there, but he decided to call at Madame Lubin's when the train had departed and see Julie at once.

He was not conscious then of any excitement. Indeed, after the hell of torment he had been through during the long night hours his nerves were numb.

There was still no word from Julie. Perhaps she would never write, never had any intention of doing so. He had called the tune and Julie had refused to play, thereby, according to his father, showing her sense.

Presently Charles stood in the semi-darkness of the station, which was like all other stations when an important train is due to start—shouts, whistles, rumbles, clanging and hissing—all making an indescribable din.

The noise irritated, but was bearable, and it came in waves of sound.

Charles stood inconspicuously apart, yet in the line of traffic from the ticket offices to the iron gates guarding the platform. His eyes flicked everywhere.

He was slightly bored because he had already decided, 'This is about the silliest way to spend a Sunday morning. I should have stayed in bed and telephoned the Lubins.'

Charles was about to move impatiently, to give up this insane quest, when he saw Julie. Her face was pale, almost devoid of make-up, and her bearing dejected, but she was chic as usual in the little black street suit that he remembered was the first dress le Gère had made for her, and which suited her pencil-slim figure so well.

Julie looked so young and lovely, so pathetically lonely, so much in need of someone to care for her that Charles felt his heart swelling with love. His nerves which had been so numb through concentrated wretched thoughts were now, at sight of her, tensed.

He thought, 'I'll do anything for Julie, whatever she thinks will make her happy.'

In his mind Charles called her crazily, his 'little mouse,' his 'leda,' his 'precious dar-r-rling.' Involuntarily he moved several paces swiftly after her retreating figure, for Julie knew exactly where she was going and was making a bee-line for the boat-train.

As he noted this, Charles's awakened love was extinguished by anger. He had been tricked.

He made a swift detour and came round between Julie and the gates. He barred her way.

"Julie!" The word sounded like the crack of a pistol.

She stopped dead. At any other time Charles would have laughed to see how her eyes widened and darkened with surprise and dismay. Her confusion would have amused him, but not now.

Julie stiffened. "Get out of my way." Her voice was brittle as broken glass. She tried to dodge past him.

"Not so fast." Charles put a detaining hand on her arm, and his flexible fingers, which could be so soft and gentle, now gripped her like a vice.

"Let me go."

"Why?"

"I have a train to catch."

"No, you are going to miss this train."

"Who says so?" How lovely and insolent she looked with her head thrown back and the light of battle in her big eyes.

"I do. You were running away. That was a mean trick."

"I never thought of you; why should I?" She contrived to speak loftily. Then Julie saw the station clock. She tried to wrench herself free, but could not do so. "Let go, or I shall scream for help."

"Do so," Charles told her quietly, but it was the calm of deep rage. "I, too, can make a scene. I shall use force if necessary."

"You would not dare!"

"Try me," Charles taunted.

"What do you want?"

"How hard you sound! But that is better. Come with me."

"Where?"

"Oh, anywhere—to the lounge of the hotel here. I want to talk to you."

Julie gave in suddenly, partly to avoid the scene which Charles had threatened to create if she refused to go with him, and which he was quite capable in his present mood of carrying out; but also because if she went quietly with him and allayed his fears that she might escape, there might yet be a chance of eluding him and catching her train.

"All right. Be quick," she told him impatiently, turning to go with him.

"Where is your baggage?"

"I haven't any."

They walked away, Charles keeping pace with Julie and still

holding her arm. They went through a private entrance to a lift, and were taken up to the hotel lounge which was built over a part of the station, and where there were big chairs, low tables and glass ashtrays, and where the carpet was thick and soft.

Charles sat down on a settee in a corner and pulled Julie down beside him. He had come to talk—explain—even cajole. He wanted to be friends. Yet now all reason fled. All he could think about was love.

A waiter came up to them, and Charles slipped a note into his hand.

"*Merci*, M'sieur." The waiter arranged a large palm near the settee which would give them extra privacy if anyone came into the lounge, then he vanished.

There was a long silence during which Julie watched the clock. But she did not move. Something—not Charles's hand—held her back.

Charles loosened his hold on Julie. She could not get away now. He turned his head to look at her. As he did so the remnants of his anger against her melted. His hand sought hers and clasped it convulsively.

"*Mignonne !*"

It was like a magic word. Quickly they passed into a hazy world of happiness.

Julie had not expected Charles to call her that. He spoke softly, and his beautiful mellow voice was jagged and broken as though he were deeply moved.

It tore at her heartstrings. Surely nothing mattered, only love ! If they could be together, sure in their love for each other, they could be happy. Why not blot out what happened, and think only of each other ?

"Don't," Julie said quickly, but she glanced at him timorously, and a shock of happiness went through her. She thought, 'Charles wants to be friends and so do I.'

"Well—dar-r-rling ! Do you like that better ?" He spoke gaily enough, but his hand was trembling.

For something to do to tide him over the emotional moment, Charles busied himself taking off Julie's gloves. He put them aside and took her hands in his, feeling their softness, letting her touch tease him.

"Forgive," he pleaded presently, raising her hands to his face, and kissing every inch of them with a growing passion which found an answering passion in her and swept it along with its tide. Explanations could wait. Only love counted just then.

"Oh, my dar-r-rling, I have been so stupid, so careless that

223

I nearly lost you. I do not know what would have happened if you had gone and left me alone." He buried his face in the palms of her hands. Then he said, "We must be married quickly. I shall not dare to take another risk like this. We will not wait to find a suitable *appartement*. We can take a furnished one, or go to an hotel. How soon shall we be married—this week?"

His impetuosity shook Julie. It swept aside everything that had divided them. How debonair and eager he was! She had the deepest and tenderest love for him. Darling Charles!

She lifted her hand and smoothed his hair, her gesture shy. "I could not be ready in a week," she told him in a shaky whisper, but there was longing in her tone.

"Then two weeks," Charles decided, his voice slurred with emotion. "I cannot wait. Julie, my beautiful, I love you so much." He raised his head to look at her, and their hands fell together in her lap. "*Chérie!* Oh, but you are so adorable!"

How soft and tender those words of love sounded!

The wan look had gone from Julie's face, and a radiance which made her seem unearthly and not of this world, but an angel from heaven, returned. Her eyes were luminous and soft as stars, her lips tremulous. She dazzled him.

Charles leant forward suddenly and kissed the little hollow at the base of her throat.

"My beloved!" His ardour was tender, possessive and passionate—tumultuous. It swept her along. He let go her hands, and putting his arms about Julie, gathered her close to him. She leaned against him and he felt her body relax. He guessed how much she loved him.

Then his arms tightened around her. "*Je t'adore*," he told her.

Julie heard the passionate cry just above her head. Unconsciously she answered that cry. Raising her face to his their lips met. . .